THE CHASE

The night wore on. Soon after midnight, while surfaced, the *Narwhal* contacted two ships astern. While he could not see them clearly, Latta sensed that they were DEs. All uncertainty ended when both vessels put on speed and one of them opened fire. The captain put all four engines on the line and ordered full speed. Then began the deadly race for safety that always develops when a submarine elects to stay on the surface and try to outrun the pursuer. In the dimly lit cavern below deck, Engineer Officer Plummer nursed his four temperamental GM 16 "270" engines up to the maximum number of turns prescribed for them, hoped for the best, and expected the worst.

THE BANTAM WAR BOOK SERIES

This is a series of books about a world on fire.

These carefully chosen volumes cover the full dramatic sweep of World War II. Many are eyewitness accounts by the men who fought in this global conflict in which the future of the civilized world hung in balance. Fighter pilots, tank commanders and infantry commanders, among others, recount exploits of individual courage in the midst of the large-scale terrors of war. They present portraits of brave men and true stories of gallantry and cowardice in action, moving sagas of survival and tragedies of untimely death. Some of the stories are told from the enemy viewpoint to give the reader an immediate sense of the incredible life and death struggle of both sides of the battle.

Through these books we begin to discover what it was like to be there, a participant in an epic war for freedom.

Each of the books in the Bantam War Book series contains a dramatic color painting and illustrations specially commissioned for each title to give the reader a deeper understanding of the roles played by the men and machines of World War II.

GUERRILLA SUBMARINES

EDWARD DISSETTE
AND
HANS CHRISTIAN ADAMSON

BANTAM BOOKS
TORONTO · NEW YORK · LONDON

GUERRILLA SUBMARINES
*A Bantam Book / published by arrangement with
the authors*
Bantam edition / March 1980

*Illustrations by Greg Beecham.
Maps by Allan McKnight.*

*Bantam Books are published by Bantam Books, Inc. Its trade-
mark, consisting of the words "Bantam Books" and the por-
trayal of a bantam, is Registered in U.S. Patent and Trademark
Office and in other countries. Marca Registrada. Bantam
Books, Inc., 666 Fifth Avenue, New York, New York 10019.*

To the gallant crews of the
GUERRILLA SUBS
and the men and women
who shared in their work

CONTENTS

FOREWORD

The story of the guerrilla movement in the Philippines during World War II and the American submarine effort to support it has never, until now, been properly recorded. At the time it was such a closely held secret that few in the military realized its magnitude.

A large part of the credit for the success of this effort must be given to the Filipino guerrilla leaders and to the American businessmen and others who remained in the Islands to act as advisors to them.

The Filipinos are unique among the peoples of Southeast Asia overrun in 1942 by the Japanese. Instead of capitulating, they fought back and, more importantly, retained their loyalty to and friendship with the nation that previously governed them. This loyalty, as well as hope, was kept alive by the frequent arrival of our submarines carrying arms, ammunition, communications equipment, medical supplies, American magazines, and, of course, the famed "I Shall Return" matchbooks. By this action, and the materials they received, the guerrillas, who had determined to defy the Japanese invaders, were able to demonstrate to their countrymen that they were, indeed, in contact with the Americans and that they had not been deserted.

The guerrilla movement could never have gotten underway without the vision and persistence of General Douglas MacArthur, his naval advisors, and the vital support furnished by U.S. submarines. But the driving force behind ultimate success was Lieutenant Charles E. ("Chick") Parsons, USNR (now a Commander, USNR [Ret.]).

As a staff officer, Commander Submarines, Southwest Pacific, I recall that when Chick first came to our headquarters at Fremantle he asked only for the use of one submarine to land two or three men and about 100 pounds of equipment somewhere in the Philippines. It was not long before he requested, and got, more submarines to land more men and more equipment.

The story told in this book is about the men who manned the submarines that supported the guerrillas, and the people, like Parsons and many others, who made the movement a success. It is one that will fascinate and inspire every reader.

Rear Admiral F. Kent Loomis
U.S. Navy (Ret.)
Washington, D.C.

AUTHORS' NOTE

We deeply appreciate the assistance given to us by Rear Admiral F. Kent Loomis, USN (Ret.), and Commander Charles E. Parsons, USNR (Ret.). Thanks are also extended to the Naval History Division of the Department of the Navy, and particularly to Captain Paul B. Ryan, who supplied us with illustrations and encouragement. The Sixth Army Research Library at the Presidio in San Francisco was also of great help.

We regret that we have been unable to comply with Chick Parsons' expressed wishes for obscurity, but the role he played in the historic drama of the interaction of submarines and guerrillas is too important to ignore.

This is not a definitive history of the Filipino guerrilla movement and does not come within miles of being one. It is chiefly an action story about a unique series of operations by American submarines in World War II who operated in enemy-held waters with the mission of equipping, supplying, and otherwise supporting the guerrillas in their harassment of the Japanese invaders.

Enough background on the guerrillas is provided to give the reader and student an idea of the nature and extent of the movement.

We acknowledge with thanks comments and recommendations by qualified submariner readers. To them we explain that some technical terms were simplified for the layman.

Hans Christian Adamson
Edward Farwell Dissette

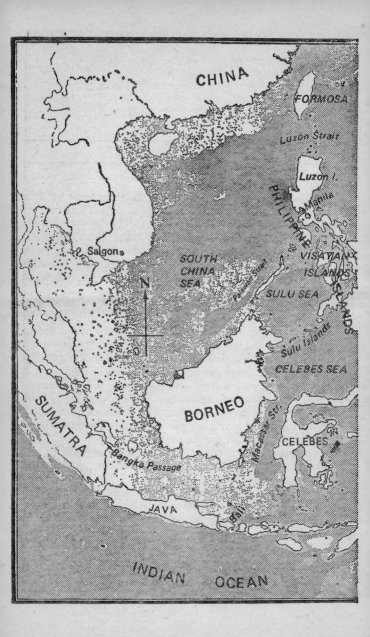

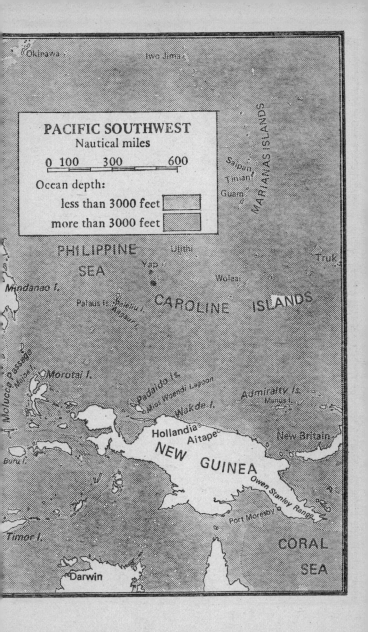

1

THE FIRST GUERRILLA
SUB RUN

The sun shone brightly on the cloudless afternoon of Sunday, 27 December 1942. The place was Fremantle, at the mouth of the Swan River, the harbor city of Perth, on the west coast of Australia. The locale was the deck of the submarine *Gudgeon;* her skipper—Lieutenant Commander William S. Stovall, Jr., United States Navy. Two days earlier the sub had taken aboard a ton of special gear for a landing party to be transported under secret orders to Mindanao and Panay, two major islands in the Philippines. All gear, except gasoline in 5-gallon cans, had been stowed under the floor plates in the forward torpedo room. The gasoline was stowed in the escape trunk, where it was safely sealed off from the rest of the ship.

Gudgeon was a fleet-type submarine, as were all her sister subs based at Fremantle, at that time under the command of Rear Admiral Charles A. Lockwood.* With a cruising radius of 10,000 miles and maximum duration at sea of 75 days for one patrol, she was hardly classed as a cargo vessel, and yet that was the kind of service she was being pressed into for the beginning of her sixth war patrol. She was 307 feet in overall length, had a beam of 27 feet, displaced 1,475 tons on the surface with full war load, and had a normal crew of 5 officers and 54 enlisted men. Her four diesel engines delivered 5,400 h.p. and produced a maximum surface speed of 20 knots. Submerged, operating on her 2,740 h.p. battery-powered

---

*Charles Andrew Lockwood graduated from the U.S. Naval Academy in 1912 and was an old hand in the submarine service dating from WW I. He was promoted to three stars, Vice Admiral, when he was appointed Commander Submarines, Pacific in February, 1943 in which post he served to the end of WW II.

motors, her maximum speed was a little less than 9 knots. Her test diving depth was 275 feet, a depth that was more frequently than not exceeded "in extremus" by many fleet-type boats.* She carried 24 torpedoes—six in her forward tubes, four aft, and the rest in stowage racks fore and aft. For surface battle, *Gudgeon* mounted a 3-inch/ 50-caliber rapid-fire rifle on deck aft (supposedly for a retreating action, or to put it more heroically, to suppress enemy pursuit), a 40-mm. Oerlikon forward and several .50- and .30-caliber demountable machine guns to repel boarders if such an unlikely event were to occur.

Fleet-type submarines were designed for a primary mission—to sink ships—and they were built to fit their specific requirements of men and material as tightly as shoes, pinching shoes, that is. There was hardly room for anything more. But "anything more" is precisely what *Gudgeon* had on board this day.

This special loading presaged a new kind of war for Shirley Stovall and for the *Gudgeon*. They had been trained to fight with torpedoes and guns, not to land people and paperback matchbooks or what-have-you. But like all good submariners—proud of their silent service and fiercely dedicated to their work—Stovall faced this unique assignment stoically, although somewhat puzzled.

The captain, lean-faced, with a pencil-line moustache, paced the deck that afternoon at the submarine docks in Fremantle, soaking up the sunshine. It would be his last sunbath for some time. The first lieutenant and the chief-of-the-boat, both old hands on board, went about their business efficiently checking the security of gear stowed topside, testing every hatch leading below, save one, to be sure they were dogged down tight. They observed the slow-motion tilting of the bow and stern diving planes as the below-decks watch checked out their systems. These were the final preparations for sea.

Topside, there was a sudden commotion at the gangway. The quartermaster of the watch blew his whistle for attention starboard. All hands on deck froze in place. Admiral Lockwood, a trim military figure in crisp, starched khaki, his garrison cap with the two silver stars

---

*Submariners invariably refer to their ships as "boats": probably derived from the early days of submarines when they were classified as "Submersible Torpedo Boats."

of his rank perched jauntily on his head, strode aboard. As he saluted the ensign flying proudly, defiantly whipping stiffly in a brisk off-shore breeze, the admiral seemed to hesitate a moment in quiet contemplation. Then he turned to Stovall and said in a clear and pleasant voice, "Carry on." The crew resumed their work. Captain Stovall stepped forward and clasped the admiral's warm handshake.

"Well, Shirley, you look fit and so does your boat, as usual."

Charles Lockwood (his commanding officers called him Uncle Charlie when he wasn't within earshot) smiled as he glanced about the clean decks of the submarine. Turning to Stovall he said, "Ready to go?"

"Yes, sir," Stovall replied.

Lockwood looked at him quizzically.

"No questions?"

The Captain hesitated, then shook his head in the negative.

"Look, Shirley, I suspect these orders kind of shook you. They shook me up a bit, too. But the fact is we're desperate for more information, more intelligence, from inside the Philippines. We're the only ones who can get in there right now and set up the works."

Stovall understood, but in his own opinion this was no way to run a submarine. He had the deepest admiration for his boss, as did all submariners who served under him, and so without hesitation Shirley went about the business of getting ready to do what he was asked to do. As for Admiral Lockwood, one might have detected a far-away gleam in his steel-blue eyes, a sort of concealed envy, a feeling that perhaps had this been an earlier era *he* might have been going out on this mission.

The admiral broke his momentary reverie with a slight, hardly perceptible shudder. With deep sincerity he held out his hand to Stovall and said:

"Good luck and good hunting."

Lockwood saluted and walked briskly down the gangplank. He didn't look back.

A few hours later seven Filipino mess boys, neatly attired in clean, faded dungarees, white mess jackets, and white hats, filed aboard and saluted the colors smartly. Ashore a kookaburra bird brayed its raucous jackass laugh as if it found seven mess boys boarding a submarine a funny sight, which it would have been under normal circumstances. However, these lads were disguised Filipino soldiers and intelligence agents under the command of Major Jesus Villamor, U.S. Army. There was no loitering on deck; one by one these mess boys slipped down the hatch to the forward torpedo room. The mission was so secret that, by order of Admiral Lockwood, the "uniforms" had been delivered direct to Major Villamor from the *Gudgeon* the day before.

Hardly had Villamor and party vanished below deck before the submarine slipped out of the harbor on the first leg of her ultrasecret voyage to the Philippines. Captain Stovall did not know that his was the forerunner of a formidable series of submarine operations that would support guerrillas in the hills, the mountains, and the coastlines of the entire Philippine Archipelago until the armed forces of the Rising Sun were driven from the Islands into the sea.

Stovall drove his ship north at full speed for the "Slot" —a narrow, dangerous entrance into the Celebes Sea. It was dominated by Japanese air cover and studded with enemy antisubmarine patrols.

Gudgeon's transit was timed to the darkness of a moonless night. He dove each dawn to get his daily trim, and thereafter only to avoid aircraft or other contacts that could disclose his presence. Too often he heard the shout "Aircraft! Clear the bridge! Dive, dive, dive!" The Klaxon would blast out the diving alarm, "Ah-oogah, Ah-ooga," and he could hear the main ballast vents slam open, releasing a swoosh of air as the boat nosed over and started down. With the main engines shut down, the motors shifted to batteries, and the comforting reports "Green board!" and from another station in the main control room "Pressure in the boat!", the captain then, and only then, could turn his attention to the immediate problem. This action all took place in less than 60 seconds.

"What was it?" he would ask the lookouts. Then, when the threat of attack seemed to pass he would edge up to periscope depth for a look. He was anxious to be up and on his way again.

"All clear. Blow main ballast. Surface. Four engines!"

Past Java, then Borneo, Stovall threaded his way through rough Makassar Strait. It was only then that

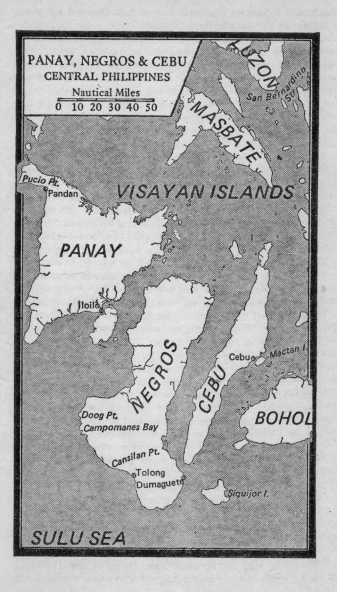

PANAY, NEGROS & CEBU
CENTRAL PHILIPPINES
Nautical Miles
0 10 20 30 40 50

LUZON

MASBATE

San Bernardino Str.

VISAYAN ISLANDS

Pucio Pt.
Pandan

PANAY

Iloilo

NEGROS

CEBU

Cebu Mactan I.

BOHOL

Doog Pt.
Campomanes Bay

Cansilan Pt.

Tolong
Dumaguete

Siquijor I.

SULU SEA

Major Villamore disclosed that he had changed his plans. Captain Stovall was rather startled.

It seems that Jesus had received information just before boarding *Gudgeon* in Fremantle that Japanese activity had taken a sharp and menacing upturn in the area he had selected previously as the landing spot. Stovall had not been included in this privileged line of communication. Now, Villamor announced, he wanted to land on the southwest coast of Negros—an island lying between Panay and Cebu. There was a safer route he could have taken, Stovall thought, had he known he was going to Negros instead of Mindanao. He didn't say anything. He just listened and fumed.

The landing place would be a little south of Doog Point, an area that was last charted about 1829. To add to Stovall's frustration—his tolerance already stretched to the breaking point—Villamor said that he had decided not to use the 18-foot wooden dinghy on board *Gudgeon* especially for this mission. The dinghy was a cumbersome piece of cargo because it could not be stowed below deck. It was, in fact, a definite hazard because it affected the diving capabilities of the submarine. But Villamor announced he would use his own rubber rafts with which he and his men had practiced. He had plywood stiffeners for the bottom of the unwieldy craft and prearranged plans for loading and unloading them.

Stovall had not been consulted about these last-minute changes in plans, and he was furious. Perhaps that is why Admiral Lockwood, on deck that departure day in Fremantle, asked him if he had any questions. Nevertheless the skipper agreed to all the changes providing that a periscope reconnaissance proved that a landing would be feasible and safe, not only for *Gudgeon* but for Villamor.

In the dying dusk of a stormy evening, *Gudgeon* reached a spot off Cansilan Point on the southwest coast of the island called Negros. The sea was very rough with a strong north-northwest wind. Stovall prudently flooded down the boat enough to slice through the heavy seas without throwing any telltale phosphorescent spray. It soon became obvious that there could be no landing that night on Cansilan Point.

Stovall backed off to look for a better landing area, hoping to find one between Cansilan Point and Tolong, a small town that lies on the edge of a bay near the southern

end of Negros. Villamor did not want to go ashore south
of Tolong. It was reportedly alive with Japanese and not-
so-friendly natives. So it was decided to reconnoiter the
beaches to the north. They found one that appeared to be
well protected despite the heavy seas from the northwest.
The only drawback was that there was a concentration of
nipa huts* along the beach. After studying the area
thoroughly through *Gudgeon*'s high-powered periscope, Jesus said that if he could get ashore undetected he had no
objection to the presence of houses. In fact, he added, he
might find some "disciples" living there.

As darkness fell, Stovall headed away from the coast
to surface out of sight and charge the main propulsion
batteries. With that completed at about midnight, *Gudgeon* turned to close the beach once again. As the sub
approached, lights began to appear until there was a solid
string of them along the shore. The lights covered all
prospective landing sites. Stovall and Villamor were puzzled. Were they Japanese patrols or was it a lively beach
party? One of the Filipino scouts aboard who was familiar
with this area explained that the lights were from torches
in boats used by native fishermen for night fishing off the
beach. Stovall was not convinced, and after a brief conference with Villamor it was concluded that there wasn't a
chance to land undetected at that spot. It was decided to
try farther north and hope that the wind and seas would
moderate enough to allow the major and his party to land
the next night on a less inhabited beach.

During the night the submarine made a surface run
well off shore. At dawn Stovall started to close the coast
in the hope of finding a spot between Campomanes Bay
and Doog Point. *Gudgeon* submerged and, for hours on
end, searched patiently for a suitable landing site. About
midafternoon it was decided that the best spot seemed to
be Catmon Point. It had a gentle sloping beach, appeared
to be deserted, and the southside of the Point was well
protected from the weather. The place was close enough

---

*A shack usually built on stilts with a rickety floor braced with
sagging cane stalks, with side walls and roof covered with nipa
palms. The usual ground floor occupants were chickens, pigs, goats,
etc. Nipa is a palm, with feathering leaves and bunches of edible
fruit, used for weaving and thatching. But best of all the nipa palm
is a source of a potent alcoholic beverage which happily led to
the untimely demise of more than one thirsty Japanese guard.

to a small village called Jinobaan, a good place according
to Villamor to make contact after landing. It suited the
major. True, the waves still marched upon the shore in
close, tall, crested ranks, but there were signs that the
wind was dying down and that the sea was losing its vio-
lence. It was agreed that a landing would be tried just
about dark to get the jump on the night fishermen, who
should not appear, if at all, until later in the evening.

The game of patience called "killing time" lasted from
1500 hours, while *Gudgeon* ran submerged at slow speed,
keeping the area under periscope surveillance, to 1854,
when the sub surfaced and crept noiselessly on electric
motors toward the dark and silent beach. As anticipated,
the wind had slackened off and the sea had flattened considerably. Stovall hove to about 1,000 yards south of the
rugged western tip of Catmon Point, a position that
would enable the landing party to take advantage of the
strong shoreward current sweeping around the end of the
island.

The submarine was trimmed down to about one foot of
freeboard to facilitate unloading. Working completely in
the dark, Villamor and his men went methodically about
their business. Stovall, as an added precaution against surprise surface attack and to cover the landing site in case
of interference ashore, had his deck guns manned.

The operation proceeded smoothly. The first two rafts
were loaded in jig time, but trouble developed when the
third and last raft could not be inflated. Captain Stovall
had had this contingency in mind after Villamor had re-
jected the use of the dinghy put aboard specifically for this
landing and offered one of *Gudgeon*'s rafts. But the Major
would not accept any other assistance. Time, he said, was
too precious to waste for any change in his landing schedule. Jesus elected to leave behind the medical supplies for
this area.

Within a half hour the two rubber rafts disappeared
into the silent black night. It was a shame, thought Stovall, to bring this amount of medical aid so far to people
who needed it and then abandon it. He was tempted to
send it ashore anyway, and he had crewmen who were
eager to try. After all, the bos'n said, they would have to
strike it below if it wasn't delivered and the dinghy would
have to be jettisoned anyway. They could get rid of two
evils at once and besides get the medical supplies where

they could be put to use. The deck hands begged the captain to let them launch the boat and take the last load in. Shirley pondered the problem. If the boat was discovered on landing it would jeopardize Villamor's mission, and it could lead to the loss of four of his crew who would be badly needed on the next phase of this combat patrol. Still, it was part of his mission. He made his decision, Send the stuff ashore.

No sooner had the dinghy been launched than the bridge watch was electrified by a dim lightbeam from the beach. It was the Morse code letter E flashed three times at three-second intervals, the prearranged signal from Villamor that all was clear ashore. That settled the problem for Stovall. It was time to get the hell out of there.

With the dinghy towing astern, *Gudgeon* crept away on quiet motors as silently as a gray ghost. Ten miles off shore Stovall pumped up to normal surface trim, brought the dinghy alongside, and ordered it riddled and cut loose. The small boat filled rapidly and slid beneath the waves. The Captain called for two engines on propulsion with two on battery charge, and cleared the area forthwith, his special mission accomplished.

Except for a handful of natives in the tiny village of Jinobaan who found that they had been joined mysteriously during the night by seven Filipino mess boys, no one knew that a United States submarine had visited the island of Negros. The date was 14 January 1943.

And so began the first operation of "guerrilla subs."

In his patrol report on this mission, Captain Stovall made a number of suggestions with respect to future operations of this nature. Among the things he recommended was that parties be limited to not more than two passengers per submarine. "More than this seriously crowds the already crowded submarine if they are to be cared for with any degree of comfort," observed Stovall.

Captain John M. Will, ComSubDiv 72, in his endorsement of this patrol report, gave *Gudgeon* a richly deserved "Well Done." But, he added, "to limit parties to two passengers per submarine is not considered practical." The division commander had no information as to what lay ahead in the nature of special missions to the Islands for Fremantle submarines. Not even Admiral Lockwood was, as yet, in on the deal. But with excellent judgment, Captain Will concluded: "The discomforts resulting from larger parties will have to be accepted as part of the price to be paid for the anticipated results."

It wasn't long before 'parties' of considerable more than two or three people became standard loads on guerrilla submarines.

2

MACARTHUR'S DREAM

The action that night of 14 January 1943, when Shirley Stovall put Jesus Villamor ashore on the island of Negros, was only the beginning. That first landing by submarine was the realization of a dream long held by General Douglas MacArthur since his days on Corregidor in the twilight hours of his futile defense of the Philippines.

The idea of establishing a militarily strong and well-organized guerrilla force in the Islands had been in the dark, secret chambers of his strategic mind ever since he realized the probability of a Japanese assault on the Philippines. It is possible that such a force had been suggested by a young American businessman who lived in and operated out of Manila and who also happened to be an officer in an Intelligence Unit of the United States Naval Reserve. His name: Parsons, Charles, "Chick," "Carlos" —he had others—and he was married to an exciting young lady of Spanish descent with the unusual name of Katsy. We will hear more of them later.

After declaring Manila an open city in late December 1941, MacArthur moved his headquarters to fortified Corregidor. He was painfully aware that he would not get enough reinforcements or outside help to repel the hordes of Japanese invaders. He probably never gave the word "surrender" more than a passing thought, but there were certain actions that could be taken, he knew, that would drive the enemy nuts.

Deep inside the damp and gloomy rock of Corregidor, the General sat in his new, unfamiliar, and (to him) most distasteful GHQ, and pulled methodically on his familiar corncob pipe. As usual, when he was pondering a problem, he was alone. His staff was standing by somewhere outside, waiting to be summoned at any moment. He was mulling over the alternatives facing him. "Give up?"— these dirty words weren't in his book. Harassment? Now that had possibilities!

Suddenly MacArthur straightened in his chair, leaned toward his desk, and methodically knocked the ashes from his pipe into the sawed-off base of a 3-inch AA brass shell that served as an ash tray. Perhaps, he had concluded, there is a way to harass the bastards. He rang for his aide. "Get me top-secret file George," he said. A few minutes later the colonel placed a manila folder on the General's desk. The file was labeled in red ink, with large block letters neat in a soldierly row. The title was underlined. "GUERRILLAS". MacArthur studied it thoughtfully.

It wasn't long before he called in his Chief of Staff, Brigadier General Richard Sutherland, and laid out his plan. The first step, he directed, would be to send couriers throughout the Islands and messages to all loyal and secure radio contacts. Encourage loyal natives to set up guerrilla units in the central and southern islands. Objective: harass the enemy and obtain intelligence.

Within a few months it was clear that the movement was a failure. It never gained momentum because there was no way to provide much-needed outside support, and there was a woeful lack of strong leadership among the natives, loyal as they might be. MacArthur realized that he had to have a man who was knowledgeable of the Philippines and their people, who was strong-willed, and who was, above all, a leader. He didn't have such a man immediately available. Even worse he did not have the means, or even an idea of how, to supply the guerrillas with their needs.

In the meantime, while he waited impatiently for his new guerrilla force to produce, MacArthur became aware of a totally new concept of waging clandestine warfare. It was the operations of United States submarines on special missions into and out of Corregidor. He was intrigued. Painted war-color gray and showing no identification on their hulls, they boldly but warily, silently, crept into and out of the Rock's anchorage. An anchorage is the best the submariners disdainfully called it. It wasn't a harbor, and it certainly was no haven. It was merely a place to off-load and reload precious cargo, including people. Under almost constant Japanese air and surface surveillance and subjected to frequent bombing attacks, it was a dangerous place for a surfaced submarine to be with hatches open and high explosives above and below deck. But the boats came in, surfaced at night, and moored to any dock that was still attached to Corregidor. Every mooring line was attended by two seamen on deck, each armed with an ax. Under air attack they would first try to slip the moorings. If that failed the lines would be chopped. The sub would back out with what dignity she had left and sink quietly to the bottom in a puddle of muddy water. They were, as submariners describe it, "pulling the blanket over our heads." When the bombs stopped dropping, the boat would rise to periscope depth and look around. If all-clear she would surface gingerly, like an oil-soaked goose in a shooting preserve, and return to the loading dock.

General Douglas MacArthur was impressed and the more he saw, the more he began to wonder if submarines might not be the answer to his problem of supplying the guerrillas.

Seawolf, Lieutenant Commander Frederick B. "Fearless Freddy" Warder commanding, was the first submarine into Corregidor after the surrender of Manila. In January 1942 Warder was given the dubious honor of delivering the first load of ammunition to the beleaguered defenders of the Rock. It marked the beginning of a new and unexpected role for the American underseas fleet. With no radar and no information about enemy antisubmarine activity, Warder crept into Corregidor under cover of darkness, running quietly on batteries. By using passive sonar he dodged Japanese surface patrols in Manila Bay. But his real concern was—MINES!

The U.S. Navy had laid a defensive minefield in the approaches to Corregidor just before the outbreak of hostilities. Unfortunately the field was not very accurately charted. In the words of Lieutenant Ted Lyster (later lost in the sinking of USS *Juneau*), the skipper of one of the small fleet of makeshift minelayers: "We'd blow the whistle and drop a mine. About half of them blew up as soon as we dropped them." They were ancient moored mines of World War I vintage.

Freddy Warder had only a general idea of the limits of

the American minefield. The question in his mind, un-
answered by Operational Intelligence at Pearl Harbor,
was: "Had the Japanese laid any others?" It was unlikely,
they all reasoned, unless the enemy expected a counter-
invasion by Allied forces from the sea. In January 1942,
that probability was extremely remote, and the Japanese
knew it. The next logical question was: "Had they thought
of a submarine coming in to Corregidor?" Warder thought
they had not and so he barreled in. He delivered the
ammo.

Seawolf's mission was a two-way street. When she departed the Rock, she had aboard 25 American aviators who
had lost their planes at Nichols Field, 16 torpedoes and
a batch of submarine spare parts. The torpedoes and
spares were desperately needed by the boats that now based
out of Australia. Warder made it to Fremantle in spite of
persistent harassment by the Japanese, who seemed to
realize that something was escaping them. But they didn't
score. Warder, and *Seawolf* and her crew did. It was only
the beginning, admittedly feeble but at least effective, and
the first of a series of strikebacks that would finally destroy
the Japanese military empire.

On 11 March 1942 MacArthur and his family—his wife
Jean and son Arthur—were spirited out of Corregidor. To
the General's credit, it must be said that he did not leave
of his own volition. He left on director orders of President Roosevelt. Although a submarine was available, Mac-
Arthur chose the PT-boats. It was a hazardous trip by
sea and air, but they made it to Australia. The submarine
supply and support of Corregidor continued even after
MacArthur's departure well into the month of May.

Probably the most unusual task ever performed by a
U.S. combat submarine was that of *Trout,* Commander
Mike Fenno commanding. She brought in a load of 3-inch
AA ammunition, and suddenly became a gold-runner, not
a gunrunner. She took out all the gold bars belonging to
the Philippine Treasury. The Japanese found nothing of
value in the insular banks when they took over the Islands.
All the gold was on Corregidor, and *Trout* was ordered to
take it out. The weight of the cargo was so great that the
submarine had to remove and put ashore most of its fixed
lead ballast. The trim dive made on leaving the bay was

scary, to say the least, Fenno mentioned in his report on the mission. Evading air and sea patrols on the surface, Captain Fenno delivered his fantastic cargo to ComSubPac at Pearl Harbor. Said he, on turning over the treasury of the crumbling Philippine government: "Never have so few carried so much so far."

The last sub run to Corregidor was an eleventh-hour rescue mission. About two months after MacArthur had disappeared from surveillance, the Japanese began to suspect they were being tricked out of something. They didn't know how it was happening, but it was.

Late one night in early May, the lights in the penthouse of the Manila Hotel were ablaze. It was MacArthur's former quarters. The room reeked of sake fumes. The Japanese officers present were being honored by their new commander, General Yamashita. For every officer there was at least one girl. No one wore shoes. Some of the young ladies had obis seductively draped about their lithe bodies; other young girls wore the traditional Philippine mestiza dress. Couples drifted in and out. The whole hotel was their playground that night. The general was very pleased. His naval advisor, Captain Inokuo, had just told him privately that the problem of the improbable disappearance of General MacArthur had been solved. It would never happen again, the captain assured Yamashita. The Imperial Japanese Navy had doubled its sea defenses around Manila. Captain Inokuo, IJN, was very drunk.

That same night, *Spearfish,* Commander James C. ("Jimmy") Dempsey skipper, a light-heavyweight boxer of Olympic caliber in his naval academy days, slipped through the drunken Inokuo's "new doubled sea defenses around Manila." As if he were back in the ring, Dempsey feinted, sidestepped, and lunged until he sensed an opening in the defense. He wasn't looking for a fight that night, he simply wanted to get through. Under cover of a moonless sky, *Spearfish,* running silently on electric drive, slid into the one remaining pier at Corregidor. Swiftly, quietly, people filed aboard and disappeared below. Dempsey didn't count them, but after he had threaded his way through the Japanese A/S patrols on his way out his exec told him that there were 12 army and navy men aboard, 12 nurses of both branches of the service, and one civilian woman.

Jimmy said later, "It was a very pleasant trip back to Australia." This in spite of, or maybe because of, the

PT-boat

overcrowded conditions below decks. He thought the ratio of male to female was just right. Dempsey gave up his stateroom and bunk to the lone civilian lady. He said he slept in the conning tower where the Captain ought to be anyway when at sea. It's a likely story.

All in all, submarines delivered about 144 tons of provisions and ammunition to beseiged Corregidor between January and May. In turn, they brought out 64 allied officers, 125 enlisted men, and 22 civilians. Almost as important as the people was the equipage the subs salvaged from the Rock: 58 torpedoes, 4 tons of submarine spare parts, and 3 tons of communication equipment. This may seem to be a paltry contribution to the total war effort then surging over the globe, but under the circumstances it was an incredible performance. These people and materiel were literally snatched from under the guns of a powerful and ruthless foe.

Although these emergency submarine operations in and out of Corregidor were not directly in support of subsequent guerrilla activities, they did lead to that beginning with *Gudgeon*'s mission in January 1943. It became obvious in later years that, while MacArthur did indeed return to the Philippines, as he had promised, the gallant Submariners of the United States Navy had never abandoned their loyal allies in the Islands. It was almost as if Admiral Dewey had returned—except this time, the enemy was not the Spanish fleet, and "Dewey's" forces were a handful of determined seamen who seemed to delight in driving around under the water. Like the old Spanish navy, the Japanese underestimated the opposition.

General Douglas MacArthur arrived in Australia late in March 1942 and was warmly received by Premier John Curtin. The Aussies were convinced that MacArthur was the man who could and would turn back the apparently unconquerable flow of Japanese aggressors into the Southwest Pacific. Australia appeared to be the ultimate target, and the Australians were worried. The majority of their men were off fighting elsewhere, most of them in Africa. Bloody few were looking out for Australia herself. It was true that MacArthur did not have an enormous army with him, or a formidable air force or a visible navy, but he did have courage and somehow he seemed to have a mysterious rapport with a Supreme Being. And he had plans.

MacArthur established his headquarters in Brisbane, a pleasant seaport on the east coast of Australia. It already had a natural submarine base—New Wharf. The General wasted no time. He wanted submarine support bases on both coasts. Fremantle, the harbor city of Perth on the west coast of Australia, was selected as the second submarine support base. The Navy appointed Rear Admiral Charles A. Lockwood to command. He was saddled with the awkward title ComSubSoWesPac. "Keerist," brayed the kookaburra bird, "how can anybody get a message to a man with a handle like that?"

Next, MacArthur settled down to the task of shoring up Australia's defenses. He drew an imaginary line across the top of the Owen Stanley Range north of Port Moresby in eastern New Guinea. He dubbed it the "They-shall-not-pass" line. Australia was no longer on the defensive, MacArthur announced. The people of Melbourne, Sydney, Brisbane, Canberra, Perth, and Hobart, where more than half the population lived, and the sheep-raisers in the great plateaus beyond the Great Dividing Range were delirious with joy. MacArthur's staff officers were delirious too—they had diarrhea. They had not been able to convince him that there were not enough troops or ships to support this plan. But the General was inconvincible.

MacArthur put together an impressive staff. Brigadier General Richard Sutherland continued as chief of staff. The land forces would be commanded by General Sir Thomas Blamey; Brigadier General Stephen J. Chamberlin, U.S. Army professional staff officer, was named GHQ operations officer. In the field Lieutenant General Robert ("Bobo" "Ike") Eichelberger came in with an Army Corp headquarters, and George C. Kenney, a major general in the army, became the commander of MacArthur's air force.

The most important appointment so far as the guerrilla movement was concerned was that of Colonel Charles P. Willoughby as chief of intelligence. Both Willoughby and MacArthur had lived for years in the Philippines and loved the people and their islands. Both shared the view that one of the primary objectives of this war was to set the Islands free. This goal was never omitted from their planning. MacArthur knew that he was in the untenable situation where, with his forces almost completely overwhelmed, he could not hit the enemy with a frontal assault. His alternative? An end around, a maneuver that required detailed intelligence of the enemy. That information could only be provided by active guerrillas operating in the midst of enemy occupied territory.

The war in the south and southwestern Pacific had been thundering a full two months since MacArthur had left the Philippines before he received the first message from a guerrilla leader. It was from Lieutenant Colonel Guillermo Nakar, entrenched on Luzon, the largest and most important island of the Philippine Archipelago. Nakar reported that he had a substantial group of stouthearted men who were organized under his command, and they were ready to fight for their freedom. MacArthur couldn't believe it. Perhaps his dream of a guerrilla force could come true. But, he asked himself, exactly where were they? And what could he do for them?

Some eight weeks later another message came in. A Major Macario Peralta, formerly of the United States Forces—Far East (USFFE) reported that he had organized 8,000 men on the island of Panay. He asked for instructions. MacArthur was exultant. His dream *was* coming true. He gave Willoughby the job of building this guerrilla force into an effective fighting organization. Willoughby in turn appointed Colonel Allison Ind, an officer who had served in the Philippines, as deputy director of the Allied Intelligence Bureau (AIB) and put him in immediate charge of Philippine affairs.

The first step Ind took was to radio Peralta and ask him what he needed to get the guerrilla movement going. Peralta's prompt reply outlined an extensive list of requirements: rifles, auto-guns, and pistols; ammunition for all weapons, as well as spare parts; medical supplies, particularly quinine or atabrine, sulfa drugs, bandages, cotton, adhesive tape and first aid kits. Other urgently needed items included tinned goods of all kinds; clothing, particularly shoes; canvas material suitable for shelter; toilet articles of all types; matches and lighters with flints and fluid; and flash-lights and batteries.

The list went on and on—from binoculars to cigarettes; from magazines, books, and playing cards to typewriter ribbons, pencils, and paper. About the only thing Peralta didn't ask for was an airplane for his personal use. He probably would have if he had had control of a good airport.

Allison Ind went to work.

When MacArthur first saw the formidable list of things the guerrillas wanted, he was stunned. But when Colonel Ind told him that he was not surprised, that he was in fact pleased that Peralta had been so conservative, MacArthur recovered. Now he was convinced that the submarine was the answer to his logistic problems. From firsthand, on Corregidor, he had seen what a submarine could do in an emergency. He had seen submarines come into hostile territory, unseen and unheard by enemy eyes and ears. Why couldn't subs support the operations of the guerrillas? Yes, why not?

MacArthur made his decision. It had to be submarines— it was the only way.

Naval advisors on his staff suggested that fleet-type subs, like *Gudgeon*, could carry 5 to 10 tons of supplies, depending on bulk, and at least six passengers on the outward-bound leg of a regular combat patrol. To MacArthur that didn't seem to be a drop in the bucket of anticipated guerrilla needs. He wanted more, and he wanted it right now. In response to that the staff recommended that the General ask for the services of large transport-type submarines. The navy had two—*Narwhal* and *Nautilus*. They were large, cumbersome workhorses plagued with engineering problems, and they dived like a falling brick. But they could carry a lot of extra people and a lot of stuff. That's what MacArthur wanted. Typically, he went to the top. He didn't bother the President, he merely asked General George Marshall, Army Chief of Staff, for assistance in obtaining the services of these particular submarines, or for that matter any others the navy could make available.

Marshall passed the buck to Admiral Nimitz, Pearl Harbor. Chester Nimitz replied that, while he was deeply sympathetic toward the project and would like to cooperate, only one of the transport subs—*Narwhal*—would be available, and then not until November 1943. *Nautilus* would have to go in to much-needed overhaul before she could be assigned. This was then June 1942.

As a substitute, Admiral Nimitz suggested using fleet-type submarines to do these special missions. He told General Marshall that these boats could carry 25 passengers

U.S.S. Nautilus

and 34 tons of cargo, if they modified their wartime load.
He added wryly that the smaller submarines would be more
handy for operations in narrow waters. This was a very
amicable exchange of communications. The only trouble
was that when ComSubPac (Rear Admiral Robert H. English) was handed the problem, he came flat out and said,
"I haven't a single submarine to spare." MacArthur was
temporarily stymied.

In the meantime an unidentified submarine skipper
sent GHQ-Brisbane, via channels, of course, a message saying that he had some rather interesting information. It included a general statement reporting that he had learned
from various sources that there was a strong probability
that numerous U.S. naval ratings were hiding in the southwestern part of Mindanao. He added that it was common
knowledge that many Japanese positions in this area were
very lightly defended and that natives were known to be
friendly toward the Americans. It is submitted, the message
continued, that:

(a) under these conditions a small group of men could be landed at night from a submarine;

(b) assembly of members of U.S. naval and military forces could be effected;

(c) a potentially valuable guerrilla force of natives could be organized and utilized;

(d) enemy morale would suffer thereby;

(e) the enemy would be forced to suffer the effects of such raids or else reinforce their garrison and outposts;

(f) Allied prestige would be enhanced;

(g) valuable information would be obtained;

(h) there is a reasonable chance of success in these undertakings.

Specifically, the anonymous submarine commander proposed that a submarine, outward bound for combat patrol from its base, land small parties of men in the southern Islands. These parties would endeavor to develop enemy dispositions, assemble naval and military personnel stranded there, and conduct such punitive raids as were feasible.

Not much of this was new to MacArthur or his staff. But at least, back in Australia, they had the feeling that there were some submarine people that believed that they could and should get into guerrilla operations. They were men whose thinking paralleled MacArthur's. He fired this information back to General Marshall. This time he got action.

A fleet-type sub, on her way out of Fremantle on a war patrol, was ordered to report to GHQ-Brisbane for further orders. It was *Gudgeon,* and Shirley Stovall in consequence of these unusual orders put ashore on a memorable night in January 1943, on an obscure island in the Philippine Archipelago, one Major Jesus Villamor and a party of seven messboys. It was the beginning of submarine support to the Filipino guerrillas.

It was not mere happenstance that Villamor was the first of a string of Filipinos to return to their occupied homeland. Even in the early days of the war, Major Villamor had won a reputation as a first-class fighter and leader. Before the war, he was the leading American-trained Filipino military flier and commanded the Filipino aircraft squadron in Luzon. For his excellent work in the early stages of the war, he was awarded the DSC (as well as the DFC) by General MacArthur. In the spring of 1942, shortly before the fall of Bataan, the major fled Manila by sailboat, and eventually, he reached Australia. There, in the course of time, he was assigned to intelligence duty by General MacArthur under the latter's chief of intelligence, Colonel Charles Willoughby.

Major Villamor's original mission on his return to the Islands was to set up a branch of the Allied Intelligence Bureau in the Philippines to be placed under the direction of Colonel Allison Ind of GHQ-AIB. However, before that could be accomplished, unity and organized leadership had to be created among guerrilla leaders fighting for expansion and control among themselves. The result was a hodgepodge of overlapping territories and conflicting leadership claims. Villamor fell heir to this bucket of worms.

3

WHO'S IN CHARGE HERE?

When Major Villamor set foot on his native soil for the first time since he had fled Manila nearly a year before, he was almost overcome with emotion. But he had no time to indulge in his personal feelings. He was aware that the guerrilla movement throughout the Philippine Archipelago was in a precarious state. This situation was due more to internal troubles in the individual guerrilla units than to enemy activities. In spite of this, the movement was making an impression. Although the Japanese controlled the towns, seaports, and most of the plains, they were not strong enough to make more than sporadic raids upon the guerrillas, thousands of them, who hid in the hills and outlying areas.

The core of these loosely organized units were former enlisted men and officers of the USAFFE. When General Jonathan Wainwright ordered the surrender of all forces in the Philippines after the surrender of Bataan on 9 April 1942, other large-scale enemy operations had been started only on Mindanao, second-largest and southernmost island in the Philippines. There were large USAFFE units on Mindanao, as well as on the Central or Visayan Islands.

Few of these soldiers had ever seen action. Practically all senior officers in the Islands complied with the surrender order. Not so Brigadier General Christie, who commanded USAFFE troops on Panay. He refused to accept the orders of an officer who was in the hands of the enemy and could be acting under duress. General Christie asked for permission to carry on in the field; this request was refused. Only then did he surrender. But the delay gave many junior officers, especially those who were stationed in isolated places, opportunity to take to the hills. On all islands, officers, noncoms, and privates, Filipinos and

Americans and a handful of other allies, by the tens of thousands, did not turn themselves in but grabbed arms and ammunition and went into hiding.

These men were too wary to be caught flatfooted by the Japanese. In turn, the Japanese developed a healthy respect for the hillmen. The latter had a nasty trick of digging road pits for trucks that carried enemy search parties, killing the soldiers, taking their weapons and ammunition, and vanishing into the woods. This practice annoyed the Japanese to a point where the rifles were chained to the soldiers to prevent quick removal of weapons from their corpses.

As for the civilian population, it was at the mercy of not only the cruel invaders but also greedy guerrilla bandits. Lack of food and funds eventually had forced the hillmen to mount illegitimate foraging expeditions in armed gangs to satisfy their needs. In these raids, an undesirable civilian element joined. There followed a wave of lawlessness, with the natives in the rural areas more afraid of the armed gangs than of the Japanese. This, in turn, resulted in the forming of small guerrilla groups which, like American gangs, were primarily concerned in defending their own territories from other gangsters. The next step undertaken by these groups was to protect their areas from the Japanese. In this, strangely enough, they met with some success because the enemy was, at that time, not prepared for local resistance of any importance.

With no access to other than strongly slanted Tokyo war news and no signs of help from Allied forces, civilian morale was at low ebb. Then, in mid-August 1942, an overoptimistic American broadcast, on a par with any of the stupid stuff ever aired by Tokyo Rose, roused the people throughout the Islands. It was to the effect that the early return of American forces could be expected. The result was a quick expansion of ready-to-fight guerrilla forces and a gradual shift from gang wars to guerrilla warfare. However, there was no concerted action. Each leader was king of his own hill. But, with the burial of the gangster image and the emergence of a fighting spirit dedicated to driving out the Japanese, many units were now being supported by civilian contributions of food and money. Some of these contributions were no doubt forced, but most were voluntary. The Filipinos, deeply loyal to the United States, were aflame with hope.

Morale among the rank and file of guerrillas was high and their spirits aggressive. They had, in fact, swung to an attitude of extreme overconfidence. It was reflected by such ideas that they wanted no help from the United States in driving the Japanese out of the Islands—only arms and support. Their confidence was somewhat blunted when guerrilla attacks on Japanese garrisons—Iloilo on Panay, and on Malabalay in Bukidnon Valley, and Butuan at the mouth of the Agusan River—failed miserably. All these attacks fell flat and brought guerrilla dreamers off their high perch. After that they settled down to sabotage and ambushing, and to gathering intelligence material and harassing small enemy garrisons. Unfortunately their efforts went on uncoordinated and were motivated primarily by the selfish interest of their leaders. The trouble lay in the lack of a definitive command structure.

A shining example of the infighting taking place among the ambitious leaders was Negros Island where Captain Abcede and Captain Ausejo, former officers of the USAFFE, had divided the island in their strife for leadership. Abcede had joined up with Lieutenant Colonel M. Peralta, strong man on Panay, and thus extended Peralta's empire to the northern end of Negros. Peralta's advantage was somewhat offset when Ausejo and his guerrillas in the southern area of Negros, threw in with Lieutenant Colonel Wendell Fertig, boss of the Mindanao guerrillas and Peralta's foremost contender in the fight for control of all the guerrilla units in the Philippines. Fertig promoted himself to brigadier general and claimed command of all the forces in the Central and Southern Philippines. Finally, to muddy the situation completely, Colonel Gador, who commanded but a corporal's guard of less than 30 rifles, decided to outdo Fertig and Peralta in both rank and jurisdiction. He promoted himself to the rank of major general and claimed supreme command, not only on Negros but on all the Central Islands. Gador, who had never fired a shot at a Japanese much less been shot at, was ignored.

Hardly had Villamor been established on Negros before a coded message from GHQ-Brisbane directed him to prepare to take command of all guerrilla forces on that island as soon as he had completed his mission to establish personal contact with other guerrilla leaders, made recommendations regarding questions of command and administration on the various islands, and set up a coast-watcher

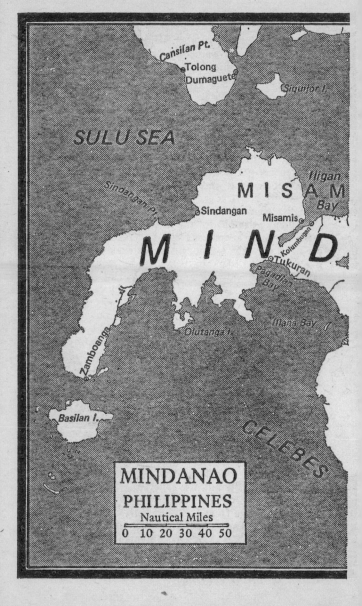

Cansilan Pt.
Tolong
Dumaguete
Siquifor I.

SULU SEA

Sindangan Pt.

MISAM
Iligan
Bay

Sindangan
Misamis

MIND

Kolumbugan
Tukuran
Pagadian
Bay

Ilana Bay

Olutanga I.

Zamboanga

CELEBES

Basilan I.

MINDANAO
PHILIPPINES
Nautical Miles
0   10 20 30 40 50

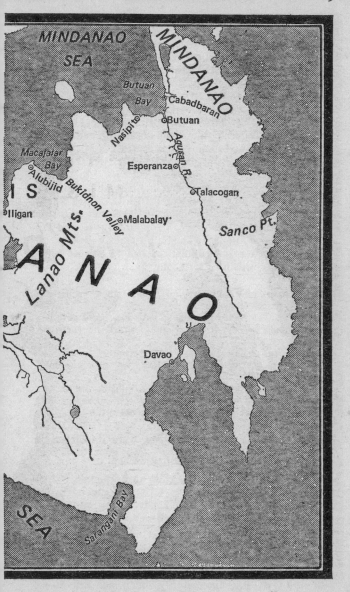

and intelligence organization on Negros with radio communications by secret code to GHQ-Brisbane.

The Philippine Bureau of the AIB was not completely unaware of the confused situation among the guerrillas in the central and southern islands, but the situation on Luzon, the northernmost and ultimately the most important island, was obscured by a band of silence after the initial broadcasts by Lieutenant Colonel Nakar. It was later learned that within a month of his first radio transmission his station had been discovered by the Japanese and he and his staff publicly tortured and summarily executed.

To face the emerging problem two major steps were taken by GHQ.

First: The islands were divided into ten military districts. Five were established on Luzon; District 6 was Panay; District 7 was comprised of Negros and Sequijor; District 8, Cebu and Bohol; District 9, Samar and Leyte; and District 10 included Mindanao and Sulu Islands.

Second: Four major stipulations had to be met before aid from GHQ would be forthcoming:

    a) Guerrillas within a military district must be united under a single command.

    b) The formations and functions of local civil government would be supported and not usurped by guerrilla leaders.

    c) Strikes against the enemy must be limited to old-line guerrilla tactics, and fruitless attacks on strong enemy positions would be ended.

    d) The primary responsibility of a military district or area commander would be to protect and strengthen his organization and to expand its intelligence net.

These instructions and directives were dispatched by every conceivable means to known loyal guerrilla leaders. Then Colonel Ind sat back and waited.

Shortly thereafter Peralta opened up on the air and announced his acceptance of the GHQ directives. He was promptly rewarded by being officially designated as Commander of District 6, Panay, and action was initiated to supply him.

Within a few days after Villamor's departure from Fremantle for the first guerrilla sub run to Negros, there appeared at GHQ-Brisbane a stocky young man with an un-

mistakable athletic build and a dark complexion that could
be easily taken for that of a native of the Philippine
Islands. He was fluent in several native dialects, of which
there are about 70. (There are so many, in fact, that until
Tagalog was decreed to be the official national language,
and education progressed, many Filipinos in one area
could not understand others, even in the same province.)

He had been summoned by General MacArthur personally. When he reported he was greeted with warmth and
affection by the General, for after all, they were old
friends from Manila days in spite of the difference in their
ages. "Chick," MacArthur said as he shook his hand, "you
just don't know how glad I am to see you!"

Charles ("Chick") Parsons was a humble man but not
necessarily shy, and on occasion had been known to be
quite indifferent to personages of rank and power. But he
had grown to know MacArthur since the days when the
General came to Manila in 1936 as Chief of Staff, Philippine Armed Forces. And MacArthur had developed a keen
respect for this American-born businessman who knew the
Islands and their people like a book. Parsons mumbled an
embarrassed reply. The reception was over. MacArthur had
finally found "His Man From Manila."

Late in February 1943, Lieutenant Commander S.
("Steve") H. Ambruster, skipper of the submarine *Tambor*, was guiding his heavily laden submersible toward the
western end of Mindanao. His human cargo included Lieutenant Commander Parsons; Captain Charles Smith, USA,
another specially selected emissary of MacArthur; and a
number of Filipino soldiers who were graduates of a guerrilla warfare school set up in Australia and conducted by
Colonel Lewis Brown, USA, an escapee from the fall of
Bataan.

This marked the first of many visits by Parsons to the
Islands. His first objective on this particular mission was
to deliver $10,000 in cash and a hefty load of ammuni-
tion to Colonel Fertig. In January 1943 Fertig had
"borrowed" a radio transmitter from Bohol strong enough
to reach Australia. He contacted GHQ and agreed to comply with the conditions established for recognition. In turn,
he was designated guerrilla commander of Mindanao and
Sulu, the 10th Military District, with the rank of colonel.
While this cut his rank from his assumed one of brigadier

general, it was actually a promotion from his official rank of lieutenant colonel. In exchange, GHQ promised Fertig quick service. Now the cargo was en route, with Commander Parsons in charge of safe delivery of 2 tons of stores. They included 50,000 rounds of .30-caliber ammunition and 20,000 rounds of .45-caliber bullets. There was also a fairly large amount of radio equipment to be put ashore for Commander Parsons' use in establishing a spy network. Its code name—*Spyron*.

Just before the *Tambor* arrived at Pagadian Bay on 4 March, Commander Parsons proposed to change the original plan of a daylight periscope reconnaissance of the Bay and a night landing of his party. While never demanding, he suggested to Ambruster that instead the landing should be made at the not-so-distant Labangan, where one of the natives in his party had a home. The reason was that he, like Jesus Villamor before him, had learned by radio that the original landing site was no longer secure. The town of Tukuran, just west of Pagadian Bay, Parsons' ultimate goal, had fallen into Japanese hands. It was one of those war rumors that filled the air like flocks of invisible birds of passage. As happened so often in the beginning of this mysterious business, the skipper of the sub was in the dark. But Parsons, being a naval type himself, shared the information with Ambruster and they agreed that they dare not take a chance on Pagadian Bay. He believed that Labangan was "safe" in guerrilla hands and proposed that a day-time contact there would be the best procedure. With reservations concerning possible Japanese air or surface patrols, or possible compromise of the mission by dissident Filipinos, Steve Ambruster agreed.

At 1850, when darkness fell on an empty sea and a desolate shore, Captain Ambruster surfaced while still far off the beach. He removed a light rowboat, or wherry, from the torpedo skids below, upon which it had been lashed, and secured it topside to have it ready and to avoid a noisy operation when the sub was closer to the beach at debarking time. At 0445, on 5 March, the *Tambor* stopped her engines about four miles southeast of Labangan. Visibility, poor throughout the night, was still bad, but under the cloak of it, Parsons and two native soldiers shoved off in the wherry. Clad only in clean but crumpled shirt and shorts, and wearing well-worn, mended shoes, Parsons looked exactly like his native companions.

On reaching the island, the boat was carefully hidden, covered with cane cuttings and other foliage. Chick Parsons then established contact with Fertig who had already learned about the arrival of the party on the incredible man-to-man bamboo wireless. On meeting Fertig, Parsons found him cooperative and ready to help in setting up a low-powered radio intelligence network in the 10th District, especially after Fertig learned that he was now the colonel in command and that supplies were on hand for immediate delivery.

The *Tambor* submerged after Parsons headed shoreward, to keep a watchful eye out for enemy patrols, both sea and air. She remained at periscope depth until late in the afternoon. No opposition was encountered. At 1637, with several hours of daylight remaining, the wherry was sighted flying a white flag as the signal that all was well. As the submerged sub closed the boat, a small power launch, also flying a white flag and towing a native lighter, stood out from the beach. Not long thereafter Captain Ambruster recognized Lieutenant Commander Parsons in the wherry, surfaced, and quickly manned all surface armament, maintaining a listening watch on his sonar gear and posting double lookouts. With the barge alongside and all hatches open, unloading began and was finished within 40 minutes, a speed made possible by Parsons' excellent planning. Without fanfare Ambruster and Parsons bid adieu, and the *Tambor* departed for more aggressive missions to the north—in search of torpedo targets.

Ashore Parsons turned to the task at hand. Fertig was pleasant enough but Parsons was disturbed by the impression that the colonel was more interested in extending his jurisdiction to other islands than in regular guerrilla operations. He seemed to regard his recognition by MacArthur as a hunting permit to expand his area of command and was actually less interested in improving his organization than in enlarging it. That this was true was eventually substantiated when Parsons later discovered that Peralta on Panay, Cushing on Cebu, and Kangeleon on Leyte were aroused against Fertig.

Mindanao is a mountainous and heavily forested island of about 40,000 square miles. At the time of surrender, the USAFFE contingent on the island was commanded by

Brigadier General William F. Sharp and numbered about
30,000 men. The forces had suffered only small losses
during presurrender combat. As on many other islands,
some officers and droves of armed soldiers escaped POW
camps by flight. One of the earliest guerrilla units on
Mindanao was formed by Luis Morgan, a former captain
in the Philippine constabulary, and a Negro named William Tait. Morgan had large dreams but small faith in his
own ability to carry them out. He wanted an American
officer to lead in this task and found him in Lieutenant
Colonel Wendell W. Fertig. The latter had spent some
years in the Islands as a mining engineer and had been a
reserve officer in the U.S. Army Engineer Corps. He was
called to active duty at the outbreak of war and had
served on Bataan.

Fertig, after getting out of Manila by the skin of his
teeth, sought refuge in the Lanao Mountains on Mindanao. Later he let it become known, for the sake of window
dressing to attract local support, that he had come up
from Australia on orders from General MacArthur to or-
ganize guerrillas in the Islands, also that he was in radio
contact with GHQ-Brisbane. Fertig established headquarters in Misamis Occidental Province, which then had
never held an enemy garrison. Morgan was promoted to
Lieutenant Colonel and made chief of staff.

As time went on, Fertig's leadership abilities were
proven when he persuaded other guerrilla leaders on
Mindanao to join his colors. Before the close of the year,
Major Robert V. Bowler and his outfit of 1,000 battle-
wise veterans were in the fold, as was Major Ernest E.
McClish with his unit of similar size. Lieutenant Selipada
Pendatun, and his smaller organization, eventually followed
suit. The first of these independents joined Fertig willingly;
the second, after some hesitation; and the third, now himself a homemade brigadier general, with a show of extremely bad grace.

Commander Parsons' first visit to the Islands began in
March 1943 and ended on 20 July of that year. During
these months he traveled from Mindanao north to Leyte
and visited the islands in between. He went on foot, on
horseback, by canoe, and always in continuous danger of
capture and death by enemy patrols. During his travels,
Parsons established coast-watch posts, met with guerrilla
leaders, coordinated guerrilla units, and made contacts

for future stations of his Spyron radio intelligence network.

At great personal risk, he entered the Bukidnon Valley on Mindanao in June. There he took part in an ambush that destroyed a strong Japanese patrol. On 26 June he was cut off in Misamis Occidental, from which Fertig narrowly made his own escape, by surprise enemy landings. Parsons had to make his way through unmapped mountainous country to rejoin Fertig's forces. According to a citation that won him the Army Distinguished Service Cross, "the brilliant daring and resourcefulness of Lieutenant Commander Parsons enabled him to avoid capture, complete his mission and return to Australia with information of great military value."

To make, if only briefly, an outline of the guerrilla situation in the Islands at the time of Lieutenant Commander Parsons' first of many visits, let us turn to Cebu and the other major islands.

Cebu (1,708 square miles) is a long, narrow finger of an almost completely deforested island that lies to the east of, and roughly parallel to, Negros. The local guerrillas were commanded by Major James Cushing, a mining engineer, and Henry Fenton, a former radio announcer. Cushing was the military commander and a good one. He spent most of his time with his band of well-armed and well-trained men in the field. On treeless Cebu there was little cover, and Cushing's guerrillas often clashed with the Japanese in open engagement, quite contrary to guerrilla tactics on other islands.

Fenton handled administrative matters. Unfortunately, he was given to executing puppet officials and suspected collaborators with or without trials. His off-handed policy brought him into disrepute, but Cushing's stock as a fighting and loyal leader was rising.

The guerrilla leadership on Bohol (1,492 square miles), where the Japanese were inactive, was, at first, contested by Major Achacuso and Lieutenant Inginiero. The latter was endorsed by Colonel Fertig as guerrilla chief. Offsetting this, Lieutenant Colonel McLish of Fertig's own outfit, endorsed Major Achacuso. Lieutenant Inginiero adroitly solved the stalemate by jailing the major for the duration.

On Leyte (3,085 square miles)—where General MacArthur was to land with his troops in 1944—several sectional and warring guerrilla groups spent more time fighting each other than in combating Japanese. The enemy, incidentally, was as inactive on Leyte as they were on Bohol.

On Japanese-infested Luzon (40,420 square miles), because of difficulties and the danger of communications, not much information was available in early 1943, the period covered by this survey. While both Commander Parsons and Major Villamor eventually reached the outskirts of Manila, they wisely refrained from venturing too far into the Japanese tiger's maws. The guerrilla mortality rate on Luzon was high, even among guerrilla leaders. This resulted not only from vigilant Japanese patrols and sharp police work, but also from the high rewards paid to informers and agents. According to the best reports, there were some 29 active guerrilla units on Luzon. These groups were reportedly poorly equipped, without communications, and, generally, badly led. Some of them were, at that time, little more than wolf packs of bandits, and some leaders were regarded as mere opportunists who tried to gain power under cover of wartime confusion. Attempts by various patriotic groups in Manila to coordinate Luzon guerrilla units had failed repeatedly because of jealousies, even betrayals, among the groups. In time, fortunately, that was to change.

On other islands, such as Masbate, Palawan, Samar, and Mindoro, there were small, unorganized guerrilla units. The largest of them were on Samar (5,050 square miles), where a four-way leadership split put the northern and southern groups widely apart.

While Parsons was unable to resolve the problem on Luzon on the first trip, it is to his everlasting credit that he successfully completed his missions in the central and southern islands. Gradually the rivalry between the various factions subsided into more orderly fighting organizations, largely the result of Parsons' persuasion, guidance, and sometimes coercion, not to mention the enticing promise of supplies to be brought in by submarine. Parsons' background was of no little significance in his success. But that is his story.

4

MANILA UNDER THE JAPANESE

Even before General MacArthur declared Manila an open city on 26 December 1941, Lieutenant Charles Parsons, U.S. Naval Reserve, who outwardly was a neutral Philippine-American business executive, had prepared to remain in the battle-ridden city to gather what intelligence he could, unless the Japanese caught him in the act. Therefore, he was not among his fellow Naval Intelligence officers who slipped out of Manila by submarine in February 1942.

Parsons was born in 1902 at Shelbyville, Tennessee. He attended the state university but left, as an undergraduate, to join an uncle who lived in Manila. There he continued his studies at the University of the Philippines. As a youth, he was secretary to General Leonard B. Wood, USA, the governor general of the Islands. After a string of executive positions that increased in responsibility as time went on, Parsons became head of the Luzon Stevedoring Company, a firm with extensive mining, shipping, and storage interests. Because of his deep concern in naval matters, he joined the U.S. Naval Reserve in 1932. In December 1941, now a lieutenant in Naval Intelligence, he was called to active duty in the old District Intelligence Office, at the Port Terminal Building in Manila.

During their victorious entrance into Manila on the night of 2 January 1942, the well-informed Japanese placed seals of belligerence on almost all the British and American business establishments in the city. The seals also included hospitals and clubs. On the streets, teams of Japanese policemen and interpreters searched all automobiles and arrested all American and British residents. Parsons had to go from his home to a hospital that morning on a small errand, but being of medium stature, slim, deeply tanned, with black hair and dark eyes, he easily passed for a Filipino. Phone calls made later to various American and British friends told Parsons that the consensus was to remain at home until the situation stabilized.

The Japanese concentrated their attention on British and Americans so heavily that they paid no heed to increased looting of warehouses by natives. In his official report, Lieutenant Parsons rather pardoned the population for these acts by explaining that native looting, oddly enough, "started when the United States Army Quartermaster, when retiring from Manila and finding that it would not be possible to remove all of the Army supplies stored in their warehouses, opened them to the public; as a result practically the entire population of Manila stormed the Port Area warehouses of the Army and were able to clean out most of the foodstuffs and clothing from these before they were set afire by the retiring Army forces on the night of 31 December."

Continuing on the subject of looting, Parsons wrote: "With the idea having been suggested by the action of the Army, the Insular Government also opened its piers and bonded warehouses to the public to permit the removal of all articles in storage, which consisted largely of foodstuffs. A day or so prior to the entry of the Japanese forces, the local Chinese merchants, who control about ninety percent of the retail grocery trade, also opened their stores to the general public. From that, it may be seen, how looting on a legitimate basis became widespread during the short period between the declaration of Manila as an open city, and the actual occupation of the city by the Japanese. This taste of looting created an appetite for illegal operations that resulted in the subsequent looting of warehouses which had not been opened to the public."

In conversations held with Japanese businessmen of Manila, such as Mr. Ikeda, assistant manager of Mitsubishi; Mr. Fukada, head of the sugar department of Mitsui Bussan Kaisha; Mr. Ishida, manager of Mitsubishi; and others, all of whom had been drafted by the military authorities to assist in handling the economic situation, Lieutenant Parsons learned that the Japanese military authorities were quite disappointed to find Manila so thoroughly stripped of its supply of gasoline, lubricating oil, fuel oil, money, and food-stuffs, all of which the public had been given a free hand to loot.

"These businessmen visited me," he observed, "at my home in search of information concerning the location of the fleet of lighters and tugboats which—it was common knowledge—belonged to the Luzon Stevedoring Company. These visits were started on the day of occupation and continued at regular intervals during the entire period of my internment at home. During the visits, I prolonged the conversations as long as possible so that I could get a general picture of the activities of the Japanese, and especially learn of their difficulties from first-hand information."

On 3 January the Japanese started picking up American and British nationals at their homes. They went from house to house with trucks and busses and advised the people to take with them a blanket and food for about three days, as they were being taken for "registration" only. As the collection went on, Lieutenant Parsons happened to remember that he was the honorary Panamian Consul for the Philippines, and decided to use that as an excuse to avoid being picked up, which would leave him in a better position to gather information.

"I found," he wrote, "a Panamanian flag among the toys of my children which I placed in the window of my residence. When the Japanese reached my house, I had already perfected the story of being entitled to diplomatic immunity, and had no difficulty in convincing the officer in charge.

"The American and British nationals were taken to Santo Tomas University, where they were advised that they should send to their homes to secure mattresses, mosquito nets and food for a 'few more days' as registration would take longer than originally thought necessary. They did not know that the policy of the Japanese was to intern 100% of the so-called belligerent nationals for the duration of the war.

"The invaders showed little or no consideration for the American and British nationals and, when picking them up for internment, they were herded into open military trucks guarded by young soldier-sentries who, in many cases, pushed the internees around or slapped them (usually when out of sight of an officer), and taken to a concentration point at the Rizal Stadium, where they were forced to remain for two days with only the meager supply of food brought by themselves, and no place to sleep. This would have been a hardship to men alone, not to mention suffering caused to the women, women with small babies, and older men and women. The young and fit did all they could for the women and children, but the manner in which the non-combatant civilians were treated was shameful, inhuman and entirely uncalled for, and their difficulties continued even when the internment camp was established at the Santo Tomas University. Only the efforts and initiative of the internees themselves made the camp a model little city, and one which would be representative of a small town in any of the rural areas of the United States."

As soon as the enemy nationals had been interned safely, the next move of the Japanese was to collect all automobiles that belonged to these people, and confiscate their homes, observed Lieutenant Parsons. He went on: "This gained for them some six-thousand units, and a number of quarters for themselves. The better ones were earmarked for occupancy by high officials of the invading forces; the smaller houses, being unoccupied by the tenants, were soon subjected to looting.

"Next, the Japanese took, with lightning speed, to freezing all business, not only of Americans and British, but also all business of Filipino and third party neutrals in the Islands. They also set up a provisional government for the city of Manila. The Japanese quickly learned their mistake in the wholesale wrecking of business in the Islands because their economic problem expanded rapidly. But, it was then too late to remedy the situation, as they had gone too far in immobilizing enemy nationals."

He continued: "Shortly after the occupation of Manila, there began to arrive there from Japan, Japanese civilians who had previously been connected with Philippine organizations. They were usually brought in by airplane. In most cases, they were assigned as civilian helpers of the Japanese Army and Navy units, and were given the task of studying the mix-up in the business of Manila, and to suggest remedies.

"I had the opportunity of talking with several of these men and they frankly admitted that their task was hopeless. First of all, they found that the retiring United States forces had effectively destroyed all existing stocks of gasoline, diesel and bunker fuels, and lubricating oils; that all vessels, which could have been used for inter-island transportation, had been scuttled; that practically all motor trucks had been requisitioned by the U.S. Army and Navy in Manila during December, and had been taken to Bataan with the forces, or had been destroyed if left in Manila. The invading Japanese forces had removed all stocks of foodstuffs from warehouses and moved them to central points for distribution to the Japanese armed forces in the field. As for the banks, they had no cash on hand and no gold in their vaults, it having been turned over to the Insular Treasury during the latter part of December for removal from Manila to Corregidor (and later taken to Hawaii by submarine) to prevent its falling into the hands of the Japanese. All factories in Manila had been closed. In order to re-open, a license, issued by the Japanese military administration, would be necessary. There were many other difficulties, all of which made the picture a rather bleak one for the Japanese civilians who were given the task of reestablishing normal commercial conditions. They found that factories could not be re-opened unless a supply of base products could be furnished, such as coconuts in the case of oleomargarine factories. Without transportation facilities, this would be almost an impossibility. Also such factories would require, in most cases, a supply of diesel or crude oil, lubricating oil, spare parts, etc., etc. At the time of my departure from the Philippines, the various departments of the Japanese economic administration, with all their experts, were still at a loss as to how factories could be re-opened."

Being Consul for Panama in the Philippines, Lieutenant Parsons was interned at his residence from the beginning of the occupation of Manila until 22 April 1942. On that date the Japanese military authorities decided that he was not entitled to a "diplomatic" status and transferred him to Santo Tomas. Fortunately, at no time did the enemy associate him with Naval Intelligence. Had he been detected, or even suspected, his life story would have been a much shorter one.

"The Swedish Consul for the Philippines, Mr. Helge Jansen, represented my interests with the foreign department established with the Japanese forces in Manila," recalled Lieutenant Parsons, "and it was through his efforts that I eventually was scheduled for repatriation in June, 1942.

"From the first day of their occupation of Manila, the Japanese claimed a desire to win the friendship of the

Filipinos," Parsons noted. "They have assured the Filipinos freedom from molestation, freedom of religious thought, and have offered them in return for their liberation from the yoke of Americanism, a place in the Greater Asia Co-prosperity Sphere. They have asked for the cooperation of the Filipinos in their efforts to return the Philippines to normalcy, promising a brilliant future when normal conditions were gained again.

"The propaganda corps of the Japanese Army has set up agencies throughout the provinces, and sent speaking groups, usually made up of well-known Filipino politicians together with carefully selected English-speaking Japanese officers. These groups outlined the 'true meaning' of the Japanese intentions, and have, in each case, pleaded for the cooperation of the natives.

"Undoubtedly some of this propaganda has had temporary results, but the Japanese could never undo the work of the Americans over the past forty years. The Japanese caused the Filipinos to be discouraged and, in many cases, to feel that they had been abandoned by the Americans, and that the Islands may not be retaken by the American forces. They were taught to feel that the Japanese were a powerful nation, and one which could not be beaten by the Americans. Such thoughts could only be of a temporary nature and would surely disappear as soon as some sort of visible effort of U.S. forces to return to the Philippines became apparent."

On the subject of atrocities, Lieutenant Parsons observed that Manila was particularly free from them. "But stories from reliable sources," he said, "continually seeped into Manila from the outlying provinces—looting of farms, rape of women, killing of people for 'military offenses,'" etc. "In cases of the more crowded centers and more populated areas, the Japanese soldiers have been kept pretty well in hand, but in some of the smaller places, and especially on isolated farms, the story has been quite different. Several executions have been published in the Manila newspaper, usually of well-meaning Filipinos caught in the act of sabotage or looting. It is also rumored, but not confirmed, that some of the members of the oil company staffs of Cebu were executed for having destroyed oil stocks.

"An item of interest is the return to Manila of Japanese who have resided and worked in the Philippines for several years prior to the emergency. One such case in particular is that of T. (Pete) Yamanouchi, who came to the Philippines about five years ago as an assistant to Bonney Powell, Fox Movietone Newsreel cameraman. Yamanouchi resigned from Movietone in Manila and took a position as art teacher at the Philippine Women's College. In addition to teaching, he opened, at his house, a minicam* [photo] laboratory. He also took assignments from commercial firms and others to photograph their enterprises for advertising and publicity purposes. He was an excellent photographer and a good artist, consequently his services were much in demand. He was also in an excellent position to record photographically strategic points throughout the Islands, as his work took him to every corner of the archipelago.

"Another case of interest along these lines is that of Mr. Yamaka (or Yamada), who called on me at my home during the month of March, after having been flown to Manila from Davao. He brought me a list of Americans and British interned at Davao, and gave me first hand information of the situation in that district. He is now residing in the house of Don Andres Soriano, who left Manila as an officer in the USAFFE forces, and says he is holding the residence for the chief of staff of the Japanese Navy, so as to prevent the Japanese Army getting hold of the house for one of their ranking officers. He told me that he was an American citizen, having been born and educated in the U.S. He and Yamanouchi do not seem to feel that they have done anything out of the ordinary in having enjoyed the hospitality of the Americans and then later taking sides with the Japanese.

"Of one thing I am absolutely certain," continued Lieutenant Parsons, "and that is that Secretary Jorge S. Vargas is loyal to President Quezon's government and to the United States. He considers that it is best that he do what he is doing for the best interests of the Filipino people, with a definite idea of preventing suffering as much as possible, than to let the Japanese authorities deal through politically ambitious Filipinos who are not loyal to the previous government.

"The majority of the members of the government, headed by Secretary Vargas, can be counted upon for their

---

*A minicam is a small camera using film of 35 mm. or less.

loyalty—in other words, they are in the same boat as Vargas is—although a few of these men have undoubtedly shown indications of being pro-Japanese."

In summarizing the situation as it existed in the Philippine Islands after occupation by the Japanese, Lieutenant Parsons wrote:

"The American, British and other Allied nationals are completely immobilized, and interned at Manila and in other internment camps in the provinces. Conditions in these camps are getting worse as food and funds get scarce, and morale is definitely deteriorating. Even so, the range of hopes for the return of American forces ran from Independence Day, 1942, the earliest, to Thanksgiving Day, 1942, the very latest day for relief to come.

"The economic situation of the country, as a whole, is very bad. Practically all commerce has been paralyzed, and chances of the Japanese being able to restore a situation that will even approximate normalcy are extremely slender. Unemployment is widespread. Earning power of the Filipinos, as well as of all other nationals in the Islands, has been reduced to an alarming low, and nothing so far has been done to remedy the situation.

"The political situation, so far as the puppet government is concerned, is satisfactory from our standpoint, as the officials charged with the administration of the government (under supervision and control of the Japanese military authorities) may be considered, with few exceptions, to be loyal to the United States.

"Treatment of nationals by the invaders, except in isolated cases, has been fair. There have been some excutions and numerous cases of people having been slapped for minor offenses, usually for failing to bow to a sentry. In Manila, Filipinos are to be found daily hanging by their wrists from trees in busy sections, serving punishment for having been caught looting. But, in general, there seems to be no concerted effort on the part of the Japanese to maltreat the people. In fact, the Japanese seem to want to gain the friendship of the Filipinos and neutrals and spend lots of time on the radio and with other propaganda to try to convince the Filipinos that their purpose is to undo all of the harm done during the past forty years by the Americans and to bring prosperity to the Philippines."

After the fall of Bataan, the prisoners of war from that sector were marched to San Fernando, Pampanga, and from there to Camp O'Donnell, near Capas, Tarlac, where they were still imprisoned when Parsons left the Philippines early in June. The physical condition of the prisoners during the early days of imprisonment he described as deplorable and the mortality rate quite high.

"Malaria and dysentery took a heavy toll in the prison camp, due principally to a lack of medicine and medical equipment, and a shortage of water," he said. "Prisoners used the dirty water from a nearby stream for drinking, bathing and washing for the first two weeks, or until engineers from the Tarlac Sugar Central volunteered to install a pumping unit for piping in a supply of suitable water for drinking purposes. The Red Cross in Manila solicited the town for medical supplies, spare clothing, and services of doctors, but had a difficult time in getting the cooperation of the Japanese military authorities to permit the Red Cross help reaching the prisoners.

"In the early days of the establishment of the O'Donnell prison camp, when the conditions were the worst, deaths among the prisoners amounted to about 350 daily, the ratio of deaths being 8.1 Filipinos to American soldiers, out of an estimated prison population of 65,000 where the ratio of Filipinos to Americans is roughly 6.1. After the camp had been cleaned up through the efforts and initiative of the prisoners themselves, and after the water supply had been improved, deaths were reduced to about 150 daily, with the death ratio between the Americans and Filipino soldiers being about the same."

Lieutenant Parsons, who winnowed every possible source of information, said that it was not very easy to get detailed data concerning the various mines throughout the Islands, due mostly to their isolated locations; however, most of the gold mines were believed to have become flooded in their underground workings, due to powerhouse shutdowns. It is understood that the Japanese stripped the powerhouses and mills of generating equipment, miscellaneous small motors, and were keen to grab tools and spare parts. As a rule, factories were not destroyed and may be restored.

"In general, it may be assumed that the Japanese invaders will reap no benefits from gold production," he observed. "Up to the present time they have shown no interest in reopening the gold mines.

"With reference to the base metals, I was approached

early after the occupation by Japanese military and civilian officials for information as to the stocks of manganese and chrome ores, as well as to the status of the Luzon Stevedoring Company's mines, from which we had supplied the largest percentage of manganese ore shipped from the Islands during the preceding four years. Also, regarding the status and stocks at our Cagayan chrome mine.

"A delegation of Japanese civilians, belonging to the Pacific Mining Company, who had been returned to Manila to take over and operate base metal mines, took me to the office of our mining department, forced me to open locked files and safe, and took all records found in the office. From these, they would gather little, if any, information on copper ore.

"After a month or so of surveying the general situation, Mr. E. Namikawa, president of the Pacific Mining Company, made me a firm proposition to join his company as a consultant at a salary of 1,000 pesos per month, with a free automobile, and freedom from internment for myself and family. This was the first such offer made to me, and I have no knowledge of an offer of employment being offered to any other American or British national.

"I asked Mr. Namikawa how he could make me such an offer, and have it approved by the Japanese military authorities. He showed me a Japanese communication, which he purported contained authority to offer me the position; but he stated that he had secured the authority on the basis that I was a Panamanian citizen and not an American. I stalled for time, thinking for a while that such a contact might place me in a position of getting much firsthand information as to the activities of the Japanese. Eventually, I decided to refuse and manufactured as many excuses as possible to have my refusal of the offer to be taken without hard feelings. I did not want to be forced to work with the organization sent to control base metals. Due to the unusualness of the offer, I can only believe that the Japanese are not capable of working out a method of reopening the base metal mining industry—not even to the extent of locating and shipping out the present stocks of base metals existing in various parts of the Islands."

Parsons was aware that the quantity of manganese and other base metal ores on hand and ready for shipment upon occupation of the Islands was much above normal stocks. This was because of the lack of shipping facilities during the last few months of 1941. "The Luzon Stevedoring Company had on hand approximately 80,000 tons of manganese ore under contract for delivery in the U.S. This ore, I feared, would undoubtedly fall into the hands of the invaders. But the actual shipment of much of it from the Islands would be extremely difficult, as it was located at points where lighterage from shore to vessel would be required. There is a shortage of lighterage equipment and of tow-boats, so that it is unlikely that the Japanese will be able to undertake shipment of the managnese ore at outports for several months."

One day, after Parsons was interned, two Japanese mining experts came to his place of internment, with Namikawa of the Pacific Mining Company. They asked Parsons to fly with them to Busuanga to show them the mining property there, to explain the operations, and how best to restart them. This, strangely, was while Busuanga Island was still in the hands of USAFFE troops. Parsons declined to visit the mine and advised them that he was only nominally at the head of the operating company. Details of operation would be the responsibility of the manager of the mining department of the company. None of them showed any interest in getting the mining department head, Mr. Russell, out of the Santo Tomas Internment Camp to give them the information. "In this case, as on previous visits," said Parsons, "they found it convenient to consider me as a Panamanian and persona grata with the military authorities. In the case of an internee of Santo Tomas, they knew that they could not secure approval by the military authorities."

Until 3 June, when Lieutenant Parsons was set free from the internment camp, he lived in fearful, hourly expectations of being seized for forced labor for the Japanese mining interests, or of having his carefully hidden Naval Intelligence identity disclosed. So many Japanese were now around who had known him in prewar days and just might recall his activities as a naval reserve junior officer. But none of them did. So it was with a feeling of deep relief when he, his wife Katsy, and their two boys left Manila aboard the Japanese hospital ship, *Ural Maru*, for Takao, with its cargo of diplomatic refugees on 4 June 1942. From there, the passengers went by air to Shanghai and boarded the diplomatic exchange vessel *Conte Verde* from which the diplomatic exchanges were effected

at Lourenco Marques, Mozambique, on the east coast of
Africa. Here the homeward-bound Americans boarded
the liner *Gripsholm* and reached New York on 12 August
1942.

Aboard the Swedish liner, Charles Parsons, feeling for
the first time really free and secure, composed his extensive and comprehensive report on Manila and the Philippines in a single-spaced, typewritten report that covered 51
closely covered pages. The report was delivered by hand
at the Navy Department in Washington, where this top secret document met with a very hush-hush but enthusiastic reception. Next he delivered on request a copy and full
verbal report to army intelligence. This was the first reliable report out of Manila since the Japanese took over
and its rich contents threw light into many hitherto
dark corners.

When Lieutenant Parsons reported at the Navy Department, he seemed as one risen from the dead. In May 1942,
he had been listed "missing in action"; now, three months
later, he was "declared safe," promoted to Lieutenant
Commander and slated for continuing intelligence work
in the diplomatic field.

"When I first arrived back in the States," observed
Parsons recently, "Naval Intelligence believed that, since I
actually became 'officially established' as a member of the
Panamanian Consular Corps, I could be developed into a
useful observer, either in Spain or perhaps in one of the
South American countries. It was thought advisable that
I spend my time in Washington with Ambassador Jaen-
Guardia, brushing up on Panamanian Consular affairs,
with the idea of being assigned to a Panamanian Embassy
or Consulate at some future date.

"In the questioning period which I underwent at the
Pentagon, handled by the FBI, Naval Intelligence and
Army Intelligence, the information was sent to MacArthur, and, as the story goes, as soon as he saw the information which I had been able to record as an observer in
Manila during the first six months of the occupation by the
Japanese Military Forces, he made an urgent request that I
be sent to Australia to join him and asked that his request
be given high priority.

"The Joint Chiefs of Staff had a ticklish ruling to
handle in my case, as it was indicated by MacArthur that
he planned eventually to send me back to the Philippines

to coordinate the activities of the guerrillas (and the Navy had in mind that I could assist greatly in establishing Coast Watcher stations to help supply submarine targets). At the time, it was contrary to the rule to the effect that once a man in the military service had been able to escape from a territory held by the enemy, he would not be permitted to return to the same territory, as he would not have the benefit of the never-applied conditions of International Military Law.

"After I had signed away any such privileges, the ruling was set aside in my case, and I eventually went out to MacArthur's GHQ. As I remember, this was all being done during the Christmas Holiday season of 1942 and I was able to wrangle a stay with my family until after the New Year so that I left Washington the 2nd or 3rd of January, 1943, arriving in Australia the 4th or 5th."

Immediately on arrival, Commander Parsons was assigned to AIB and placed in charge of an ambitious project to establish high- and low-power radio units in guerrilla forces all over the Islands. These would transmit their coded information to an advanced Navy radio station to be installed on Mindanao. There the data would be sifted and either forwarded to GHQ-Brisbane or passed on to fleet units for operational information. Commander Parsons would also continue the work begun by Major Villamor, to strengthen and unify guerrilla leadership in all Central and Southern Islands to a point where they would be eligible to meet the standards set by General MacArthur for recognition.

It was Parsons' iron nerves, cool daring, and sublime skill that made the end products of the submarine guerrilla runs bear full fruit, created a radio spy ring (dubbed Spyron) that covered the Islands, and helped make a proud fighting force out of a ragged bunch of Filipinos who proudly proclaimed themselves "MacArthur's Own."

5

HOW TO GET A SPY
INTO MANILA

While Parsons roamed the Islands, guerrilla submarines were not idle. Delivery of supplies and equipment to the recognized military district leaders was stepped up as fast as submarines became available.

The *Gudgeon* under the command of Lieutenant Commander Stovall had made the first guerrilla sub run putting Major Villamor ashore on Negros island. Now *Gudgeon* made her second and last visit to guerrilla land in April 1943, this time commanded by Lieutenant Commander W. S. ("Bill") Post, Jr. She carried 6,000 pounds of equipment to Panay to supply the forces of Lieutenant Colonel Peralta, officially designated commander, 6th Military District. Aboard, as well, was a military party consisting of Second Lieutenant Torribio Crespo, U.S. Army, and three enlisted men. All were of Filipino descent.

Lieutenant Crespo turned out to be quite a character. In the words of Skipper Post: "Crespo led his men well and was a good shipmate. Upon our departure from Fremantle he was a gay swashbuckler, but as we approached Panay he became more serious. He studied and restudied his orders, and tried to prepare his group for any imaginable contingency. A day or two before the landing he asked, 'What shall I do if my orders get wet?' Our gallant and resourceful Lieutenant Tex Penland, who was to give his own life a few days later, had the answer. He stepped to the medical kit, found an appropriate rubber prophylactic, and handed it to Crespo. The wardroom roared. Crespo's problem was solved, and he recovered his derring-do before his D-Day."

While Panay bound from Fremantle, Post was shocked to discover that none of the army men had the slightest conception of how to load or handle a rubber boat. He took time out long enough to give them a rudimentary course in boat handling in Exmouth Gulf, at the top of western Australia. As the skipper describes it: "The rehearsal at Exmouth Gulf was a mini-scale version of a rehearsal for an amphibious landing. Each of Lieutenant Crespo's men and every submariner assigned to the landing party had his station in an inflatable rubber boat, and specific cargo he was to stow and discharge. We flooded *Gudgeon* down so that the deck was almost at a level with the boats. The cargo was loaded, the boats away, and backloading accomplished according to plan."

Once again underway for Panay all was serene until on the thirteenth day out of Fremantle, while running on the surface in the early morning twilight, the skipper, who was asleep in the conning tower, was jolted awake by the cry of a lookout: "Object on the starboard bow!" Post grabbed his binoculars and hit the bridge. There in the distant haze was a large tanker, a prize target.

"Clear the bridge! Dive, dive, dive!"

At periscope depth he began an approach for torpedo attack. After running for over an hour at full speed he still was not able to close the radically zigzagging target. Exasperated, he decided to surface and try an end around to get into position ahead of the tanker. With his batteries badly discharged from the high-speed submerged run, he was able to put only two main engines on propulsion while the other two were put on battery charge. This combination unfortunately did not give him enough speed to overtake the target, so, reluctantly, he broke off the contact.

Much has been said and written about the torpedo problems that plagued our submariners in the early stages of World War II. Here is a typical example. In his patrol report Post wrote: "Upon securing from this unsuccessful attack, torpedoes in the tubes which had been flooded were pulled and checked.* It was found that out of six torpedoes: two exploders, three gyros and five afterbodies had been flooded. Spent most of the day working over torpedoes and trying to dry out exploders."

It was a wise decision, because just before midnight

---

*As a submarine approaches the firing point the outer doors on the selected torpedo tubes are opened, flooding the tubes. If the fish are not fired they are usually pulled and inspected. (Authors' note.)

Gudgeon ran into another contact. Post began tracking. The target was making 17.5 knots on a base course of about 190°, zigzagging 40 degrees on each side of base course every five minutes. He tentatively identified the ship as the *Kamakura Maru*. One hour and fifteen minutes after contact, Post fired a spread of four torpedoes, the last he had in the forward tubes. Twelve minutes later he watched the *Kamakura Maru* sink.

In his report on this action, Post wrote that he returned to the spot where the *Maru* went down. "Came abreast about a dozen lifeboats, floating debris, oil, and swimming Japs, all covering several acres. Sounded like Dante's Inferno. We have been having radar interference* all day, the boat was already overcrowded, and we still had our special mission to accomplish, so decided that rescue of survivors either for humanitarian reasons or to furnish more positive identification of ship sunk could not be accomplished without detriment to our mission. Submerged to give crew a day of rest."

On 29 April, two days after the successful torpedo attack, the *Gudgeon* reached her objective, the vicinity of Pucio Point, and submerged a mile and a half off Pandan. Post spent the entire day running at periscope depth one mile off the coast between Pandan and Pucio Point, conducting submerged reconnaissance in accordance with his special instructions issued by Rear Admiral Ralph Christie, Commander, Task Force 71. Following a conference with Lieutenant Crespo, it was decided that the best landing spot was 3.7 miles east of Pucio Point. After sunset *Gudgeon* surfaced 1800 yards off the selected site. Lieutenant Crespo went ashore with Sergeant Orlando Alfabeto in a rubber boat, which they handled fairly well, for close reconnaissance and to make contacts. As they did not return with morning twilight the sub went under to await nightfall. During the day the *Gudgeon* patrolled off the town of Libertad.

Captain Post hardly expected to see Crespo come out in broad daylight and yet he secretly hoped that he would show some signs that he and everything ashore was all right. He got no such assurance, and as the day wore on, he began to worry. On surfacing just after dark at a pre-

---

*Radar interference is an indication that other ships or aircraft are in the vicinity, the range cannot be determined and it is almost impossible to determine if it is friend or foe.

selected point, Lieutenant Crespo, much to Post's relief, returned. The Lieutenant reported that he made his first contact ashore in the early morning of that day, when he met up with a beach patrol of Peralta's Volunteer Guards. He was taken to their nearby headquarters where he identified himself and was given a cordial welcome. In the course of the day he established contact with army authorities and obtained some very vital, secret information which he passed on to the skipper.

"I discovered," said Crespo, "that it was possible for a Filipino to enter Manila by taking a sailing boat from some Jap-occupied area and, posing as a merchant from that area, land at Batangas, go to the Municipal building of Bauan and at the cost of one peso get a residence certificate. With this certificate, one may enter Manila—after being searched at the city limits by armed guards."

Crespo paused briefly and continued, "I was told that enlisted men have entered the city by riding in the cab of a loaded truck. No identification is required to obtain a residence certificate. However, the applicant must say he is a merchant from occupied territory and is 'playing ball' with the boys from Nippon."

The lieutenant also reported that the Japanese had installed heavy guns, 10 inches or larger, along the beach at the once-popular Los Tamaraos Polo Club on Manila Bay facing west toward Corregidor. Los Tamaraos was once the playground of the wealthy Spanish-Filipino aristocracy. Before the war it had even boasted a talented and popular photographer—one Pete Yamanouchi, a Japanese. No doubt he had surveyed and photographed these beaches where the guns were now emplaced.

This intelligence, simple as it seemed, was nonetheless priceless to GHQ-Brisbane. Unloading of the cargo from the *Gudgeon* began soon after Crespo returned. By using two seven-man rubber boats, and two five-man boats, plus all hands working energetically, the cargo was taken on deck, loaded, and rowed ashore, all in one trip.

The off-loading accomplished, Lieutenant Crespo returned to the *Gudgeon* with a Major Garcia, the senior guerrilla officer in the vicinity, and his second, a Filipino army captain. Post was particularly impressed with Garcia, whom he described as "an exceptionally intelligent and capable officer." The major told the Skipper that the Japanese were, for the time being, treating the Filipinos in the

outlying provinces very well and making strenuous efforts
to restore normal trade conditions. Garcia was proud. Post
reported, of the fanatical morale and achievements of his
troops in minor combat, but deprecated their lack of
equipment. "He stated confidently," Commander Post
wrote, "that with 1000 rifles and 500,000 rounds of ammunition they could retake Panay."

After transferring torpedoes from aft to the forward
torpedo tubes, a hazardous operation because the submarine was rendered incapable of diving for about four
hours, Captain Post aimed his ship northward and proceeded at full speed to his assigned hunting grounds. He
radioed CTF 71, "Mission accomplished."

He left highly enthusiastic about the guerrillas and
with "renewed confidence in our allies behind the lines and
admiration for the zest with which they handled their
arduous and hazardous tasks." His report closed with the
observation: "As long as a torpedo shortage exists, it
seems feasible and highly desirable that every submarine
bound for the Philippines or the South China Sea carry
what men and equipment it can to these troops who are
on the spot and capable of seriously harassing the enemy."

In May and June, Lieutenant Commander A. H. Clark,
commanding the *Trout*, made two quick, successive guerrilla runs. On 26 May 1943 she delivered a party of six or
seven army men, $10,000 in Japanese Occupation money
and 2 tons of equipment on Basilan Island in the Sulu
group, which lies southwest from Mindanao, and was part
of Colonel Fertig's 10th District. These men were to extend Spyron's secret intelligence network in the Sulu and
Zamboanga areas. In addition, they were to set up coast-
watchers and arrange for delivery of supplies to guerrillas.
Clark encountered no opposition on this mission.

The second run was not so uneventful for *Trout*.
The mission was to land a party of two army officers and
three soldiers under the command of Captain J. A. Hamner, USA, near Labangan, Pagadian Bay, on the southwest
shore of Mindanao.

On the morning of 11 June, one day before the scheduled rendezvous, *Trout* was running submerged to avoid
detection as Clark approached the landing site. On a routine periscope sweep a small Japanese observation plane
was sighted. Apparently the submarine was not detected
and Clark passed it off as an insignificant incident. That

night, running on the surface (showing no lights, of course), *Trout* suddenly encountered two patrol boats in Illana Bay, which was too near the rendezvous for comfort. One of them opened fire and Clark dove to avoid the attack. Now he *was* suspicious that his operation had been compromised. Perhaps, he thought, it was not mere coincidence that first there was an air patrol in the area, then later at night, surface patrols near the prearranged rendezvous. While the opposition could not be called formidable it was, if nothing else, significant.

At dusk on 12 June Clark sighted the proper security signals on the beach and shortly thereafter cautiously surfaced. All clear. A small steam launch appeared out of nowhere and after a brief exchange of recognition signals by dim, hooded flashlight tubes, the launch moored alongside. Unloading of cargo and ammunition began immediately. The ubiquitous Chick Parsons appeared on board, much to Clark's astonishment.

The skipper took the opportunity to warn Parsons of the possibility of prearranged rendezvous being compromised. He related his experience of the previous day and night and suggested that perhaps too many natives knew about the clandestine submarine landings. Parsons seemed slightly amused but agreed when Clark urged that different landing points should be used for future missions. Parsons did not mention that, even this early in the game, patriotic Filipinos were building morale in the Islands by assuring the early arrival of the American Army of Liberation and using as proof the delivery of American and Australian goods by submarine. This was absolutely contrary to the U.S. policy of strict secrecy concerning these operations. But the Filipinos argued that since the Japanese could not patrol 7,000 islands, mostly surrounded by deep, unminable waters, the desperate need for morale-lifting propaganda offset the danger of compromising a submarine mission. They apparently did not consider the potential danger to the submarine itself. Anyway, they were grateful but did not remain silent. Parsons was powerless to muzzle them and he worried that this development would reach the ears of the submariners who might balk at making future contacts with the guerrillas.

This mission completed, *Trout* proceeded on combat patrol in an assigned area not too distant from the Philippine Archipelago, with orders to wait for future instruc-

tions. These came within three weeks. Clark was directed
to contact Commander Parsons at a designated point on
the west coast of Mindanao, take aboard his party and
proceed to a rendezvous in an area southeast of Olutanga
Island south of Mindanao.

As usual when operating with Parsons, the contact was
made exactly on time and without a hitch. Parsons knew
the necessity of being punctual when keeping a date with a
United States submarine. The commander and four U.S.
naval officers came aboard. It was 9 July.

Welcoming ceremonies over, as informal as they were,
and introductions made, Clark headed south wondering
"what the hell this was all about." Parsons did not offer
any explanation nor did Clark ask for any. However, during the course of conversations en route to the rendezvous,
the commander revealed that on 26 June Japanese forces
had made a surprise landing and occupied Misamis in
the northern end of Mindanao—and incidentally (or was
it?) the location of Colonel Fertig's headquarters. The
colonel fell back to a prepared position but it proved untenable. He was driven out of it by a Japanese force of
some 150 to 200 men, which does not sound overwhelming except when one considers that the defenders numbered a mere handful of men. Fertig made for the hills in
the nearby province of Lanao, his old home. Parsons, with
his usual modesty, did not mention that he too had been
cut off by this surprise landing and had had to beat his
way back through unfamiliar and unmapped rugged mountainous country to rejoin Fertig.

With a note of disgust Parsons disclosed to Clark that
the internal strife among certain self-proclaimed guerrilla
leaders on Mindanao had erupted again.

As mentioned previously, when Colonel Fertig was officially designated Commander, 10th Military District, he
appointed as his chief of staff Luis Morgan with the rank
of Lieutenant Colonel, a rank Morgan could never have at-
tained elsewhere under any other circumstances. Later it
became evident that Morgan regretted having relinquished
to Fertig his early advantage as the self-proclaimed leader of the largest guerrilla group on Mindanao, even though
he had fervently hoped that such a man as Fertig would
come along and take over the responsibility for which he
felt inadequate. Morgan was a man of great ambition and

little ability. His timidity grew into animosity as Fertig demonstrated his leadership by consolidating his command. Morgan began playing around with the several dissident factotums who fancied themselves as commanders of potent guerrilla units. As a matter of fact their units were insignificant as to strength and effectiveness, and were being exploited only for their leaders' personal gains. One such chief had gone so far that, in a huff, he had surrendered his entire unit to the enemy. Another, a Major Limona, who had led a long-standing mutiny, fell into line with Morgan. But Fertig retained control of his command and his internal dilemma was partially solved when Morgan was finally persuaded to get out of the Islands by submarine and go to Australia (a sop to his vanity), from where he was never heard of again. Order was eventually restored to the guerrilla ranks when the last of the renegade leaders threw in their lot with Fertig. Parsons did not say how or who engineered it, but Clark had his own private opinions. It is possible that some of the tempting array of weapons, bullets, and supplies being consistently supplied by American submarines had something to do with it. Parsons did not elaborate.

Arriving at the rendezvous at dawn, Clark dove *Trout* and conducted periscope reconnaissance of the area. In the late afternoon a small launch belching heavy black smoke, unmistakably from a wood-fired boiler, was observed steaming aimlessly in the vicinity of the rendezvous. She was camouflaged with tree limbs but boldly flew the American flag. Parsons took a look through the periscope and, smiling engagingly, turned to Clark and said: "That's my boy!"

When the *Trout* surfaced at sunset five miles northwest of Liscum Bank, Parsons and party transferred to the launch and departed for destination unknown. Clark suddenly felt lonely and wished he knew where Parsons was going. But he didn't, and he never found out because seven months later, on the last day of February 1944, *Trout* went down to enemy action and Commander Albert Hobbs Clark, U.S. Naval Academy, Class of 1933, graduate number 11255, went with her, and with him he took some very intimate thoughts, probably not the least of which concerned his feelings about the guerrillas and his admiration of them and of Parsons.

After leaving *Trout* Parsons seemed to disappear from the face of the earth. All of a sudden, toward the end of July, he reappeared at GHQ-Brisbane. How he got there was quite mysterious, but that was par for the course for Lieutenant Commander Charles Parsons.

6

SEWING MACHINE NEEDLES AND PADRE KITS

When Parsons returned to Australia from his first lengthy trip to the Islands, he found that the intelligence setup at GHQ had undergone a radical change. At the time of his departure in February 1943, Philippine affairs had been in the hands of the Allied Intelligence Bureau headed by Colonel C. G. Roberts, an Australian intelligence officer. His deputy was Major Allison Ind, a U.S. Army Air Corps intelligence officer who had seen service in Manila. Between the two of them they could muster a better-than-average understanding of the Philippines, and it was adequate in 1942. But in 1943 the accelerated activity and volume of reports from the Islands brought increasing pressure on AIB, whose responsibilities mushroomed into the entire area from Saigon to the New Hebrides. MacArthur came to the conclusion that this operation needed a change.

The opportunity to make it came in the late spring of 1943, when Colonel Courtney Whitney arrived in Australia from the States. With his broad understanding of the Islands, keen perception, and energetic initiative, he was tailor-made for the job of heading MacArthur's new Philippine section, a semi-independant extension of Colonel Willoughby's intelligence department. Major Ind continued as his deputy. Time proved this change highly beneficial to the guerrilla campaign in the Philippines. Whitney was open to new ideas and had a strong desire to get results. He was also a top-hole intelligence officer, a masterful interrogator, and a fine judge of men, with a great capacity for getting along with people. His former associates described him as "rugged and aggressive; a fearless leader."

Parsons reported to Whitney immediately upon his arrival in Australia. He told him of his successes, and failures, in establishing coast-watcher stations and the Spyron network. He briefed him on the guerrilla leadership problem and enthusiastically endorsed the establishment of definitive military districts. He also strongly supported the stipulations, promulgated by AIB before Whitney's arrival, that guerrilla leaders had to comply with in order to receive support from GHQ, but he warned that certain chiefs might give only lip service to the regulations and would have to be watched closely. Whitney wasn't fooled —he sensed that Parsons was paving his way for an early return to the Islands. He was quite right, of course.

The colonel listened attentively, nodding his head occasionally in approval. He was not surprised at Parsons' successes, or his failures, and least of all at his inherent modesty. Whitney had known him for many years in Manila and had watched him grow into the successful businessman that he was.

Now it was the colonel's time to speak. He leveled his piercing gray-blue eyes directly at Parsons, and said:

"Chick, you've done a grand job but there is much more to be done as you well know. But you worry me a little bit. You're rather reckless. You know, don't you, that the Japanese have put a price on your head? A hundred thousand dollars? I wish to God you'd become more cautious, and with that kind of money you'd better be careful with whom you associate. Will you give me a written report on this trip?"

Parsons' report was not stilted in crisp military lingo. It was more narrative than a formal report. He wrote:

It is obvious that we have to rearm the guerrillas quite generally. On this trip I found that some had Army rifles while some had only bolo knives; other had home-made guns called paltiks. The latter were made of pieces of metal piping that would take a shot-gun shell loaded with zero-zero pellets. This is mounted on a stock on which a sharp nail takes the place of hammer and trigger. For firing, the loaded end of the tube which can be moved slightly along the stock, is jammed against the nail and the gun goes off, sometimes in all directions. Even so, the weapon served its purpose better than no weapon at all and Double-O shotgun shells were, for a long time, standard guerrilla ammunition. Now, light, effective carbines are being supplied to replace the paltiks. To help fuel and oil production we are supplying small copper stills in addition to limited deliveries of fuel oil and gasoline. These items are difficult and dangerous to carry by submarine.

I believe we must all credit General MacArthur for what I consider his cleverness and great foresight in realizing that, if he could maintain the loyalty of the Philippine people to the Allied cause—the loyalty which was so prevalent in the Philippines for the many years we Americans have been there—he could count on a friendly populace upon his return. He had this in mind when he sent me back. In addition to the basic program of setting up coast-watcher stations as observation posts spotting ship movements, primarily to finger targets for submarines patrolling in the area, he thought of the civilians and placed great emphasis on taking care of them. For instance, when I arrived on Mindanao, I found the natives suffering from an epidemic of malaria which had taken the lives of many people, which could have been prevented had there been quinine available. I also noted the prevalence of skin ulcers, probably the result of defective diet. Quinine was not available in any quantity but atabrine was, and I urgently requested the delivery of massive quantities of the tablets. Delivery started with the next submarine supply run. Sulfanilamide was next in priority.

On Mindanao the Catholic priests, for lack of flour, were extending their supply of religious wafers by reducing the size considerably, and literally using eye droppers to stretch their ceremonial wine supply. Neither wheat nor grapes are grown in the Islands. I have contacted the head man of the Catholic Church in Australia and he is making available the supplies required. We are packing what we call "Padre's Kits" in five gallon kerosene tins, made up of about three quarters of wheat flour and a half dozen bottles of Mass wine. Packed in between are religious medals and other items which the priests can make good use of. These tins are wrapped in burlap, another useful item, bound by rope, and to identify them a Roman cross is secured to the package. When these kits are delivered to the priests throughout the Philippines I am sure they will serve an important function in maintaining the morale and loyalty of the Filipinos; as much perhaps as items necessary to health such as atabrine, sulfanilamide, etc.

I am confident that the operation to destroy the value of the Japanese occupational currency used in the Philippines (a printing press currency) by counterfeiting the bills will eventually be very effective. This effort should be escalated and a good supply of it should be landed on every submarine trip. It is used for maintaining guerrilla activities and for the benefit of the people in the occupied

areas thus diluting the money issued by the Japanese and
the Puppet Government.

On a scouting mission with Major Villamor as far north
as the outskirts of Manila we learned that the Japanese
had decided that they could not uproot the guerrillas by
military action and that a more effective way to bring them
in line was to cut-off their local sources of essential food
supplies. Areas in which guerrillas are believed to be operating have been designated "Bandit Zones," and the civilian population ordered to move out on-the-double or
else. On the heels of these orders mass executions of civilians, young and old; men, women and children became
the order of the day. This terror campaign had its effect
because many survivors are reluctant to risk their lives in
supporting the freedom fighters. But it also had an adverse
effect. These atrocities only strengthened the guerrillas' determination to wipe out as many Japs as they can.

After studying Parsons' report, Whitney called him in
and outlined his plan of action and areas of responsibility.
The colonel asserted that his job was to provide arms for
the guerrillas and trained personnel, as well as equipment,
for radio stations, coastal ship and plane watchers, weathermen, and so on. The technical specialists, most of them
selected from volunteer Filipino servicemen in Hawaii
and the U.S., would be trained at a supersecret base in
Australia, known as Tabragalba. The schooling was under
the direction of Colonel Lewis Brown, USA, who had
escaped when Bataan fell. Parsons' task, Whitney decreed,
was to obtain equipment necessary to extend Spyron and
the coastwatcher stations, and the use of submarines to
deliver the goods and men. It was up to him to locate and
"liberate" the wanted materiel.

Parsons looked at Whitney intently, then broke into a
broad grin. He realized that he had found a man who
would not interfere in his operations. Chick was de-
lighted and exuberant.

To assist him, Parsons secured the services of Captain
George Kinsler, USA, and Tom Jurika, Captain USAFFE,
both to handle procurement. Jurika had arrived in Australia only recently after a fantastic escape from capture
in the Islands. Both of these men had proven themselves
adept at the art of "procurement" although their methods
were not always strictly orthodox.

At the outbreak of the war Jurika was serving with the
U.S. Army Transportation Service, which handled all

coastal shipping throughout the Islands, with headquarters in Cebu City. When in May, 1942 surrender was imminent, Jurika, who wanted no part of that, persuaded Brigadier General Chenowitz, commanding U.S. forces on Cebu, to give him a letter releasing him from the Cebu command and authorizing him to join any unit he thought would continue resistance. No doubt General Chenowitz agreed to this unusual arrangement because he knew that Jurika was born and raised in the Islands, and for him to be captured by the Japanese meant certain torture and death.

Jurika figured that the commander on Leyte was least likely to give up so he took off for that island just as the Japs took over Cebu. It wasn't long before he realized that he had misjudged the Leyte commander. When the enemy moved in on his HQ, the Colonel ordered his men to lay down their arms and surrender. "And that includes you, Captain Jurika!"

"The hell it does," was Jurika's reply, and as the Japs walked in the front door he walked out the back. The conquerors foolishly had failed to surround the building.

He struck out through the cane fields keeping low and moving stealthily until well clear. There was a narrow trail almost obscured by the tall canebrakes on either side. He soon found it and turned south. Within a short time he demonstrated his knack for "procurement." He came upon a native merrily riding his bicycle along the hidden trail, and Jurika asked politely in Tagalog if he could borrow it. The astonished Filipino asked, equally politely, where he was going. "Australia," replied Tom Jurika as he pedalled off. It took him almost two years to make it.

For the next several months he continued to improve his procurement technique, living off the land and the natives as he made his way south. He sometimes joined roving bands of guerrillas when it seemed appropriate, such as when eluding Jap patrols. His greatest coup was when he came into possession of a 70 foot, two masted sailing outrigger banca. He recruited a small crew of natives, adroitly procured provisions, and shoved off on his final stretch to freedom—Australia. With no navigational equipment except a cheap wrist watch, and no charts, he had to rely solely on his and his crews' knowledge of the Islands.

Jurika's hopes were high, and the outlook was promising

for awhile. Few Jap patrol boats were encountered and those that did get curious went away bewildered when the crew of the banca, dressed in poor native fisherman garb, would jabber away in their native dialect, thoroughly confusing and frustrating the inquisitive sailors. But it finally happened. The unpredictable elements did them in.

A sudden violent storm dismasted the banca, blew out her sails and tore away the rudder. It was all the hapless crew could do to stay afloat. "When the storm subsided," Jurika told me years later, "the sea was wild but we managed to jury rig a jib, and just went where wind and seas took us." Miraculously, after days and nights that seemed an eternity, they were cast up through an angry surf onto an island, and they were alive! It was Mindanao, where Jurika was born.

For over a year he roamed the mountains and the valleys of the island that he knew so well, operating with the guerrillas under Colonel Fertig's command. Eventually, at the urging of Chick Parsons, and only after concluding that he could do more for the overall guerrilla movement down in Australia than he could on his native island, Jurika agreed to leave. And so, in March, 1944 he stepped aboard the ubiquitous *Narwhal* in Butuan Bay and not long after found himself in Australia on the staff of his brother-in-law. In what capacity? Procurement of course.

Parsons completed his staff with Lieutenant Lee Strickland, USN, and another Navy man, Ensign Bill Hagan, an American born and raised in the Islands. They were given the responsibility of the warehouses and loading facilities at Darwin, a forward base which became a major staging area for passengers and cargo.

Parsons promptly ran into difficulties. While he was in the Islands he had not realized what a tough time Allison Ind had had getting the few supplies together, and the submarines to deliver them. Chick grimly faced his new tasks with unceasing vigor. He was determined to get his job done so he could get back to the Islands.

One problem that Parsons faced was the number of high command channels that had to be navigated. He suddenly developed a brand new aptitude. He became a champion channel swimmer. One of his most common stretches was the channel between Colonel Whitney and Captain Arthur

H. McCollum, USN, who was Whitney's opposite number on the staff of Vice Admiral Arthur S. Carpender, chief of MacArthur's own navy—a term exceedingly distasteful to most senior naval officers. Later, under Admiral Kincaid, this force became known as the Seventh Fleet—a designation more palatable to the Navy.

"Captain McCollum," said Parsons, "worked and cooperated beautifully with the various 'opposites' on Gen. MacArthur's staff, including Col. Whitney. Capt. Richard Cruzen, Chief of Operations for Carpender, was also another important contact who helped make our submarine trips possible. In fact, between the two of them I was able to hitch rides for myself, my people and my supplies to the Philippines with more frequency than I had ever dreamed possible. Without them, their belief in the project and their help, my efforts would have gone down the drain.

"I soon discovered that the Navy in the Southwest Pacific was not in complete harmony with Uncle Doug. However, they did cooperate very well when they could. I also soon found out that the Navy took a dim view of using the very limited number of submarines available for patrols at that time for the delivery of supplies to the guerrillas in the Philippines, but their ears perked up when we described our successes in establishing coastwatcher stations and how they would supply information on targets to these same submarines when in Philippine waters. It paid off very well for the submariners in the long run."

To get Spyron going at the home base actually took more push than had been required in the field, Parsons soon discovered. "The stuff we needed," he recalled, "in the line of radio equipment light enough to be portable, yet strong enough to stand up to rough service, dampness and mildew, was not available." But Colonel Allison Ind went to his Australian AIB contacts, and soon a battery-powered radio small enough to fit down a submarine hatch was developed in Australia. The limiting dimension was 23 inches across the longest diagonal of any one package. These consisted of four boxes—one contained the battery; another the transmitter; the third the receiver; and the fourth a collapsible 40-foot antenna, ground wire, and all accessories to make the set functional, as well as spares to keep it operating for at least a year. All of these metal boxes were completely water-tight and could have been thrown overboard and recovered later and still be usable.

In the meantime, the New Guinea campaign was going full tilt and Parsons was hemmed in by walls of priorities higher and wider than the Great Wall of China. "I found it very difficult to get the type of supplies that I felt were essential to the Filipinos," wrote Parsons later. "You can imagine what happened when I asked the supply people to let me have a large quantity of sewing machine needles, at a high priority. The worst they could do was growl 'What the hell! Don't you know there's a war going on?' In the Philippines, almost every house or Nipa shack in small towns had a sewing machine, and as the occupation wore on and replacement of essentials were out of the question housewives found it necessary to make clothing for the family out of rice bags, upholstery from chairs, curtains and any other cloth, even the burlap wrappings from our packages smuggled in by submarine, which was available. This took a heavier than usual toll of sewing machine needles so, as ridiculous as it sounds now, they went to the top of the priority list."

General MacArthur finally realized that Parsons knew what he was doing and gave his group a preferential method of getting supplies which did not follow any standard organizational charts. As a result they were able, eventually, to requisition some rather unique items which were of the greatest value in the Philippines.

As time went on Whitney and, of course, Parsons found themselves involved in psychological warfare. That branch in MacArthur's family not only pushed the delivery of phony occupational money, but they hit upon the idea of sending in small packages of cigarettes, chocolates for the children, and many other things, all bearing the imprint: "I Shall Return." These items were so treasured that when the contents were consumed by the lucky persons who received them there was a ready market for the purchase of the empty containers. They even went so far as to mark every orange delivered to the Islands "USA" even though they had been grown elsewhere.

For some time American counterpropaganda had met Japanese propaganda head-on—the Japanese shouted almost hysterically that the Americans would never try to come back to the Philippines, while the United States

pushed the slogan: "I Shall Return—MacArthur!" It was
very effective. Later a 5 P.M. newscast from Australia's
most powerful radio station covered the Islands like a
blanket. It always began with: "This is General MacArthur
—I Shall Return!" Then the Philippine national anthem
was played, followed by an hour of news, international,
national, and local. Finally MacArthur's voice: "I Shall
Return!" Then the air went silent.

While Parsons labored at his shore-side tasks, sometimes
longing to be back in the Islands, there was still some submarine activity. The August and September runs of the
Grayling and *Bowfin* to Panay and Mindanao, respectively,
were "milk runs"—untouched by the slightest ripples of
trouble.

Bowfin did have an amusing incident while unloading
cargo on 2 September about 1¼ miles east of Binuni Point,
Mindanao. With much pride Captain Joe Willingham, the
skipper, saw to it that the working party of natives on
deck were served a lunch of coffee, sandwiches, and pie.
The sandwiches were thick slices of freshly baked bread,
richly buttered and each containing a generous slice of
pink, beautiful ham. To the captain's unhappy surprise
the natives did not eat the ham. He learned that they
were Muhammadans. However, they required no substitute for the meat. None of them had tasted bread or butter
since the start of the war, and the hamless sandwich was a
major treat in itself.

At the end of her war patrol, in keeping with radio
orders, the *Bowfin* surfaced at nightfall late in September
off Iligan, Mindanao. Along came a banca and aboard
came Colonel Fertig with a party of nine officers for
transportation to Australia. Among them was Luis P.
Morgan, former chief of staff to Colonel Fertig, who bade
him a hearty farewell. This marked the end of Fertig's
internal problems and signalled as well a new day in the
progress in Mindanao's fight for freedom. He went ashore,
happy in the thought that now he could devote more
time to fighting Japanese instead of fellow guerrillas.

Bowfin's return to base in Australia was uneventful
except for a few alarms triggered by unidentified air and
sea contacts, one of which turned out to be a friendly submarine unaware of *Bowfin*'s mission. This unhappy situation was faced by our Special Mission subs more than once
because of the ironclad policy of absolute secrecy about

Banca

their movements, even to the point of withholding such information from our own forces. Subsequently this led to the tragic loss of one of our own guerrilla subs, and near misses for several others.

In the meantime GHQ-Brisbane and the submarine command at Fremantle got a shot in the arm. A large submarine, specially designed to carry relatively big cargoes and a number of personnel was on its way to relieve the pressure on the combat-bound boats that had been pressed into service to supply the guerrillas. It was the beginning of the formation of a Special Mission Unit which was to do yeoman service in helping MacArthur carry out his ambitious plans for the Philippines.

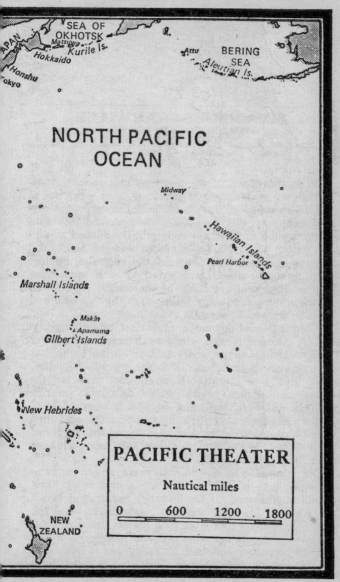

SEA OF
OKHOTSK
JAPAN
Matsuwa
Kurile Is.
Hokkaido
Honshu
Tokyo

Attu
BERING
SEA
Aleutian Is.

NORTH PACIFIC
OCEAN

Midway

Hawaiian Islands

Pearl Harbor

Marshall Islands

Makin
Apamama
Gilbert Islands

New Hebrides

PACIFIC THEATER

Nautical miles

0   600   1200   1800

NEW
ZEALAND

7

SUPERSUBS—NARWHAL
AND NAUTILUS

While the efforts of the fleet-type submarines in supporting the guerrillas were significant, they were not in themselves sufficient. They were limited in cargo and passenger capacity, they were limited in time, and they were in short supply. After all, their primary mission was to sink ships. What was really needed was the services of cargo submarines. The needs of the guerrillas, Spyron, and the coast-watchers had grown to such proportions that the piecemeal operations by the combat subs out of Australia were completely inadequate. The *Narwhal* and *Nautilus* were sorely needed.

When it seemed that cargo submarines, as earlier promised by Admiral Nimitz, would never reach Australia in 1943, Manuel Quezon, the President of the Philippines in exile, who was familiar with the guerrilla situation, went directly to President Roosevelt and explained the urgent need of their services exclusively on the guerrilla run. He told FDR the entire fascinating story of MacArthur's radio spy net and the fighting guerrillas supported by submarines. Roosevelt was so intrigued that he issued orders to the navy to dispatch at least one large submarine to Brisbane without delay.

The *Narwhal* and the *Nautilus* were supersubs, commissioned in 1930 when the navy went giant-hunting. Their overall lengths were 371 feet and they had extreme beams of 33.3 feet. They had standard displacements of 2,780 tons, almost 1,000 tons more than regular fleet-type subs. Their complements were 8 officers and 80 men. Both carried 26 torpedoes and had 10 tubes, two 6-inch deck guns, and ample machine guns. Their surface speeds were 17 knots; submerged they made 8 knots.

Since the outbreak of war, the *Nautilus,* with Lieutenant Commander W. H. Brockman as skipper, had put marines on the beaches of Makin Island, and evacuated civilians from the Solomons. Both subs had disembarked army scouts at Scarlet Beach on Attu Island in the Aleutian Chain to drive out Japanese invaders. *Narwhal,* captained by Lieutenant Commander Frank D. Latta, had bombarded Matsuwa Airfield in the remote Kuriles, close to the Japanese homeland. *Nautilus* had made extensive photographic reconnaissances in the Gilbert Islands and later, before landing a unit of marines on Apamana Island, had narrowly escaped destruction by an American warship.

In 1943 the two percherons of the deep had creaking bones and their cranky engines were given to breakdowns. Even so, old and tired as they were, these veterans of hard and dangerous service from the equator to the Arctic seas were still worth the weight they could carry. The *Narwhal,* commanded by Latta, was ordered to report to MacArthur's navy. The sub had completed her sixth war patrol with a long run from Pearl Harbor to Brisbane, where she arrived on 2 October 1943.

During a sorely needed refit at New Farm Wharf, Brisbane, all torpedoes, except the ten in the tubes, were offloaded along with all torpedo skids and handling gear. This provided space and weight compensation for about 92 tons of ammunition and stores, which was loaded aboard in preparation for her first guerrilla run. Half of this cargo was to be put ashore with Commander Parsons at the western end of Paluan Bay; the remainder was to be delivered to Colonel Fertig on Mindanao. Paluan Bay lies under Cape Calavite at the northwestern tip of Mindoro, only some 75 miles south of Manila Bay, much too close to Japanese scrutiny to be pleasant. The hour of departure was 2000 on 23 October. Half an hour before that, Chick Parsons and a party of nine, four officers and five enlisted men, came aboard.

The cruise north was uneventful until 1 November, when a large unidentified (but unmistakably enemy) plane was sighted by the submerged *Narwhal.* At noon, a Japanese "Mavis" flying boat was spotted. Air activity in this area was on the increase, Latta observed. The next day more enemy planes were contacted and avoided by timely dives.

The smooth passage continued until 9 November, when

"Mavis" Kawanishi H6K

the *Narwhal* passed through narrow Surigao Strait from the Pacific Ocean into Mindanao Sea. This was a new approach for guerrilla subs into Philippine waters. Previously all boats transited Celebes Sea to reach their destination. But this was the beginning of a whole new series of support operations and it was decided to start it with a fresh course of action.

On the surface the next evening, *Narwhal*'s soundmen picked up torpedo meat at a range of 12,000 yards. Latta found himself in a good position and quickly changed course to bring the target astern, manning his tracking stations as the sub swung ponderously to the new heading at low speed to reduce the phosphorescent wake. Polished by brilliant moonlight, the sea was like a mirror. As the target closed the range slowly, it appeared to be a large tanker of about 10,000 tons accompanied by three small destroyer-escorts. *Narwhal* dove to commence the attack. Exactly seven minutes later the crew heard and felt the shock wave of a distant depth charge. Another blast followed seconds later. Latta did not believe that he had been sighted and concluded that the ashcans had been dropped at random by the escorts. American submariners disdainfully dubbed this tactic an "embarrassment attack," a tactic frequently reverted to by the Japanese when they sensed danger but could not pinpoint the source.

At any rate he pressed home the attack and fired four torpedoes. He missed. No torpedo explosions were heard even though sound tracked them as hot, straight, and normal. *Narwhal* was subjected to a brief and rather half-hearted depth-charge attack. Latta reasoned that the wake of the tinfish in the moonlight alerted the escorts.

Safely out of this venture, although empty-handed, the *Narwhal* was destined to face a busy night. Several hours after the abortive attack, while proceeding on the surface, lookouts spotted a peculiar elliptical cloud in the bright moonlit sky. Called to the bridge, Latta and two other officers studied it intently. Had they been in friendly waters they would probably have shrugged it off as nothing more than a cloud, and certainly no threat. But they were not in friendly territory, and absurd as it seemed to Frank Latta, he reluctantly concluded that it was a blimp and decided to dive. On the way down the skipper asked himself, "Who ever heard of a blimp flying around at night alone, especially with no apparent base nearby?" But then he would argue, "Who ever heard of a submarine delivering supplies and people into occupied territory right under the very noses of the enemy?"

At periscope depth Latta searched the sky meticulously and found nothing. He accepted it as just "another one of those things that happens out here." He surfaced and proceeded on his assigned mission.

This reaction to the unknown was not uncommon among submariners, operating alone in hostile waters far distant from their home base, who had little or no timely intelligence on enemy activity in their areas. Communications, for security reasons, were practically nonexistent.*

---

*Under Admiral Lockwood, a broadcast system of sending information to submarines on combat patrol was perfected. At four-hour intervals, on a schedule known only to the submarines, shore-based high-powered radio stations would transmit a series of numbered coded messages. Submarines did not acknowledge receipt of the transmissions, maintaining radio silence. These broadcasts were repeated for at least 24 hours to insure that everybody got the word. Since the serials might contain information of vital importance to a particular submarine, each boat had to break (decode) each message, a task that placed a heavy burden on the communication officers. But the broadcasts were looked forward to eagerly by the men at sea. Sometimes the CommOff would be startled in the midst of his decoding chore to learn that he had just become a father—"mother and son are well."

It was not a matter of being easily frightened by anything —spook, phantom radar contact, or real danger—it was, instead, a matter of being dedicated to completing an assigned mission in spite of all odds. Contrary to many people's belief that submarines operated underwater all the time they were at sea, our World War II boats spent about 90 percent of their time on the surface and submerged only to avoid attack or detection, or to set up a submerged torpedo attack. The lookouts, enlisted men and officers who stood deck watches at sea, were trained to report anything they saw of a suspicious nature. The ultimate decision was up to the skipper—was it a legitimate target? was it a friend? was it a threat? It was never an easy decision.

The night wore on. Soon after midnight, while surfaced, the *Narwhal* contacted two ships astern. While he could not see them clearly, Latta sensed that they were DEs. All uncertainty ended when both vessels put on speed and one of them opened fire. The captain put all four engines on the line and ordered full speed. Thence began the gut-tying race for safety that always develops when a submarine elects to stay on the surface and try to outrun the pursuer. In the dimly lit cavern below deck, Engineer Officer Plummer nursed his four temperamental GM 16 "270" engines up to the maximum number of turns prescribed for them, hoped for the best, and expected the worst—an engine breakdown.

On the bridge, Captain Latta and Commander Parsons saw the splashes of the exploding shells coming closer and closer.

"More power," Latta demanded of Plummer. "Tie down the damn throttles!"

Below, anxious Lieutenant Plummer gave his galloping horses their heads. And lo! a miracle happened. One by one the turns increased until they reached a full 15 rpm above the rated full-power output and the recommended maximum revolutions. For three to four hours the race went on. During that time the pit log read 19.2 knots, an unbelievable speed for the old girl whose best speed was supposed to be 17.

The DEs never caught up, but before the chase ended the *Narwhal* had the unpleasant experience of being exposed to star-shell fire, which forced the captain to zigzag at top speed, a maneuver that did not tend to increase the gap between the submarine and her pursuers.

"These star-shells," Latta observed in his report, "retain much of their forward velocity instead of falling directly down when close overhead. They appear like aircraft with brilliant landing lights coming in in a steep glide."

Commander Latta, who, like most men of the sea, had a religious turn of mind, regarded the giving of wings that night to *Narwhal* as a divine gift. In gratitude, he at once named each of the four engines after four of the Apostles: No. 1, Matthew; No. 2, Mark; No. 3, Luke; and No. 4, John.

But, to return to grim reality, in the haste to escape and dodging around islands, Latta found himself lost in unknown waters dotted with islands that could not be told apart in the dark or by means of any chart. However, Commander Parsons came to the rescue. When a well-lighted town came into view, he had it spotted. It would take a well-informed and local sailor to know that the bright electric lights had to be those of Dumaguete City, the only town in that area of Negros Island that boasted electricity. Latta's problem as to his whereabouts in a watery island wilderness was solved. He thanked the good Lord for the presence of Parsons.

Captain Latta pressed north, past Negros and Panay and onward to his landing site on Mindoro. By this time Parsons and party were becoming restless and eager to get ashore. The skipper was equally eager to complete this phase of his mission. He had another date elsewhere and he was falling behind schedule. As he approached the disembarking spot on the surface, in the pale yellow light of a waning moon, the *Narwhal*'s radar picked up a surface contact at 4600 yards. Latta slowed and commenced tracking, not with the thought of attacking but to evade. In a short time it was determined that the vessel, whatever it was, was stopped in a position about two miles off the landing site. The skipper and Parsons agreed that it probably was a patrol boat. Latta shifted to electric drive to silence his noisy engines and crept into Paluan Bay dead slow as the moon went down. He got in undetected. Early in the morning of 13 November Parsons and his men departed in a rubber boat and disappeared into the pitch-black night.

As *Narwhal* cleared the bay, she held the enemy vessel

again on her radar. The Japanese evidently smelled trouble but did not know what or where. The vessel was underway now at slow speed wandering aimlessly around her former position. Against the island, the submarine was practically invisible in the darkness. Undetected, *Narwhal* crept out to sea where Latta took her down in the early morning twilight. According to plan, he returned to Paluan Bay submerged. There was the patrol boat back on station, but as Latta kept his periscope trained on her he had the satisfaction, eventually, of seeing her up anchor and steam off in the direction of Manila.

In the late afternoon a rubber boat, flying the proper security signal, was observed inshore in the bay. The *Narwhal* surfaced and the boat stood out to meet her. Chick Parsons came aboard. Following his directions Latta took the *Narwhal* into the shallows of the bay and moored, of all places, alongside a schooner, the *Dona Juana Maru*, flying the Japanese flag. Unloading was commenced immediately under the supervision of Major L. H. Phillips, AUS. As the sun set, all visitors were ashore and the cargo unloading completed. Captain Latta wasted no time clearing the schooner, and headed for the relative safety of the open sea. Commander Parsons remained aboard.

The *Narwhal* made knots heading southward toward Mindanao and Butuan Bay. The bay lies at the mouth of the Agusan River in a wild, mountainous region on the northern coast of the island. After an uneventful run, the sub lay to on the surface off Butuan Bay in the blinding glare of a midafternoon sun. It was not long before a small boat stood out carrying Colonel Fertig. With him as a pilot, the sub entered Nasipit's small harbor. She promptly ran aground on a soft sand shoal. Captain Latta prayed silently that there would be no air patrols that afternoon. After much sweat, including "sallying"* ship using the offwatch and the passengers led by Chick Parsons, she backed off into deeper water. The natives ashore must have thought the Americans had gone crazy as the men rushed back and forth from beam to beam on deck.

Fertig may have had his troubles, but even so, a uniformed Filipino band struck up a lively rendition of "Anchors Aweigh" and other pulse-raising tunes to welcome the visitors as *Narwhal* moored to a decrepit pier.

"*Sally: to rock a ship from side to side by rushing the crew from beam to beam in an attempt to get a grounded ship moving."

They even broke out cold beer for all hands. The unloading of cargo was completed in six hours, and shortly thereafter 32 evacuees including 8 women, 2 children, and one tiny baby were herded aboard. The *Narwhal* headed for sea and Australia, leaving Parsons and Fertig ashore. It had been a nervous time for Latta, who had learned that there were Japanese only 3 miles inshore.

One of the busiest men aboard during the return journey was Pharmacist's Mate Thomas J. Fitzgerald. He not only had an unusually high percentage of sick crewmen to handle, but each evacuee required special attention, from tropical ulcers to cigarette burns on the baby. Some 16 were ill from lack of nutrition. All of those showed marked improvement after several days of vitamin pills and good food.

Two days later, "Matthew," main engine No. 1, broke down with a broken head bolt. The submarine made way on three engines until Matthew was restored to duty within six hours. Otherwise the journey to Fremantle, the *Narwhal's* new base of operations, was uneventful.

During this mission the *Narwhal* made six enemy surface contacts, attacked one convoy without success, and played blindman's buff with a Japanese patrol boat that exposed her to hostile gunfire. She also brought 32 ill and badly undernourished evacuees to safety in Australia. She traversed 4,345 miles from Brisbane to the Island area and back, 1,364 miles in Philippine waters and 1,850 miles in transit to Darwin where the evacuees were disembarked.

In his report the captain noted that, referring to the engines, which needed almost constant babying, the vessel would soon have completed one year of continuous service since overhaul.

"During this time," Captain Latta wrote, "the *Narwhal* has cruised from the eastern Pacific to the Sea of Okhotsk, from the Bering Sea to the Indian Ocean, covering more than 85,000 miles. Credit for this excellent engineering performance is due the Engineer Officer, Lt. J. E. Plummer, USN."

While at sea on her first war patrol in the Philippine area, in October, the *Cabrilla*, Lieutenant Commander Douglas T. Hammond skipper, received orders directly from GHP-Brisbane to make for Doog Point on the west coast of Negros, to be on hand on the 19th to pick up

Major Jesus A. Villamor, USA, and a few other army officers, for transportation to Australia. She was to arrive early in the morning and make a daytime periscope survey. If conditions were right, a white sheet would be shown on the beach. The passengers were to come out in a sailboat flying white pennants in the bow and stern. If no contact was made on the first day, they would try again the following day.

No contact was made at first, but a small Japanese coastal ferry passed close aboard. Hammond elected to let it go, although it was a tempting target. After that interesting encounter the *Cabrilla* stood offshore to survey the enemy patrol activity, which seemed to be increasing in the area. Meanwhile, the major and his party sat in their boat, one mile off the beach, from the time the ferry passed by, for what seemed an eternity, waiting in deep dejection for the submarine that never came. When the moon rose at 0400, no sub could be seen. The trouble was that neither an exact time for contact nor a specific rendezvous point had been designated. But Hammond was game to keep looking for a "needle in the hay stack" and closed the coast again in the afternoon in a flat, calm sea. He might as well have been flying a battle flag from his periscope for the wake it left, even at dead slow speed.

Late in the afternoon he sighted a boat. It displayed some kind of signal but it was not the proper one. Hammond approached the questionable craft with some reluctance, looked it over again, then made a "battle surface," manning the deck guns the instant the submarine emerged. He was not sure that this small boat was friendly, and even though it was too small to carry weapons that could really hurt, it could be a lookout for a more formidable vessel lurking inshore.

It turned out to be an unnecessary drill. With his machine guns trained on the banca, Hammond signalled it by hand to come alongside. It approached gingerly and as it neared the *Cabrilla* the skipper recognized an American among the passengers. Being new on the guerrilla route Hammond wouldn't know Villamor from any other Filipino, but reassured by the presence of an American in the boat, *Cabrilla's* guns were secured and the boat came alongside. The American turned out to be Major Meider, USA, and he introduced Villamor and Captains Torres and Gabangbang of the Philippine Army.

After conferring with Meider and Villamor, Captain Hammond ordered a quantity of supplies put aboard the sailboat, but the articles most needed by the guerrillas, guns and ammunition, had not been included in the loading bill for *Cabrilla* on departure for this patrol. Nobody, least of all Hammond, had expected the *Cabrilla* to be pressed into guerrilla service. But this shortcoming was partially remedied in the last moment before leaving the island by the donation of a Tommy gun and ammunition. Then the *Cabrilla* departed without further delay.

The captain regretted, when too late, that he had been in such a hurry to get away. But this was the *Cabrilla*'s first war patrol and Hammond was eager to get her into combat. He had taken her out of Portsmouth, New Hampshire where she was commissioned in May 1943. She was yet to taste the blood of a Maru, and this guerrilla bit was completely new to her officers and crew. The skipper reported later that the guerrillas could have received more needed help from *Cabrilla*—arms, ammunition, atabrine, and flour—had he been more aware of the needs of the natives before he sailed. Still, who could blame Captain Hammond. His orders were to pick up the party of four, bring them to GHQ-Brisbane and p.d.q.

When Major Villamor, who had consolidated the renegade guerrillas on Negros into an effective fighting group under a single command, left in *Cabrilla* he turned the leadership over to Captain Abcede, an able and well-trained officer. GHQ regarded Abcede as only acting commander, even though Villamor was not slated to return to Negros. For a time the stream of supplies to Negroes was shut off. Not until February 1944 did GHQ designate Abcede a lieutenant colonel and commander of the 7th District. This decision left both Peralta and Fertig out in the cold so far as running Negros was concerned. That month a 45-ton shipment of carbines, ammunition, and radio equipment was delivered to Abcede by submarine.

Chances are that Colonel Abcede had Colonel Gador to blame for those months of trials and suspense. "Major General" Gador had slipped over to Bohol late in 1943. There, by hook or crook, he got access to a radio transmitter that could reach Brisbane. He got in touch with GHQ and advocated his own claim for leadership on Negros so adroitly that AIB was giving his case serious

M-1 Carbine

consideration. By good luck a party of responsible Americans, familiar with the islands, reached Brisbane early in
1944. They gave General MacArthur and his staff a new
view of the situation on Negros. Gador was immediately
sidetracked and Abcede given the go ahead.

On her second run to the Island, in November–December
1943, the *Narwhal* had an uneventful trip to Cabadbaran on
Mindanao's Butuan Bay. On 2 December she lay alongside
a 150-ton barge on which Captain Latta landed the two
army officers and several enlisted men who had been his
passengers. The ever-present Commander Parsons came
aboard with Colonel Fertig and remained while 90 tons
of ammunition and stores was being off-loaded. The sub

then picked up seven evacuees. They included one woman and an eight-year-old girl. Fertig left but Parsons remained aboard. From a portable radio station aboard the barge, Captain Latta received orders to pick up a group of refugees at Alubijid, Macajalar Bay, west of Butuan Bay on the north coast of Mindanao. While en route, Latta was warned that the evacuation was considered impossible and advised to scrub it. Now in the Sulu Sea, the sub skipper decided to investigate Malocanan Bay on Negros for future reference and then head back to the Mindanao Sea to try to do the impossible. He was against scrubbing evacuees. At 0148 on 5 December, due to the fine work of Bob Managhan as navigator, a bonfire was sighted at Macajalar Bay and Latta set out to tilt his lance against whatever dangers the darkness might hold and to rescue the refugees. It had been raining heavily, but the downpour had stopped. The sky, however, was heavily overcast. On electric motors, the sub closed the coast to 450 yards; Latta flashed his own security signal toward the bonfire, wondering if the people had been warned that the mission was off. But, as usual, communications had been bad. The bonfire was built to guide in the still expected rescuers.

Soon after the *Narwhal* disclosed her presence, Second Lieutenant Noble, PA, came alongside in a dugout canoe. Unfortunately, he had not arranged a signal to the shore to verify that the sub was there to pick up evacuees. He had to return to the beach to tell his good news. A full hour passed before the first boat-load of evacuees came aboard. Latta, usually cool and collected, was irritated by the delay, and the small craft, when empty, was returned with all the vituperations the captain could muster to produce more haste. He had been warned that Japanese patrols were vigilant and frequent in this locality. Pips were popping up all over his radar screen like a rash and Latta scented potential danger in all of them. Least of all, did he want a tussle with an enemy destroyer while he was anchored off a lee shore; small patrol boats, however, could be handled by his deck guns. The second boat-load of refugees, at long last, came just before dawn. It was escorted by a flotilla of Filipino barrotas. Enough, as Latta gloomily thought, to have brought all the evacuees at one time in the first place. Two minutes after the last person was aboard, he stood out of the bay at full speed. Not long thereafter he encountered an unescorted *Omi Maru*-type 4,000-ton freighter and attacked her by gunfire from both his 6-inch deck guns at a range of 4,500 yards. The third salvo hit and stopped the Maru cold in her tracks; fires broke out and explosions thundered in the hull. The sub went to periscope depth and approached the flaming wreck to see her sink and look for survivors, of which there were none. This successful attack relieved some of the tension built up in the crew of the *Narwhal* over the senseless delay in sending out the last boatload of evacuees. Latta was justifiably incensed over the obvious inefficiency of the guerrillas responsible for the arrangements at Alubijid. "This kind of thing and the endless monotony of delivering cargo and people in the dark of night under the constant threat of discovery and attack, with little opportunity to get into combat," said Latta, "was more nerve-racking than a barrage of depth charges."

Darwin-bound, all went well until 10 December, when Mark, the No. 2 main engine, blew a head gasket just before dawn. It was not back on the line until early afternoon. Even so, the *Narwhal* reached Port Darwin before midnight, where the evacuees were dropped. On 13 December, en route to Fremantle, Luke, the No. 3 main engine, suffered a broken head bolt. Again time and sweat were expended on six hours of repairs. But Fremantle was reached on 18 December.

The old gang in the *Narwhal's* wardroom always referred to the submarine as the *Inchcliff Castle Maru* and to John Plummer, the engineer officer, as Colin Glencannon, the fictional chief engineer of the fictional rundown tramp steamer that—with noisy engines and many troubles invented by author Guy Gilpatrick—steamed almost weekly through the pages of the *Saturday Evening Post*. These stories were widely read and very popular in the navy.

In his patrol report, Captain Latta noted that the assistance of Commander Parsons had been very valuable on his patrol and the previous one. Parsons' knowledge of Philippine waters and enemy installations, he observed, "makes his presence on missions of this sort an asset greatly appreciated by the commanding officer."

The *Narwhal* was given credit for sinking the 4,000-ton freighter *Himano Maru* and complimented on using gunfire instead of expending scarce and expensive torpedoes.

Even in submarine warfare, thrift was appreciated in high places.

"We were able to unload the cargo, take on passengers and stand out to sea exactly one hour and fifty minutes after surfacing," he noted, with pleasure. There was no driving pressure for speed on this occasion, but the skipper believed that urgency was a great factor in remaining afloat and alive.

Frank Latta was so right! It *was* of the utmost urgency for him to keep *Narwhal* afloat and alive. The poor old aching workhorse was the only one operating on the guerrilla circuit in December of '43. Of the original four boats designated to form the newly established Special Supply Unit organized in October, 1943 *Narwhal* was alone. *Nautilus* was still undergoing a major and sorely needed overhaul, and the aging fleet-type subs, *Seawolf* and *Stingray* had not yet been released from combat duty. And so the fleet-type boats continued to be pressed into guerrilla service on their way to or returning from combat patrol areas.

8

PART 1—THE CASE OF
THE SLAMMING DOOR

Christmas came and went, not unobserved, but with no change in pace of the relentless demands of war. At Fremantle, repair crews worked feverishly to overhaul *Narwhal's* ailing engines. The good people of Perth and Fremantle organized game parties and dances for the Americans in their midst. Chaplains of various faiths held services aboard ships on Christmas eve and again on Christmas morning. In the pleasant summer weather a makeshift altar was put up on the spacious afterdeck of the supersub. An enterprising crewman scrounged up a portable organ and led the worshipers in singing traditional Christmas hymns. At night *Narwhal* glowed like a Christmas tree with a string of varicolored lights hoisted from stem to stern over the periscope shears. There was little threat of an air raid here.

By 18 January the *Narwhal* was ready for sea. The first war patrol on the guerrilla circuit of 1944 began that day when the sub headed north. Her mission was to deliver 45 tons of ammunition and stores to Colonel Peralta on Panay, and a similar amount to Lieutenant Colonel Abcede, by now designated permanent commander of Negros. The passage was made without incident. On the return journey, the submarine carried 6 evacuees from Panay and 28 from Negros, including 8 women and 9 children. But something new had been added—a supercargo in the form of Commander F. Kent Loomis of the Fremantle staff, who had boarded at Darwin, where Latta had stopped enroute north. Loomis took over the job of supervising the human cargo, dividing his charges between the two torpedo rooms.

The Submarine Force Commander at Fremantle had instigated a practice of letting each submarine officer on his staff make at least one war patrol to break the monotony and rigor (mostly social) of shore duty and to let them see and experience at first-hand the problems that faced the boats on the guerrilla circuit. Incidentally, this also gave these officers the privilege of wearing the coveted Submarine Combat Insignia, a miniature submarine silhouette of silver, pinned under their dolphins (the gold medal which distinguishes an officer who is "qualified in submarines").

After a quick turnaround at Fremantle, *Narwhal* was once again ready for sea, or at least as ready as she could be without a much-needed major overhaul.

This was *Narwhal's* tenth war patrol, her fourth special mission, and it was one of grinding frustrations and thrill-packed action. It started quietly enough as Matthew, Mark, Luke, and John, under the critical eyes and ears of her engineer officer, Lieutenant Plummer, pulled her over the guerrilla trade trail from Darwin toward the Islands, starting 16 February 1944.

Near sunrise two days later, the tops of a Japanese cargo ship were sighted at 14,000 yards. It was escorted by a Chidori-type destroyer, a deadly antisubmarine vessel that had earned the respect of American submariners for the ferocity and accuracy of their depth-charge attacks. The target was within 2 miles of Buru Island and, as bad luck would have it, disappeared into a sheltered harbor. Captain Latta shook his head in disgust. It wasn't a very good beginning.

In the late afternoon of 21 February another radar contact was made, and Latta went after it with a vengeance. The target was never clearly sighted because of a low-hanging haze. After tracking for a short time Latta realized that he was in the unfortunate position of being astern of the contact and therefore confronted with a stern chase or an "end around" situation. He refused to give up, and cranked up full speed but, despite the strenuous efforts of the engineers sweating it out below, the engines smoked so heavily that she left a thick black trail worthy of the *Inchcliff Castle* and so conspicuous that Latta feared he would be sighted. He did not believe he had yet been seen so he closed the target track

slowly. By sunset *Narwhal* was in good position for a
night radar attack, and flooded down to radar depth.
Suddenly they were engulfed in a blinding rain squall
and the target disappeared from sight, sound, and radar
as if it, too, had submerged. The heavy rain made such
a racket on the surface of the flat sea that it drowned
out the sound listening gear, and the deluge probably
had something to do with the radar set suddenly becoming sick. The target was never picked up again. A
frustrated Latta surfaced and headed for the first rendezvous.

The next morning the sub approached Mantabuan, a
small island south of Mindanao. She cruised along the
coast all day at periscope depth but saw no landing
signal. Latta took a chance and surfaced before sunset,
hoping the guerrillas would see him and be ready the next
day. No such luck. The next day brought the same dis-
couraging results. Being unable to deliver his cargo or
passengers—one U.S. Army and two Navy officers with
four Filipino Army enlisted men—he saw nothing else
to do but be on his way to Mindanao and Tawitawi for
other deliveries. Everything had gone sour so far. Sometimes it seemed a sub skipper just couldn't earn his pay.

Early on the morning of 26 February the submerged
Narwhal stole into Pamutsin Cove in Paluan Bay on
Mindanao. No sailboats anywhere; no activity or sign of
life along the shore; no security signals from Fertig or
his men. Another no show? Latta was getting fed up. At
nightfall, *Narwhal* slipped out to sea, surfaced, and put in
a quick battery charge. By midnight, under a bright,
starlit sky, the sub returned to the cove on the surface.
Still no dice; no signal. Latta cleared the area and headed
to sea again to report the situation to his boss in
Australia. At dawn, he reentered the cove submerged
and patiently waited all day. Again no action ashore, so
he returned to sea and surfaced for a charge that juiced
up the batteries but did not give Latta a lift.

Later that night, on 28 February, he received, with
great relief, radio orders to make contact on 2 March
at Cabadbaran in Butuan Bay, about 15 miles from Nasipit
on Mindanao where the band had played so merrily on
an earlier occasion. Here Latta's luck turned for the
better. The proper security signal was sighted on the
beach in the morning of the designated date.

The sub lay submerged until dark, then surfaced. Promptly, a two-masted outrigger came alongside and Lieutenant Commander Wilson, Lieutenant Colonel McLish, and Major Childers came aboard. They told Latta that Colonel Fertig was at the mouth of Agusan River, in waters too rough to tow the barge into the bay. Could not the *Narwhal* move to the barge's position? She could not! But to be of as much help as possible, Fertig could get a tow to haul his barge a small way up the river to quieter waters if Latta would move his sub to the same place. This plan, while it differed little from the first proposal, was grudgingly accepted, even though it entailed entering the mouth of an uncharted river.

The night was murky, with too many unidentifiable peaks for good radar navigation. Captain Latta headed into the river channel, took his vessel as near the river mouth as he dared, and lay to. To save time he rigged for unloading topside while under way, and stood ready to put his own boats in use for delivery of cargo to Colonel Fertig. When, after a long wait, the colonel came aboard, he wanted the *Narwhal* brought closer to the barge. Latta refused. Next Fertig proposed to delay unloading until the next day. Again Latta had to decline. The cargo, which included two 26-foot diesel whaleboats, was finally unloaded into the barge, which was towed into place by a steam launch. At 0225 on 3 March, the unloading of 70 tons of supplies was completed. It was replaced by 20 servicemen and 8 civilians, including 2 women. Latta, grateful for small favors, was glad there were no children. Four minutes later, the sub was off for Tawitawi, onetime base of the U.S. Asiatic Fleet, and now being built up as a major Japanese naval base and staging area.

A heartwarming incident occurred later that morning. The sub was running on the surface when it passed a small sailboat close aboard. The five Filipinos aboard it doused sails as the sub approached, lined up as for inspection, and with expressionless faces, began solemn and continuous bowing.

When Latta waved from the bridge and the natives saw they were Americans, not Japanese as they had expected, the Filipinos broke into ear-to-ear grins and loud cheers. "We passed in an aura of good fellowship," noted the captain. "Still later in the morning, another sailboat passed close aboard and the same experience was repeated. We tossed them some cigarettes and became boon companions."

Late that afternoon Latta saw a sight that quickens any combat submariner's pulse. Contact! Masts and the tall cylindrical stack typical of an ancient coalburning vessel so prevalent in the Japanese maritime fleet loomed over the horizon. Latta was in perfect position. With the range down to 16,000 yards *Narwhal* dove and commenced the attack approach. The target, a 3,600-ton transport, seemed unescorted. She was zigzagging and making very slow speed as she came out of the channel between Negros and Siquijor Islands, apparently from Cebu. The skipper was determined not to let this one get away. At 1200 yards, as the target zigged away, he let go a four-torpedo spread. He watched eagerly as the torpedoes sped toward the unsuspecting Maru. Sonar reported that all four fish were running hot, straight, and normal. With stopwatch in hand the quartermaster called off 10-second intervals. At 45 knots, with a calculated torpedo run of 1500 yards, the first hit should erupt at 60 seconds. The seconds ticked off while Latta stood by the housed periscope. There was deathly silence throughout the boat, except for the low whine of the electric motors and the constant hum of the ventilating blowers, as all hands hoped and prayed for a hit.

"Five-oh seconds," droned the quartermaster.

"Up 'scope!" Latta ordered.

"Mark sixty."

Nothing happened for what seemed an eternity but was probably only a few seconds, then: *"Baroom!"* There was a violent explosion in the fore part of the target. The sub crew, hearing the hit, cheered. *Narwhal* shuddered as the shock wave hit her. Latta waited for the other torpedoes to reach their mark, but there were no more explosions. The captain turned over the periscope to the exec for a good look to verify a hit and identify the target. A heavy black smoke cloud obscured the entire target. When it cleared away moments later the vessel was dead in the water but on an even keel. The bow had vanished as far aft as the bridge. Latta changed course and increased speed to take position for a second salvo, when the target opened fire from the fantail with a well-aimed 5-inch gun. On a sweep around, Latta discovered a small escort-type warship coming up. It seemed as if the latter was coming to the transport's assistance when suddenly, at full speed, she turned toward the *Narwhal's* periscope and ran hell-for-leather toward it. The skipper decided that he was in no position to stop her with torpedoes. All Latta could do was to pull his 'scope down, turn away, rig for depth charge, and go deep. This he did promptly. For the next 40 minutes, the *Narwhal* was closer to Davey Jones's locker than she had ever been. That gunboat might have been hard to hit with a torpedo, but when it came to dropping depth charges deadly close, she loomed like a battleship. The enemy must have detected the *Narwhal's* change in course as she went deep.

The first depth charge was dropped fairly close. The second came a minute later and was the most violent of the two hundred-odd depth charges the *Narwhal* had chalked up on previous war patrols. The sub bounced and bobbed up and down; hatch wheels spun; lights went out; the Torpedo Data Computer jammed; fuses blew; the port annunciator went crazy, swinging uncontrolled from Full Ahead to Emergency Back; cork insulation rained down from stem to stern. All that saved the *Narwhal* from utter destruction was the common Japanese "fault" of never setting their depth charges deep enough.

Number three charge was close aboard but not as close as number two had been. Two more explosions followed at greater distances. Latta went in search of a hiding place and, luckily, found a soundproof water temperature gradient at 220 feet where his bathythermograph* took a sharp dip on the scale. In his own words, "we pulled the blanket over our heads."

All hands met the trial well. The crew took it in their stride; the passengers did not panic. There was absolute silence and no unnecessary movement in the sub as the next charges were awaited. They were heard, from far away, at 1910. All aboard breathed easier but not for long. Within two minutes peculiar noises, as of gravel dropping on deck, were heard. *Narwhal's* people had a

---

*A device that measures water temperature at the sub's keel depth and continuously records it on a tape in the Control Room where the diving officer can observe it.

few bad moments waiting for something to blow up. There is no fear like the fear of the unknown. Silence reigned for the next half hour, until the ninth and, quickly following, tenth depth charges were heard from some distance. That was the last *Narwhal* heard from the sub hunters. Latta came up to periscope depth, looked around, and found himself in the clear. Surfaced, the skipper, who had kept his passengers informed on what was going on throughout the ordeal, was told by the soldiers that they liked foxholes better.

On 5 March, as per schedule, *Narwhal* was off Bohi Gangsa on the northern coast of Tawitawi. The proper security signals were sighted on the beach and after dark Captain Latta surfaced. Soon a small banca with Captain Hamner aboard came alongside. Since only two small boats were available, four of the sub's rubber boats were made ready. Tawitawi—soon to become the hideout of Admiral Ozawa and his huge flattop fleet preparing for a sneak attack on American forces invading the Marianas—was a sensitive, heavily patrolled spot. In preparation for trouble, Latta manned all deck guns and broke open all carbine cases so that guns could be handed out quickly if necessary.

During unloading operations, radar detected an oncoming vessel at 8,500 yards. Reluctant to pick a surface fight with any warship larger than a patrol boat, Latta cleared the decks of people, saw to it that all his men were aboard, closed loading hatches, and ready on engines, started a swing to open out from the islands.

The *Narwhal's* batteries were low on juice so Latta remained surfaced, charging on two generators and going ahead full on the other engines. Meanwhile, the first ship had been identified as a destroyer-escort and soon two additional DEs were sighted. Surfaced, Latta saved as much of the deck load as he could by striking it below through the engine room hatch as they ran from the DEs. Meanwhile the *Narwhal* was smoking like hell wouldn't have it and was clearly visible in the bright moonlight. At a range of 3100 yards the closest DE turned broadside to the sub and opened fire with her deck guns.

In an even voice, Latta ordered: "Stand by to dive."

Then came the two blasts of the diving alarm. Again the hoarse blast of the klaxon, "Ahooga, Ahooga," rang throughout the boat. The expert coordination of a well-trained crew was quickly and quietly demonstrated as the sub dove and went deep. Routine reports from all compartments poured in over the "talker's circuit." The captain knew instantly that his boat was secure. Then, and only then, he turned his attention to the game of chess between him—the Black Knight—and his opponent, the White Queen. Waiting for the sound of fast screws and echo pinging which would herald a depth-charge attack, the Black Knight rigged for silent running and plotted his evasive tactics. But, oddly enough, nothing was heard from the pursuers. With this turn of events Latta, after a short period of silence, rose to periscope depth even though moonset was still three hours away and his periscope wake would be like a red flag waved in the face of a charging bull. He looked around in both high and low power on the 'scope. All clear and absolute silence. But the skipper was an old hand at this business, and he did not accept the absence of any tangible evidence of would-be attackers at face value. He cautiously remained submerged but stayed at periscope depth. About an hour later he heard echo ranging far astern, and four distant depth charges. He went deep again, suspecting that there was a "sleeper" somewhat closer. Within ten minutes he heard fast screws astern and got set for real trouble when sonar detected echo ranging right on the beam. The pinging increased in intensity and when the hunters shifted to short scale it was the signal that the enemy was coming in for the kill. Latta swung the ponderous *Narwhal* to port in a slow spiral dive keeping her stern, her smallest target that could be presented, aimed at the attackers. Nothing happened. The Japanese were apparently befuddled. Probably confused by the "knuckle" *Narwhal* left in her wake as she went deep with hard left rudder (a favorite tactic of our combat-wise submarine skippers), the enemy shifted their echo-ranging onto the false target. The hunters turned away and diligently pursued the bucket of bubbles that they thought was a submarine.

An hour went by in complete silence and Latta came up to periscope depth. He walked the 'scope around but saw nothing; however, as in all cat-and-mouse games, the mouse could never afford to assume he was safe. About 0400, there were four distant charges. So Latta went deep again. Bob Managhan, the executive officer, suggested that the sound could have been the slamming of a door topside between the bridge and the forward machine-gun platform. Believing this possible, Latta started back up but was halted by three distant explosions. Were they depth charges, or caused by a slamming door on *Narwhal?* Next, five explosions. Again, were they depth charges, or the damned door? The skipper decided that they were not charges and surfaced. The door was examined; it was closed and nothing seemed wrong. He headed north, away from Tawitawi, in what seemed the safest direction to go, and poured on the power. He did not return to Bohi Gangsa to deliver the 6 tons of cargo that remained below deck. As for the cargo still topside, it was dumped into the sea. Much of it remained afloat. A few days later, the Zamboanga newspapers reported that a former American gunboat, captured and now operated by the Japanese, had sunk an American submarine, and cited the floating cargo as proof.

On completing battery charges in the Sulu Sea, the captain swung south and, after nightfall, entered Sibutu Passage. As he passed the hot spot, Tawitawi, on his port hand, Latta kept his eye peeled for enemy ships lurking in the dark in wait for him; but, if they were there, he did not see them, nor was he seen by them. On the rest of the trip to Darwin, where he discharged passengers, and then on to Fremantle, there were no troubles of any kind.

On thorough inquiry, the door in question was held blameless for the depth-charge-like slamming. It was laid instead to the door on one of the 12 torpedo tubes installed on deck for torpedo storage but now used for other storage purposes. All 12 doors were checked. There were no more imitations by a slamming door of distant depth-charge explosions aboard the submarine.

The *Narwhal* was credited with damaging a 3,600-ton transport. After the war this assessment was revised downward by a Battle Damage Review Board made up of personnel who were long on statistics but short on combat experience. Latta was finally credited with having sunk the 500-ton river gunboat, *Karatsu Maru*. Similarity in silhouettes caused the mistaken identity, if there was in fact a mistake. Postwar Japanese records of ship sinkings were not particularly reliable. In any event, the *Narwhal* took quite a shellacking for a mere stink pot. Commander Frank D. Latta did not live to learn of this reversal. He went down to enemy action in his new command, *Lagarto,* in the treacherous South China Sea.

PART 2—THE COAST-WATCHERS AND THE MARIANAS TURKEY SHOOT

"By early summer, 1944, the massive work of creating the *Spyron* network had been done, as had the manning of the various weather, coast-watcher and plane observer stations," recalled Commander Parsons. "All that now remained was to continue training guerrilla combat personnel and build up ammunition and similar reserves.

"There was a general feeling that the Big Day was in the offing but, of course, no one could even venture a guess as to when that day would be, nor where the blow would hit. The Japanese, like most of us, believed that the Americans, when they came, would land on southern Mindanao. That had been Admiral Mineichi Koga's invasion concept and his successor as chief of the fleet, Admiral Soemu Toyoda, had not changed it. The Japs kept sending planes and troops to southern Mindanao but General Kenney's aviators kept mowing them down as fast as they came in."

The impact of *Narwhal's* astounding capability to carry tons of cargo and large numbers of persons to the Islands was evident within a few months after she started her regular runs. As the months went by in early 1944 the delivery of arms and other supplies by submarine increased significantly, and the business of distributing them within the respective military districts became correspondingly difficult. Water transport—native dugouts, bancas, under sail or some with outboard engines—was the most efficient means of getting the material to points otherwise isolated from the off-loading ports. Transport overland was arduous and dangerous and sometimes impossible because of the rugged terrain and frequent Japanese patrols. But it was imperative that the coast-watcher and Spyron stations be kept supplied, and guerrilla units in remote areas be armed with modern weapons. More and more native boats were pressed into service.

"The Japs," recalled Parsons, "were neither stupid nor blind and, eventually, the increasing number of native sailing craft in Island waters aroused their suspicions. They began, as the phrase went, 'to hook' the sailboats for inspection. Since most of these captures occurred in 10th District waters, Fertig took counteraction by running his boats under the protection of armed convoys. This, in turn, led to demands upon Brisbane for heavier and heavier weapons. We ran up through twenty mm to fifty mm machineguns, to bazookas and twenty mm deck-type cannon."

20 mm Oerlikon Gun

The armed convoys must have amused the enemy, but his force of small patrol boats was spread so thin throughout the Philippine Archipelago that he was unable to put an end to the guerrilla supply lines. Armed convoys might have been the answer but there is no record of any naval engagements between them and the Japanese.

In May 1944 Chick Parsons' efforts in the Islands began to pay off. In fact his spy net hit the jackpot. Early that month Japanese activity in the anchorages of Tawitawi went into high gear. Coast-watchers, noting this, began to bombard GHQ-Brisbane with numerous reports of the arrivals and departures of enemy warships. At first GHQ was inclined to discount this information as relatively insignificant, but a situation worth watching. On 16 May the staff at Brisbane was jolted into action, by a submarine contact report. It confirmed the coast-watchers' observations. *Bonefish*, Commander T. W. Hogan skipper, tracked and trailed a large enemy fleet unit, which included a carrier guarded by screening destroyers. It led him straight to Tawitawi. There he stumbled on a huge concentration of heavy ships made up of carriers, battleships, cruisers, and a host of DDs and support ships. It was Admiral Jisaburo Ozawa's First Mobile Fleet.

This news was flashed to Brisbane, Washington, and Pearl Harbor and passed on to all force commanders who had a need to know. Admiral Christie's reaction was quick and decisive. From SubSoWesPac, submarines were dispatched at full speed to form a ring around the Japanese stronghold, and other boats were placed on guard in the Celebes Sea and off Luzon's west coast. ComSubPac stationed his subs in Luzon Strait southeast of Formosa, off San Bernardino Strait north of Samar Island, and off Surigao Strait south of Leyte. These were the only avenues of egress from the west through the Philippine Archipelago into the Philippine Sea.

The Japanese had dreamed up a rather extravagant plan. It was to lure the enemy into a battle situation in selected decisive battle areas that were, in the words of the battle plan itself, "roughly prearranged." These areas were concentrated on the Palau Islands and the western Carolines (Yap, Ulithi, and Woleai). Island-based aircraft and carrier planes would unite to wreck the American task force, which, as the order said, "will be attacked and destroyed for the most part in a day assault." The Marianas, which, unbeknownst to the Japanese were about to be attacked and invaded by the

Americans, were brushed off with the casual comment: ". . . when the enemy maneuvers in the Marianas . . . the enemy will be attacked by base air forces in that area."

To lure the Americans into the predetermined areas, the traps would be baited with small naval forces designed to trick the enemy into underestimating Japanese naval strength in the area. When the Americans took the bait and stumbled into the traps, Ozawa's First Mobile Fleet, which included nine flattops and formidable gunpower, would sortie from the Sulu Sea, enter the Philippine Sea "without a trace" and slaughter the unsuspecting enemy. But in planning this attack the Japanese high command overlooked the opponent's submarines and the tight invisible ring they had formed around Admiral Ozawa.

Coast-watchers and submarines joined to keep track of the Japanese forces' movements. On 13 June they reported the sortie of the enemy fleet from Tawitawi, a move that puzzled, but did not immediately alarm, Admiral Raymond A. Spruance, commander of the United States Fifth Fleet, then busily engaged in softening up Saipan and Tinian in preparation for invasion. But a close watch was kept on Ozawa's movements as he maneuvered in the Sulu Sea.

When the First Mobile Fleet burst through San Bernardino Strait, ready to do battle with the Fifth Fleet, coast-watchers flashed the alarm to Brisbane. It was 15 June 1944—D-Day on Saipan. Shortly after the coast-watchers' report, Commander R. D. ("Bob") Risser, skipper of the *Flying Fish* cruising off the strait, blasted off a contact report to Pearl on the same force. From then on Ozawa, proceeding east at 20 knots, was in a glass cage.

Spruance accepted the battle challenge and at the appropriate time dispatched Task Force 58, Admiral Marc Mitscher, to meet the enemy. On the morning of 19 June the American force was proceeding west at 24 knots, and at 1000 hours Ozawa's force was within striking range. Thus began the action that became known as the Marianas Turkey Shoot. TF-58 fighters claimed 366 enemy planes downed. Another 19 were shot down by task force gunners. During the air battle two large Japanese CV's were torpedoed and sunk by submarines.

While the coast-watchers never saw any of the action of this unprecedented naval air battle, they certainly earned their pay and their laurels on that 15th day of June 1944.

That the coast-watchers did not rest on their newly won honors became evident at firsthand to Commander E. F. Dissette, commanding *Cero,* on 4 August 1944. While on combat patrol off the east coast of Mindanao, he attacked with torpedoes an escorted tanker close inshore. He saw two hits, heard two more, and observed the Maru exploding and breaking up. Forced deep by the escorts, he was obliged to dive under the sinking tanker. He made good his escape from the escorts and after dark surfaced to send an action report. Before he could get the message on the air a ComSubSoWesPac serial was being copied. One coded message said: "Nice work CERO. Coast watcher reports sub sank 10,000 ton tanker off coast your assigned area. It had to be you." It was.

9

COMBAT SUBS TO THE RESCUE

In the spring of 1944 American pressure on the Japanese moved relentlessly to the west. In April, MacArthur's forces launched assaults on and occupied the main ports on the north coast of New Guinea—Aitape, Hollandia, Wakde—and at the same time stormed and took the strategically important island of Manus, lying to the northeast of New Guinea.

While these operations had no direct effect on the activities of the guerrillas in the Philippines, they did hamper the gathering of supplies and arms in Australia for them because MacArthur's requirements were given top priority. With *Narwhal* virtually out of commission while undergoing major engine overhaul in Fremantle and the demands on other combat submarines to support the overall western Pacific drive, there were no boats available to deliver cargo anyway. So the guerrilla submarine operations took a sudden turn in reverse. Combat subs nearing completion of patrols in the vicinity of the Philippines were commandeered to rendezvous with guerrillas and bring out people—not deliver them, or cargo.

One of the first missions in this new role fell to the spanking new fleet sub *Angler,* commanded by Lieutenant Commander R. I. Olsen, who had taken her out of the Electric Boat Company's shipyard at Groton, Connecticut, late in 1943. This was the *Angler's* second war patrol. On 18 March 1944, while at sea on patrol, she received radio orders "to rescue about 19 U.S. citizens" from a signaled rendezvous position on the west coast of Panay Island. It was with mixed emotion that Olsen headed toward his destination. But the old "can do" spirit of the Silent Service soon asserted itself. At 0900 on 20 March the *Angler* approached, submerged, within one mile of the rendezvous and Swede Olsen saw a large crowd of people walking behind the tree line on a narrow beach. Soon the prescribed signals were hoisted in trees along the water's edge. *Angler* stood out to sea to await nightfall but by midafternoon Olsen became impatient and turned back to the .point, still submerged. At sunset he made a "battle surface" about 1,000 yards off the shore. Soon a small boat carrying Lieutenant Colonel Garcia and Captain Hawley, both of the Philippine Army, came aboard. He was immediately rewarded with the sight of many people, many more than the 19 mentioned in his radio orders, gathered in groups around three rather large native sailboats, their wrapped-up belongings stacked among them.

Colonel Garcia said there were 58 evacuees, not 19, most of whom had walked a long way to get there. Hesitantly, he asked Olsen if he could handle them. The skipper gulped, and after recovering from the initial shock replied bravely that he could. Vastly relieved, Garcia sent an affirmation signal ashore by flashlight and soon the evacuees began to come on board. They made a heartrending sight as one by one they boarded the submarine—a ragged, barefooted mixture of old men and women, returning officers and soldiers, young civilians—men and women, and children from their teens to mere babies. One woman was eight months pregnant but looked so much closer to delivery time that Captain Olsen was deeply concerned. All were aboard before the evening twilight darkened into the black of night. With passengers and their small belongings taken below, the *Angler* steamed out to sea, made a trim dive, surfaced, and shaped course for Darwin.

The entire ship's company was berthed in the `after battery room except for torpedo-room watch-standers. Fore and aft, the boat was crowded like a huge tin of canned humanity, but no one minded. All hearts, from the captain to the mess boys, had gone out to the sturdy band of evacuees, and nothing aboard was too good for them. The *Angler* was doing her limited best to show hospitality. Men and boys were lodged in the after torpedo room, women and children in the forward torpedo room. A CPO was assigned to each room. The CPO quarters were occupied by one mother with her two-month old baby, one pregnant woman, two elderly women, and Gwendolyn Whitney, age 12, a very sick little girl who had gone through the vicious wringer of war.

In addition, the ship was immediately infested with cockroaches and body and hair lice. A large percentage of passengers had tropical ulcers, plus an odor that was unique in its intensity. Two meals a day, with soup at midnight for all hands, was put in effect at once because there was not enough food aboard for a full three meals a day. The passengers ate ravenously at chow time.

"Conditions forward of the Control Room resembled the 'black hole of Calcutta,' " reported Captain Olsen. "It resulted from children urinating on, and otherwise fouling, the deck [Olsen is a very delicate man with the printed word]; body odors and forty or more persons sleeping forward of the Control Room were other factors. In spite of a constant, but discreet, watch on the head [water closet], it became impossible to teach our passengers how to use this vehicle, a rather complicated pump, because after all they had spent two years in the hills and were not acquainted with modern plumbing.

"The first night aboard, an enterprising Army Captain paid a ship's cook 100 pesos for an apple pie. While attached to Colonel Garcia's guerrilla army, the captain had printed the money personally to compete with Japanese Occupation 'pesos,' which were not very popular. The ship's cook could have cared less.

"One for the book was seeing a two-year-old baby smoking and inhaling a cigar while feeding at his Filipino mother's breast. Also a sight to remember was that of two little girls, perched in an upper bunk, picking lice out of each other's hair and cracking them with their finger nails.

"On arrival in Darwin and after disembarking passengers, we spent two days rehabilitating the ship, moving mattresses topside into sunlight and scrubbing down completely with hot soap and water and carbolic acid disinfectant. Numerous cockroach and lice bombs were used in both torpedo rooms and in the CPO quarters."

Thus the mission of the *Angler* was completed. It had been hard work for all aboard, not least of all for the pharmacist's mate, "Doc" Needlinger.

Among the passengers, the men seemed to have suffered more with their feet than did the women. Going

barefoot over the trails—especially through the sharp
Coogon grass, so common on mountain trails, after always
having worn heavy shoes—was a painful experience.
Many suffered from tropical ulcers on their feet, which
were swollen and sore. The women had fared better
despite their thinly soled shoes which were badly worn.
Although most of these people had spent more than two
years in the mountains, fleeing from one hiding place to
another like hunted animals, the general health of all
was good. To be sure, they were malnourished, thin as
rails, and victims of boils; their nerves were on edge,
like banjo strings; but their morale was actually very
high.

Harry G. Heise, an elderly Spanish-American War
veteran, born in Brooklyn, New York, was tense and
nervous, as he came aboard. His mind had become confused in January of that year and turned worse as time
went on. When he came aboard the *Angler* he was in
almost hysterical high spirits. He wanted to shake hands
with everyone and boasted of his wealth and influence.
He had lost his dentures and glasses on the trail. To the
great joy of his wife, Mr. Heise seemed to improve with
rest, good food, and medical care. Toward the end of
the trip he was able to get up, wash, and act as any
normal person. Evidently a submarine trip was just what
the doctor ordered.

Then there was Martin Waldo Luther, a jittery lad of
four. His sight was damaged by an unrelenting sun while
he was adrift at sea with his family in a small boat
for many days. He was totally deaf in his right ear
because of a bomb explosion near him on Nichols Field,
Manila. Martin's father, Lieutenant A. W. King, USA,
was killed in action in 1943.

"Doc" Needlinger was kept busy by a wide assortment
of patients. In addition, he really had a problem keeping
Gwendolyn Whitney alive. On the evening of 21 February
1943, she and all of her four younger sisters and three
younger brothers had been rushed from their home on
Panay into a bamboo thicket to hide from an approaching Japanese patrol in force. The enemy came later that
night and killed, among others, Gwen's maternal great-
grandmother, who had remained at her home. The mur-
der of her great-grandmother threw the girl into a state
of shock. Her tension grew when the Japanese fired

machine-gun bursts into the area where the Whitneys were hiding. When the family, after months of hiding, finally hiked through the jungle-dense mountains to reach the submarine, Gwen was carried in a hammock most of the time. Occasionally it was necessary for her to walk when the trail became heartbreakingly difficult.

When Gwen came aboard the *Angler,* she was near the end of her frayed rope of endurance. With a temperature of 102 degrees the Doc took over. On the second day, despite the medic's intensive care, her temperature shot up to 104 degrees. From then on for ten days, the child's temperature hovered above 100. Then suddenly it dropped to normal, and on the twelfth day Gwen ate breakfast in the mess hall.

This proved the mettle of which navy pharmacist's mates are made.

All of the evacuees had been living for months on a monotonous diet of rice and fish, with some little meat and chicken at infrequent intervals. The change to submarine chow, the finest in the navy, was not too good for the many children in the group, so they were fed steamed rice until the supply was exhausted. By then, they could eat the regular food—and loved it.

Baby Susan Fertig, three-month-old daughter of Major Claude E. Fertig, USA, and Mrs. Fertig, of all aboard, stood the trip best. She gained three quarters of a pound, slept much, cried little, and did not seem to suffer from the low percentage of oxygen on long submerged runs. Her father, a native of LaJunta, Colorado, had boils on his bruised legs and tropical ulcers on his feet. His wife, born in Stoutland, Missouri, was in poor condition as the result of the recent childbirth.

The *Angler* had enjoyed freedom from enemy interference on its homeward voyage of mercy. Not so lucky was the *Crevalle,* Lieutenant Commander F. D. Walker, Jr., commanding.

Crevalle, a fleet-type boat, was commandeered by Com-SubSoWesPac, and tied up to New Farm Wharf in the western Pacific. It was a new deal for Walker and his crew. Instead of sinking ships and killing people, *Crevalle* was going to save some. Ordered to rendezvous with Colonel Salvador Abcede on Negros, Walker cranked on the power. His own words tell the story.

The markers for the rendezvous appeared exactly on time and in the exact positions where we expected them. The orders given *Crevalle* called for surfacing at dusk. However, we decided our chances to escape a possible ambush were much better in daylight and therefore we surfaced at sunset, about thirty minutes early. Colonel Abcede's party appeared immediately.

My orders stated that we would bring out twenty-five passengers and no baggage, and Colonel Abcede had the selected twenty-five in the first canoe. He also, however, had sixteen other refugees in a second canoe, with a small load of baggage, lying off. He said that he did this because he hoped to persuade us to carry more than twenty-five, since many of the refugees were children. We agreed quickly to take them all and called them alongside. At the last minute, an American missionary decided not to come along and returned to the banca after a tearful farewell to his wife and children.

Abcede, dressed in a freshly laundered and starched khaki uniform, boarded with the first load and immediately established his own lookouts, bow and stern. He said he had lookouts in the hills who would give us warning of the approach of aircraft from the other side of the island. We loaded the party through the after battery hatch which was attended by the Chief of the Boat, "Hook" Sutter. The operation was complicated because Abcede wanted to get as much from us as he could and, as a result, it was a two-way affair. We gave him all our small arms and small arms ammunition and a number of assorted tools and other miscellaneous items which his ubiquitous crew wrangled from us. Unfortunately, because of our added load of passengers, we could not give him much food. I learned later that one item which he requisitioned was a new typewriter ribbon.

We established the refugees in the forward torpedo room (which was empty of torpedoes), allowing them to use the wardroom as a lounge. The Chiefs evacuated the CPO Quarters, which provided the women with a space with a door for privacy. We fed them in the crew's mess room, which required trooping them through the control room. This fascinated some of the children, who took to straggling and playing with the switches. The chief of the watch solved this by putting a sign on the switchboard reading, "Any children found in the control room without their parents will be shot." The mothers read this gravely to their kids, who seemed to take it as a matter of course. Considering that some of them could not remember when they were not fugitives, perhaps this is understandable. We entered Molucca Passage about dawn and shortly after, we were forced to dive from aircraft. My memory is that we surfaced and were very quickly driven down again. We had started a battery charge before dawn but our battery was lower than we would have liked. We only had two torpedoes left (in the after tubes) and we were not looking for anything but a quick passage home.

After the second dive from aircraft, we sighted a large convoy on the horizon. At first, it appeared that it would pass us by and we set a course to try to cut off the last ship in the column. However, very suddenly the convoy zigged and started right for us. I have often pondered the reason for this maneuver. My superiors in Perth had the opinion that the second aircraft had stayed in the vicinity of our dive and had sighted our periscope. In any case, this put us in front of the convoy and very close to two escorts who bore down on us. There was no opportunity to shoot and I flooded negative and went deep. We were at about 90 feet when the first escort passed overhead. For what seemed to be a long time, nothing happened and indeed I ordered negative blown to hold the depth. At this moment, however, the first pattern (I think there were only four) of the depth charges exploded. They were very close and were followed in very short order by a second pattern of equal severity. These were the only two attacks made but they left us in a very bad way. It was, without a doubt, the most severe depth charging I have ever experienced.

Our sonar gear was knocked out and for a while there were no more attacks. We thought that our pursuers had abandoned us. However, as soon as we got the sonar fixed, we found they were right on top of us. For the rest of that long day, they hunted us while we gradually crept away. When we surfaced that night, they were still there —searching.

For the passengers it was a most traumatic experience. One of the charges must have exploded very close to the forward torpedo room because when we were docked later we found that the hull was slightly dished-in on the starboard side. When the first charge went off the vent risers from the forward ballast tank opened their joints at the shock and showered the refugees and the room with water. When we finally got down to our running depth, we were heavy and carried a large up angle, which added to the passengers' discomfort. The necessary cutting down of lights and shutting down auxiliary machinery created a dark and eerie stillness. The atmosphere within the boat became very foul and the entire experience must have been horrible. I've often wondered how many of them thought they would never again see dry land. In my report

I said their conduct was magnificent, and it was. We had no trouble with them at all. Our only troubles were with the Japs and with our damaged ship.

When we surfaced, we found everything on top side smashed. This included both periscopes and the radar, which essentially rendered us blind and prevented us from getting into more trouble. We immediately put distance between us and the Japs and charged our very first battery. The trip to Darwin was without incident.

On 3 May 1944, the *Nautilus,* sister ship of the *Narwhal,* passed from the command of ComSubPac, Pearl Harbor, to that of Rear Admiral Ralph Christie, ComSubSoWesPac, and tied up to New Farm Wharf in Brisbane after a not-too-smooth run from Pearl Harbor. Her new skipper was Commander George A. Sharp, USN. Down the long run from Pearl, the new captain of the famous old amazon trained his crew intensely in diving, day and night gunnery practices, and other operational and combat techniques to integrate his three new officers and twenty-two green crewmen with the more seasoned *Nautilus* personnel who had remained aboard. The drills produced a finely honed team. At the same time, the veteran submarine showed the same engine deteriorations that haunted her sister ship the *Narwhal. Nautilus* had 11 broken head studs and 7 cracked liners, with a total loss of 60 engine-hours, by the time she reached Brisbane. Later, northbound to Darwin from Brisbane, the engines managed to produce 3 broken head studs, 2 cracked heads, 1 timer casualty, and a broken vertical drive shaft. Total loss—98 engine-hours. Under normal conditions, the submarine would have headed for dry dock, but, as previously mentioned, there was a war on and *Nautilus* had a job to do. At Darwin, she stripped down by unloading fourteen torpedoes, leaving 10 in the tubes. She also unloaded all torpedo handling gear in both torpedo rooms. Having unloaded this and other items, she took on 92 tons of cargo and Lieutenant John D. Simmons, USNR, all bound for Loculan, Iligan Bay, Mindanao. There had been no time to complete repairs at Darwin; war waits for no man, and repairs could be completed at sea.

The *Nautilus* left Darwin, northbound on her first special mission on 29 May 1944 on three engines; No. 2 engine was still out of commission. The following morning she had an airplane contact by radar but could not see it; she dove just the same. When the sub passed 90 feet going down, all aboard plainly heard a steady hail that sounded, as Sharp remarked, "like we were being raked by machine-gun fire." An hour later the *Nautilus* surfaced; Sharp saw the plane and dodged with another quick dive. Those repeated practice dives while running "down under" certainly paid off.

Number 2 main engine finally was back on the line on 30 May. But this had hardly been accomplished before there was a crankcase explosion on No. 4 that shook all aboard. It was followed by a stubborn fire, but no one was injured. Airplane contacts came in too consistently. It was dive, surface, dive, surface, and so on in wearisome succession. At dawn on 2 June, she surfaced and shortly thereafter sighted a small patrol craft. The enemy opened fire. Captain Sharp tried to shake him off at three-engine full speed, but the Japanese closed the gap and *Nautilus* started the day with another dive. The sea was glassy calm, and the sub was kept submerged until darkness, because the constant presence of patrol craft radar was noted whenever she attempted to surface. The day that followed was free from planes and patrol craft. This gave *Nautilus* a chance to recharge her hungry batteries and for her crew to gulp some fresh air and rest in the sunlight. But on the next day, near her landing spot in Iligan Bay, she again ran into trouble. While surfacing in heavy rain, Sharp saw an enemy cargo ship appear out of a rain squall at 4,500 yards. It was a tempting target, but the Skipper felt he was too close to his landing spot to jeopardize the mission. The problem was settled for Commander Sharp when two Japanese escorts barged out of the squall and headed at high speed toward the *Nautilus*. Sharp pulled the plug, and *Nautilus* went down and deep. Then she took the first and only attack from this particular group. Five depth charges were dropped, but none were very close, and that ended that brief encounter.

At daylight on 5 June the proper security signals were sighted on the beach. This was a new game for Sharp, but he had held a few hot poker hands before, so he played it close to his vest. Submerged, the sub cruised in and out past the beach twice during the day. At least 1,000 people crowded the shore. As soon as the

Nautilus surfaced after sunset, Colonel Robert V. Bowler, USA, came aboard with a party of ten men. It was not long before some 30 bancas, outriggers, and rafts of all sizes came alongside to receive the cargo. By about three in the dusky, dark morning, within minutes of the typical southwest Pacific early dawn, all cargo and personnel had been put ashore and the sub stood out to sea at flank speed. Shortly thereafter an enemy patrol craft drove the *Nautilus* down.

A type of action more to Sharp's liking happened in the early evening of the next day. A two-masted schooner was picked up on radar. Sharp closed to 13,000 yards on the surface and prepared to open fire with the forward 6-inch gun. But the target fired first with flashless powder. Its salvo fell about 1,500 yards short. The target, having a land background, was hard for the *Nautilus* gunners to see, and even radar lost him. Both deck guns were brought into play but after each had fired three salvos, Sharp broke off the action with nothing but observed near-misses to show for his work. After more plane and patrol dodgings, *Nautilus* completed her mission on arrival at Darwin, on 11 June 1944.

About the same time, the *Nautilus* began her first venture into the gunrunning business from Darwin, the *Redfin*, a standard combat fleet sub, commanded by Lieutenant Commander M. H. Austin, USN, was diverted from her Japanese ship hunt and pressed into service for the guerrillas. She was ordered to deliver to Ramos Island in the Sulu Sea 6,500 pounds of Spyron radio equipment, miscellaneous cargo, and personnel: First Sergeant Amado S. Corpus, USA, and five enlisted men trained at Colonel Whitney's private school.

Also aboard, and stowed in the engine room, were four seven-man rubber boats. In line with orders, *Redfin* stopped in Exmouth Bay long enough to show the army men how to handle and disembark from rubber boats. Radio and important personal gear had to go into the first boat. Sergeant Corpus discovered that gasoline to start the radio generator had been forgotten in Fremantle. Enough to fill the bill was obtained at Exmouth Bay. Packed in the starboard ammunition locker, the fume-spreading gasoline containers were a distinct hazard. "The locker was aired every day," Captain Austin recalled, "but I could not help wondering how the explosive fumes would react to a close depth charge. Not exactly a pleasant thought and I kept it to myself."

But the gods of the war smiled upon the *Redfin*. The nine-day run from Australia to Ramos Island was untroubled. Encampment Point, the landing spot, seemed well chosen. The sub surfaced early at night, 600 yards from the beach. Instead of oars, the boatmen pulled themselves by a manila line stretched between ship and shore. The wisdom of this arrangement was revealed when, toward the end of the operation, oars would have been unable to propel the huge, awkward rubber boats against the swift, tidal current. At 2225, the *Redfin* was under way. Lieutenant Commander Charles K. Miller, USN, and Chief Torpedoman William H. H. O'Hara were roundly commended for their good work in rehearsing and executing the unloading operation. Incidentally, the manila line that saved the day had been borrowed en route from Captain Sam Dealey, famous destroyer-killer and skipper of the equally famous submarine *Harder*.

By mid-May *Narwhal* was once again ready for duty. She had a new deal in her command echelon—Lieutenant Commander J. C. Titus became CO, while Frank Latta went ashore on some well-earned leave and to command a new sub still under construction. Executive/Navigator Officer Bob Managhan and Engineer/Diving Officer J. E. Plummer were also to be relieved. But, unhappily, Managhan's successor, Lieutenant Charles R. Gebhardt, did not reach the ship before sailing time. Since an officer with experience in big boats was needed, Lieutenant Plummer was named to fill the Executive vacancy. While he had spent two years in the *Narwhal* as engineer officer, he was brand new to the much bigger job of executive/navigator officer.

"We sailed from Fremantle," said Plummer (now Captain, USN [Ret.]), "and soon after we cleared the harbor we made a trim dive. On that dive, the stern diving planes jammed at a depth of 290 feet. Also, every soul aboard heard a loud, cannon-like crack.

"After nearly losing the boat, we blew up to the surface, stern diving planes still jammed. We returned to Fremantle and went into an ARD, a mobile floating dock, for emergency repairs. When the *Narwhal* sat on the heavy timber blocks, she broke them, fore and aft, as if they were orange crates. It was determined that she was 'hogged,' which means bent in the middle. This was probably caused by the concentration of loading the heavy guerrilla cargoes in both torpedo rooms, 45 tons or more, in each. While in dock, the planes were freed. This 'hogging' could have explained the cannon-like crack heard aboard the submarine at the time the diving planes jammed. Those repairs took several days, during which Lieutenant Gebhardt reported aboard."

In ordinary times, it is doubtful that higher authorities would have permitted the ship to go to sea in her decrepit condition. But this was war and the need for her highly specialized services was demanding. So she sailed northward, prepared to deliver precious guerrilla cargo and fight such Japanese shipping as came along.

One morning, on 21 May, she was in Philippine waters when her starboard main motor flashed over at the forward commutator but, luckily, quickly burned itself out. About this very moment Commander Titus was preparing for a radar attack on a large enemy convoy and his exec did not believe the time propitious for reporting troubles down below. So nothing was said as Captain Titus crossed ahead of the column of enemy ships and took station for tracking at some 12,000 yards on the enemy's starboard bow, against a backdrop of dark land and cloud background that made the surfaced submarine virtually invisible. At 11,000 yards the weather was so thick that no one on the sub could see the bridge, stacks, or details of the nearest ship in the convoy. From an occasional glimpse in a momentary letup in the weather they could see that one target had the long, low, flat lines of a tanker. Other shapes were dimly seen in the fading light of a gathering storm.

Storms meant nothing to the warwise *Narwhal* and her battle-trained men. At 0220, although it was pouring rain and wild winds whipped the waves into frenzied turmoil, the *Narwhal* had the convoy's speed nailed down at 8 knots and zigzagging at from six- to ten-minute legs on a base course of 165 degrees. To take advantage of the rain and poor visibility, Commander Titus started to go in for the kill, with all torpedo tubes ready. At 0310, he fired four bow tubes and swung to starboard so as to bring stern tubes to bear.

After a brief wait, two heavy explosions rolled across the roaring seas and the skipper considered this sufficient evidence of two hits so that he decided against the stern shots. It was his first torpedo attack since taking command, and Jack Titus was highly pleased. All hands had performed excellently in the critical eyes of the new captain. Later, he gave special credit to Lieutenant (jg) J. W. Curtis, USNR, for his masterly operation of the Torpedo Data Computer, the heart of the attack apparatus. Curtis had handled the complicated device with the easy skill of a concert pianist, performing on his instrument. At ten-second intervals, tubes No. 4, 3, 2, and 1 had been fired in such a manner that the fanning spread would hit different ships. All four tin fish ran hot, straight, and normal toward their targets. Torpedoes No. 4 and No. 1 produced hits. The explosions were so overwhelming that the sub's engines slowed down because of jarring of the governors on the main engines.

"This explosion was strong enough so that I could feel it in my knees as I stood in the conning tower," recalled Titus. "I felt as if the entire ship rose from six inches to a foot, something like a small boat riding a wave. I remember holding out my hand to feel the flow of air down the conning tower hatch so that I could tell when the engines came up to speed again. When the explosive shock hit us the flow of air to the engines nearly stopped."

At the same time, radar reported enemy escorts were approaching the submarine rapidly. Titus increased speed to 17 knots and began evasive action. It looked bad for a moment. The fast escorts seemed to increase their speed at the same time and they intensified their search tactics. The weather was so thick that they could not be seen from the submarine at 1,000 yards. At this moment, the radar failed and the gadget became useless. Titus decided to run while the running was good. Not until then did he learn about the starboard motor. Titus took *Narwhal* down and stayed submerged all day to repair the motor and fix the radar.

The *Narwhal* later claimed two hits on two different ships. CTF 72 credited her with damaging two 4,000-ton vessels. On 24 May, the *Narwhal* delivered 28 men and 25 tons of goods to Major C. M. Smith, AUS, at Alusan Bay, on the northeast coast of Samar. She then made for Sanco Point, Mindanao, to deliver mail and to pick up evacuees and captured documents. But disappointment awaited her. She failed to make contact in two days of trying.

Titus wrote in his patrol report: "Whether this was due to difficulties in navigation caused by a 2 knot current setting along the coast and by overcast skies which prevented starsights, or by the shore people being chased away by the enemy is not known. It could well be both as we probably were not there the first night, and the second night when we were there the enemy might have chased off the shore party."

On she went for her final assignment on this trip to Tukuran, Mindanao, where Colonel Robert V. Bowler, AUS, came aboard. Here she delivered 16 men and 25 tons of supplies. All very prosaic, except for the unhappy fact that the *Narwhal* was now leaving a giveaway oil slick wherever she went, and worse than that, the engines were smoking more and Titus enjoying it less.

"For some time I had been campaigning with the engine room to reduce smoke. They had improved to the point where smoke was noticeable only when we increased speed rapidly," Titus recalled. "After unloading I backed clear of the beach and went ahead on the engines, at the same time swinging clear of the coast. There was bright moonlight, and a good deal of smoke which persisted. As I sent word to the engine room to knock off the smoke, the helmsman reported that the gyro compass had stuck. Since we had been having intermittent gyro trouble, I assumed that this was a compass failure and ordered the helmsman to steer by the magnetic compass. Shortly thereafter, the yeoman who was on the bridge as a lookout, reported: 'Captain, the water ain't going by!' Then I realized that we were aground, and that the smoke had been caused by the unusual load on the engines. I was somewhat embarrassed."

Stopping the engines and putting the low-pressure blowers on the main ballast tanks to blow out residual water and lighten ship, *Narwhal* was able to back off without difficulty and work her way around the sandbar. During the unloading period she had drifted down the beach so that the sandbar was between her and the open sea. In the future the new skipper made it a practice to partially flood the main ballast tanks in order to

increase the draft of the ship and have more leeway
in getting off sandbars.

Perhaps it was the oil slick on a glassy, calm sea—
maybe not—but at 0640 on 3 June, while submerged,
the sub was suddenly attacked by a plane. One bomb
came fairly close. It knocked off some cork and grounded
the bridge diving alarm. Now this was highly unusual.
The approved submarine technique of watching out for
planes and ducking them, without waiting for friend or
foe signals, and which had been highly successful so far,
had been strictly adhered to in this instance. When radar
contacted the plane at 9 miles, Titus promptly submerged.
The attack was a complete and unpleasant surprise. After
lying dogo* for two hours, the submarine swung her
'scope preliminary to surfacing only to discover another
Japanese plane—a "Pete"—close aboard. *Narwhal* went
to 120 feet. A good hour later she sneaked up to peri-

"Pete" Mitsubishi F1M2

scope depth and found "Pete" was still there; she went
deep again. Same situation at 1205. Back to 120 feet.
"Pete" was persistent.

Now, if a submariner must have one special virtue,
among many, it is patience. And Titus had plenty of it.
The dull hours passed in the coal-black depths until

---

*Dogo: navy slang for lying silent and inactive, usually on the
bottom.

1412, when sonar reported fast screws approaching. Evidently "Pete" had sent for reinforcements. Soon the screws were slowed and stopped. The Japanese aboard the enemy vessel obviously were listening, there was no pinging. Captain Titus rigged for silent running and a depth-charge attack. He discovered a density layer at 120 feet and went under it to avoid observation.

Narwhal's bent keel had, so far, caused no troubles, nor had the stern diving planes. Sound heard no more screw noises during the afternoon as *Narwhal* sneaked away from the area. At sunset, a periscope survey revealed an empty sky and a glassy, empty sea. Titus surfaced and continued on a southerly course heading for friendly waters. On the mid watch, in Bangka Passage, in the Indonesian Islands, a Chidori-type torpedo boat was sighted by the OOD and lookouts, at a range of 12,000 yards. The skipper, either because of fatigue or poor night vision, could not see the enemy. Anyway, if the Japanese mission was to block the passage, it failed. Titus stalked the boat for a few hours, and after determining that it was, indeed, trying to close the narrowest gap in Bangka Passage, *Narwhal* dove. In view of the turn things were taking, Titus decided to run submerged for the next two days to avoid detection and give his bone-weary crew a much-needed rest. On 9 June he moored to the boom jetty at Darwin, glad to see friendly faces in a friendly port.

In his report, he referred to the increase in both quantity and quality of enemy air search and complained of unstable operation of the governors on engines No. 1, 2 and 4. There were difficulties in starting and stopping them. He also mentioned the mysterious oil leaks. Finally, there was that everlasting smoke trail to contend with. Praise was bestowed upon Lieutenant G. C. Atkinson, Jr., Commissary Officer, who was able to improve the low culinary standards, despite the poor quality of the ship's cooks. Rear Admiral Ralph W. Christie, ComSub's SWPA, awarded the *Narwhal* the Submarine Combat Insignia and congratulated her skipper on damaging 8,000 tons worth of enemy shipping.

With wry humor, Captain Titus told how the natives at Spot Three on Mindanao had been ready to take to the hills when they heard the *Narwhal's* noisy surface approach in the night.

"They believed," he reported, "that an enemy fleet of motor launches was approaching. Colonel Bowler reassured them that the Japs did not have anything that made as much noise as did our submarine. We knew that our engines were noisy, but we did not know that they were *that* noisy."

Perhaps Captain Titus could have claimed that the *Narwhal* was the navy's only heavy-weather submarine because she actually depended on high winds to scatter her smoke trail, and roaring seas to wipe away her oil slicks and hide the penetrating noises of her engines.

10

GUERRILLAS IN ACTION

The guerrilla movement in the Islands had been mainly a hollow front when Commander Parsons, Major Villamor, and the submarines began their work. Even so, the people of the Philippines had made a better fight against the invaders than had other peoples in the Far East. For that they deserve full credit.

On analyzing the guerrilla situation in mid-1944, experts in GHQ Australia determined that the lack of trained officers to provide military discipline was being relieved by the importation of graduates from the school at Tabragalba; also, the lack of everything from weapons to food was being filled by submarines.

The leadership situation, thanks to Parsons' intensive efforts, had also improved. There were now nine recognized leaders in the ten military districts. Their names, districts, and respective strengths as of about 15 July 1944 follows:

6th Military District—Panay—Lt. Col. M. Peralta
.... 18,000 (probably high)
7th Military District—Negros—Lt. Col. Salvadore Abcede
.... 8,000
8th Military District—Cebu—Lt. Col. James Cushing
.... 5,000
8th Military District—Bohol—Maj I. Inginiero
.... 3,000
9th Military District—Leyte—Lt. Col. Ruperto Kangeleon
.... 2,500
9th Military District—Samar—(Not recognized)
10th Military District—Mindanao & Sulu—Col. Wendell W. Fertig .... 35,150 (decidedly high)

| | Total 71,650 |

Actual strength was probably about 60,000 to 65,000 men, which, any way one looks at it, would be a big lump for the Japanese to swallow in their stride. The beefing-up process begun by the *Gudgeon* in 1943 and taken over recently by the giant *Narwhal* and *Nautilus* was to be stepped up. The number of guerrilla radio stations was to be increased although they had now reached an impressive number; so had the number of coast-watchers, plane spotters, weathermen and radio operators.

A quick review of the internal situation in July in the military districts seems called for at this point to bring the reader up to date.

Late in 1943 Colonel Peralta had been driven into the mountains of Panay by a strong enemy force that topped its drive by murdering 3,000 civilians. But Peralta seemed to flourish on adversity and reorganized his men into an even stronger force after the Japanese threat diminished.

In June 1944 the enemy paid a surprise visit to Negros but Colonel Abcede withdrew his forces without suffering serious damage.

Meanwhile, on Cebu other events had transpired. In September 1943, Lieutenant Colonel Estrella, who had either planned a coup while Major Cushing was absent on a call to Negros or had sold out to the Japanese, killed co-leader Fenton. On his return, Cushing court-martialed Estrella and executed him. The major, in January 1944, was promoted to lieutenant colonel and named area commander of Cebu but not recognized as commander of the district, which then included Bohol. He was supposed to receive supplies from Peralta but none were forthcoming.

On Bohol, Major Inginiero was recognized as district commander in November 1943. His leadership was neither energetic nor productive. When the Japanese landed in force on Bohol in June 1944, with decidedly hostile intent, Inginiero's forces ran away and took refuge on Cebu. The Japanese left Bohol on 8 July with a lot of valuable combat loot and automobiles captured from guerrilla sources.

While one Japanese force was working over Bohol, another struck Misamis on Mindanao on 26 June 1944, and Fertig lost his headquarters there. He retreated to

the mountainous area of Lanao. From there he moved
across Mindanao to the town of Esperanza on the Agusan
River, where he was to narrowly escape from two Japanese columns. Fertig and his men vanished in the jungle
and headed for Talacogon in the hinterland of the Agusan
River's headwaters. In July, Fertig reorganized and
claimed to have six divisions of 35,150 men, a figure
that GHQ took with a grain of salt.

Among the unrecognized areas, where strife among
leaders continued, the largest was Samar, where a man
named Merritt led some 1,000 men in the north under
Peralta's protection. There were two additional local
candidates for leadership. The situation was finally settled
by placing Lieutenant Colonel Charles Smith, USA,
temporarily in charge on the island. Under his leadership, order was brought to guerrilla operations on Samar.

Masbate had two conflicting groups, one headed by
Major Janciongco, a Peralta protege, the other by a
native named Villaojada. On Palawan was a force of
about 200 guerrillas, armed by Peralta; on Mindoro a
similar armed force, but without leadership, existed.

The guerrilla situation on Luzon was still confused
and ultrahazardous. Heroic attempts to unify and or-
ganize them had failed. But in midsummer 1944, it
seemed as if military leaders, such as Colonel Russell
W. Volckmann, would stop and reverse the tragic and
turbulent guerrilla record of Luzon.

Before completing his first tour of the Islands in July
1943, Parsons put the finishing touch to his job of unify-
ing the various dissident groups of guerrillas and selecting
and recommending to GHQ-Brisbane district commanders. One of the worst situations was on Leyte, as mentioned in Chapter 3. Parsons resolved this by persuading
Colonel Roberto Ruperto K. Kangeleon, a Filipino
plantation owner, to come out of retirement and take
over the leadership of all the factions on the island. He
convinced Kangeleon that unity on Leyte depended on
such a move. The elderly plantation owner gave his
consent reluctantly, but once he had taken charge, he
assumed full and vigorous command. GHQ-Brisbane confirmed Kangeleon's designation without delay, and the
local war on Leyte was ended.

In the meantime the guerrillas and their supply subs were not idle.

Early in April 1944, a two-plane flight of two huge enemy Kawanichi (four-engined flying boats) left Palaus, south of the Marianas, for Davao, Mindanao. Admiral Koga, Chief of the Imperial Combined Fleet, was moving his headquarters. He was in one plane. In his head were plans for future fleet operations based on the anticipated American invasion of the Philippines prior to a direct attack on Japan. To insure against their loss, copies of the plans were in the briefcase of Vice Admiral Shigeru Fukodome, Koga's chief of staff, in the other plane. Koga's aircraft was lost in a violent storm and never seen again. The other plane, battered by severe weather, was driven off course and sank after making a rough landing off the coast of northern Cebu. Fukodome was captured by Cushing's guerrillas who had been concentrated on that end of the island by Japanese pressure.

In a postwar interrogation, Vice Admiral Fukodome described his ordeal:

> The crash occurred around 0230 in the morning, and . . . when it became daylight I saw a chimney of the Asano Cement Plant, and hence felt I was in fairly safe territory. The actual position of the crash was about 4 kilometers off-shore. We started to swim but progress was slow because of the strong cross current. As I continued swimming shoreward, two or three canoes came out to me, but I hesitated to be taken on because I was not sure whether they were friends or enemies. I finally decided to take a chance and be rescued. When I was taken ashore there were five or six natives who immediately surrounded me and told me to follow them. I went with them into the mountains. The atmosphere there was such that I feared we would be killed. . . . It was late in the afternoon when we got there, and about three hours afterwards there arrived a native non-commissioned officer who spoke fairly good English, and who said: 'We thought you had a pistol when you landed. What have you done with it?' . . . I explained the circumstances of the trip and the accident. When they learned that, contrary to their belief, our plane had not come to attack the island or the natives, they made me wait several hours, and then suddenly their attitude changed. They offered to take me to a hospital, seeing that I was badly injured. . . . I was placed on a simple, primitive stretcher, was carried through the mountains for

seven days, and on the eighth day . . . I was carried into
a fairly good native home where there were two Filipino
doctors and nurses to attend to me. . . . Then there came
to this home a Lieutenant-Colonel Kooshing who said that
he had control of Cebu, and that as long as I was in his
hands, I was safe. . . . At midnight of the 9th [the next
day] Kooshing came to me suddenly, saying that there had
arrived some Japanese Army men to recover the party
[Fukodome and several officers and men of his staff] and
they were causing trouble to the natives. He promised to
release me and my party if I would send word to the
Army that they should not kill or injure the natives. . . .
A message [was] sent through by Kooshing, to which the
Army apparently agreed, so that I was again placed on a
stretcher and taken to Cebu.

Cushing ("Kooshing" in Japanese) had intended to
send the prisoner to Australia by submarine but with
the Japanese threatening the natives (Cushing's wife was
a Filipino), and knowing that he held the low cards, he
delivered the prisoner reluctantly. But the briefcase, and
its precious contents, was sped to Australia by submarine
and aircraft where the plans of the IJN were quickly
encoded and forwarded to all top commanders. Now
they knew how the enemy was thinking, and what were
his latest plans for the defense of his homeland.

This valuable intelligence contribution probably improved Cushing's status at GHQ. Recognition as the 8th
Military District Commander, including Bohol, since
Inginiero had chickened out, was quickly forthcoming
and the pace of submarine deliveries of various badly
needed stores was stepped up.

For some time Manuel Roxas, one of the outstanding
political leaders in the Islands, had been under strong
Japanese pressure to lend his prestige to the Japanese-
created puppet government. Early in 1944 the pressure
became so intense that he decided to follow the pleadings
of his friends and leave the country. Through underground
channels, Roxas got in touch with Chick Parsons. It was
agreed that Parsons, aboard the submarine Narwhal,
would pick up the Filipino leader at the pier of a sugar
plant near Calatagan in southwest Luzon.

In the interest of safety, Mrs. Roxas and their children
would remain in Manila, but Roxas made the mistake of
informing his friend, General Vincente Lim, of his plans

during a visit to him at the Philippine General Hospital. Lim pleaded with Roxas to take him along, and he finally promised to see what could be done. Through Parsons, he asked MacArthur if he could bring General Lim along. The answer was a firm "No."

On his own Roxas told the disappointed Lim that he should go to Paluan Bay on Mindoro's northwest coast and, when Parsons arrived with the sub, plead his own case. This the general decided to do. On the appointed day, about 25 February 1944, Lim left Manila and on arrival in Batangas boarded the *San Carlos*, a large sailboat, which was to take him to Mindoro.

Aboard the *San Carlos* were members of an intelligence network operating in Manila that had been set up by Parsons before he left the Islands in June 1942.

Parsons' plan was to pick up intelligence data from his unit aboard the *San Carlos* at a rendezvous on Mindoro, and confirming that Roxas was ready at Calatagan, Parsons and the sub would head for the pickup point. There was no advance information on the coming of General Lim. Meanwhile, word had reached the Japanese that an important Filipino leader was planning to escape from the country and patrol boats kept vigilant watch over the waters between Luzon and Mindoro. Thus it was that General Lim's boat was stopped and all papers examined. They seemed to be in order and the boarding party was just about to leave the *San Carlos* when one inspector reported that he had found two revolvers in the luggage.

That was a criminal offense and the boat, with all aboard, was taken to Calapan, Mindoro, where Lim was recognized. He and his unlucky shipmates were taken to Fort Santiago prison and executed.

When Chick Parsons learned about the capture of the *San Carlos*, he was ashore, and he had a difficult time getting back aboard the *Narwhal* through the Mindoro woods, which were thickly populated by Japanese patrols. At this time, Major J. H. Philipps, an undercover radio operator on Mindoro, was ambushed and killed by Japanese troops. Lim's capture naturally blew the rescue mission sky-high. Roxas, on hearing the news, returned to Manila posthaste so as not to be caught off-base.

"Eventually, I got back aboard the *Narwhal* safely," reported Commander Parsons. "After we were out of the area, Captain Latta received, on his routine radio schedule, advice from Australia to the effect that there were reports that I had been captured and killed in Mindoro. Actually, the person who was killed in the exchanges we had on Mindoro with Japanese patrols was Major Philipps who was in charge of a local group. Apparently, he had a signet ring with the initial 'P' on his finger. The Japanese patrol, in querying local inhabitants as to whether or not this was Parsons, had been told that it was."

The dramatic part of this incident aboard the *Narwhal* was a very serious message from Australia that read something along these lines:

"If Parsons is aboard your submarine and in good health, proceed to a point several miles away from your patrol area and, at midnight, come on the air and broadcast only the number of fish still in your forward tubes."

This is apparently the same procedure that was set up when the enemy advised that one of our submarines had been sunk. Without breaking radio silence to a dangerous point, the submarine operations base can verify whether or not the information is correct.

"We broke radio silence and sent the figure which would indicate that I was okay and the next radio schedule from Australia brought us one of the nicest messages I think the Navy could have sent, and it then clarified the original message by saying that the reason this was asked was that Tokyo Rose had advised that I had been captured and killed in Mindoro and, since she knew that my mission took me to Mindoro, there might have been some truth in it."

The broadcast of this news by Tokyo Rose was picked up and published in the United States resulting, said Parsons, "in a few nice obituaries."

On 4 July 1946, Manuel Roxas took office as the first president of a free Philippine Republic. Chick Parsons, who by then proudly wore the Philippine Medal for Valor, was to become his naval aide and liaison officer.

On 30 June the *Nautilus* departed Darwin on a threefold mission. She was to disembark one navy officer and 22 enlisted men and 10 tons of supplies at the mouth of the Amnay River, Mindoro, which showed that the hands-off policy of GHQ-Brisbane toward guerrillas with unrecognized leaders was softening. Ten tons of war supplies was not much, but it was better than nothing to the guerrillas concerned.

En route she was to discharge two Filipino Army enlisted men and 30 tons of stores at Canayeon, Bohol; two U.S. Army enlisted men and 30 tons of goods were to be put ashore at Lagoma on Leyte.

At dawn on the first morning out, the sub's radar detected a plane at 5 miles and closing. The plane was recognized as a friendly Beaufort. But this pilot had

Bristol Beaufort

unfriendly intentions. He dove toward the startled bridge watch and lookouts on the submarine's weather deck periscope shears. Fortunately, the pilot allowed too much lead as he dropped a bomb. It hit the water and exploded too far ahead to do damage. His strafing, from two .50-caliber machine guns set in the wings, was also sloppy. The heavy steel pellets ripped into the sea 100 yards off the sub's starboard side. For reasons known only to himself, the pilot did not press the attack but broke away.

Later that day the radar had a rash of plane contacts. Again it was dive, surface, dive, surface. The run continued; some enemy ships were sighted, but none worth sinking. The unloading at Mindoro was quick and without events—except the hearty welcome given the Americans by the local guerrillas. The landing at Bohol was called

off by radio orders because of a sudden Japanese occupation in force.

Captain Sharp passed through narrow and twisting
Surigao Strait, entered the Pacific Ocean, and cruised
northward to Leyte through placid waters.

Since no contact could be made at the number one
rendezvous at Lagoma, Leyte, Captain Sharp made for
the alternate place off San Roque where the expected
security signal was sighted on 14 July. After sunset he
saw a small banca, displaying a brand new Stars and
Stripes and carrying four men, stand out to sea.

The *Nautilus* surfaced and Lieutenant Colonel Kangeleon came aboard. Many boats of good size were on
hand, and one was always ready for loading. The colonel's
organization won warm praise from the submarine commander. If the guerrilla leader worked under pressure,
he did not show it. The Japanese were ashore and fighting in the streets of Lagoma, only 6 kilometers away.
Small wonder that there were no security signals there.
Captain Sharp learned this only just before he sailed
from San Roque. Just after midnight all cargo was clear
of the ship, and the sub set course for distant Sibutu
Passage by way of island water routes. En route she
narrowly escaped disaster when, because of a sluggish
dive, she was attacked by a plane that dropped a bomb.
It was fortunate for *Nautilus* that the pilot was a third-
rate bombadier, for the bomb was wide of the mark and
exploded harmlessly nearby. When she surfaced again,
she soon discovered the same plane and made a running
dive. This plane was as persistent as a New Jersey
swamp mosquito. It continued to hang around and kept
the *Nautilus* down the rest of the day. It was believed
that the plane actually dropped a depth charge instead
of a bomb. This could have been a hit if it had not
been set for a depth too shallow to reach the submarine;
it exploded far overhead. The *Nautilus* stayed under till
sunset.

The missions to Mindoro and Leyte were accomplished
without further incident, but the landing on Bohol was
aborted because the Japanese had landed in force on that
island. The return voyage was quiet except for a few
alarms, all of which were triggered by false contacts.

On arriving at base Sharp pointed with pride to the
fact that his boat had been underway 87 days and

steamed over 20,000 miles in the 94 days since last
refit. He praised J. F. Goodman and N. A. Bruck, chief
machinist's mate and leading motor machinist, respectively, for maintaining an effective plant in spite of chronic
weaknesses and unreliability.

By the time *Nautilus* returned to Fremantle in late
July 1944, General MacArthur, with land forces under
General Walter Krueger, and his Seventh Fleet, commanded by Vice Admiral Thomas C. Kinkaid, had conquered the north coast of New Guinea, and the General
was off for a conference in Hawaii with President
Roosevelt, Admirals King and Nimitz, plus other high staff
officers. Purpose: to decide how to aim for Tokyo. In
the discussion, Admiral Nimitz stood by his old plan of
bypassing a Philippine occupation and heading for Tokyo
by way of Formosa. On the other side, MacArthur insisted that the liberation of the Filipinos en route to Tokyo
was not only humanely correct but also a military
necessity. The decision was left open. In Washington
later, a divided Joint Chiefs of Staff split the issue. The
army, headed by General George C. Marshall, supported
General MacArthur; the navy, led by Admiral Ernest J.
King, was in Nimitz's corner. Nothing was decided. The
plan was held in abeyance for the big Allied conference
in Quebec in September.

Meanwhile, Douglas MacArthur, whose devotion to the
Philippines had never abated, recognized that the tempo
of delivery of supplies and men to his guerrillas would
have to be stepped up. He was counting heavily on
guerrilla intelligence in preparation for his dreams of
assault on the Islands. Accordingly, he urgently requested
reinforcements for his guerrilla sub force. He was aware
that guerrilla intelligence reports sent to GHQ by Spyron,
or brought out by submarine, were locating targets,
particularly in the southern islands, for his own army
airmen, under General George C. Kenney, who bombed
Japanese installations from Mindanao to Mindoro, from
Leyte to the Sulu Sea. MacArthur was rewarded when,
in July 1944, the fleet subs *Stingray* and *Seawolf*, both
of 1938 vintage, were ordered to augment his Special
Mission Unit.

While not specifically assigned as a guerrilla sub, the
Flier, Lieutenant Commander J. D. Crowley skipper, was

traversing regular guerrilla sub areas when tragedy struck on the night of 13 August 1944.

The night was serene, though the sky was overcast, as Lieutenant Commander Crowley drove his submarine from Fremantle to Saigon on her second war patrol. She was heading from the Sulu Sea into the South China Sea, by way of Balabac Strait, which lies between Borneo and Palawan Island. The sub ran smoothly on the surface at a steady 15 knots and the bell had just struck 2200 in the evening watch when the vessel hit a submerged mine. Chaos began with a volcanic eruption up through the conning tower that shook the ship violently and pelted the bridge watch, including Captain Crowley, with debris. A great column of air literally shot from the conning tower through the bridge hatch and carried the exec, Lieutenant J. W. Liddell, who had been standing under the open hatch, with it. He was quickly followed by a line of men who, having left their stations, crowded up behind him. The sub was still doing 15 knots but settling deeper and deeper in the water in what was virtually a running dive to eternity. By Commander Crowley's estimate, the *Flier* sank 60 seconds after she hit the mine. Only the bridge watch, including Crowley, and a handful of men on watch in the conning tower managed to escape the sinking sub.

The 13 men who found themselves miraculously alive and afloat were all strong swimmers. At first, the captain tried to keep them together. He knew that Balabac, a small island just south of Palawan, lay to the north, and he led off in that direction. When the moon rose at 0300, it became easier for the determined survivors to maintain course, but nothing eased the long hard pull. By then some of the swimmers had been swept away by the tide; some of the injured men, unable to go on, had to give up; others just too tired to continue stopped their tired legs and arms and gave themselves to the sea.

Captain Crowley told the survivors with him that land was in sight but it was every man for himself. At 1330, after a 15-hour swim, Crowley and four men staggered ashore where they found two swimmers who had landed ahead of them. Eventually they were joined by two other crewmen. After five dreary days of worried waiting—wet, hungry, and thirsty, and mourning for their lost ship and shipmates—the party was discovered by native fishermen.

In short order the survivors were delivered to a coast-watcher station on Palawan, where they were given food and drink and comforting. Fremantle was notified and the *Redfin,* a part-time guerrilla sub commanded by Lieutenant Commander M. H. Austin, was called off her war patrol west of Balabac Strait to perform a double rescue mission on Palawan—the *Flier* survivors and nine other persons marooned at Sir John Brookes Point on Palawan. As things turned out, it proved to be quite an unusual expedition.

Redfin reached the rendezvous on 30 August and spent most of the day keeping a close periscope watch on the shore, where, at 1305, a small Japanese sea-truck of the cargo type proceeded toward Brookes Point from the north. The truck anchored and *Redfin* crept to within 3,000 yards of the ship to investigate by periscope. Captain Austin saw no armament and concluded that the truck's coming was entirely incidental. But the Japanese had radio equipment and the situation demanded caution. As darkness fell, *Redfin* drew away and surfaced with manned battle stations. But there were no shore signals; only a confusion of radio calls that never made sense bombarded the *Redfin* from shore.

At 2255, hoping for some kind of action, Captain Austin went within 4,000 yards of the anchored ship and flashed "AA" four or five times by blinker tube. No answer. Rather discouraged, Austin secured from battle stations and set out to sea to charge batteries. But, at 0037, radar discovered pips that indicated that there were two small boats in a spot 5 miles from the point. At 0100, the boats passed close aboard and hailed the sub. Fortunately Austin recognized the voice of his friend, Commander Crowley. On board came not only the *Flier* survivors but also the other party of nine.* The flap ashore seemed to have been caused by the close presence of the Japanese ship, which filled the evacuees with consternation. Some of the latter described the anxieties of that night as "hair-raising!" Austin told the coast-watchers who came aboard that he proposed to shell the Japanese ship when he departed and asked them to capture escaped crewmen. To his pleasant sur-

---

*This party consisted of two army enlisted men (escaped POWs), one naval enlisted man from PATWING 10, four British subjects, one American civilian, and one Finnish citizen.

prise he learned that two of the coast-watchers had been landed, with all their radio equipment, from the *Redfin* on her June 1944 run to Ramos Island. In return for their hospitality, the men from Palawan received rifles, machine guns, pistols, and ammunition from the *Redfin*, as well as cigarettes, medicines, playing cards, food, and radio tubes.

Alas, the shelling of the sea-truck was a miserable failure. The vessel escaped in shoal waters too shallow for the *Redfin* to enter. But the spectators had a good time watching the gunfire while it lasted. By radio the coast-watchers reported the completion of the rescue mission and added that Alastair D. Sutherland, six-year-old son of the Reverend A. M. Sutherland (a missionary in Palawan) jumped with joy as he yelled, "Kill the Japs! Kill the Japs!"

On 30 July, Lieutenant Commander R. S. Lynch, CO of the gallant *Seawolf*, was relieved by Lieutenant Commander A. M. Bontier, an old hand at submarine warfare having made a dozen combat patrols. *Seawolf* left Darwin at 1800 hours on 1 August 1944 on Bontier's first guerrilla run. This was the second guerrilla trip for the famous fighter credited with sending 71,609 tons of enemy shipping to the emperor's fast growing ocean-bottom merchant and warship fleets, but Bontier's first. He was to deliver Lieutenant Konglain Teo, four radio operators, one weatherman, and 14,540 pounds of supplies to Tawitawi to reinforce an intelligence party headed by Captain Young, AUS. She was then to land Sergeant Cabias with five radio- and weathermen on Palawan to set up a coast-watcher station.

The run to Tawitawi held no thrills or spills. Once they stalked a submarine. It turned out to be a tree stump. Bontier blasted it with gunfire. At the landing point, Captain Young came aboard, followed by his aide. The latter was armed with a veritable arsenal of knives and guns. With all his paraphernalia, he could barely get down the 24-inch hatch. In the wardroom, Captain Young told tall guerrilla stories and consumed a stack of sandwiches hungrily. He looked, said Bontier, half-starved.

The men had a hard time unloading the cargo because of the ebb tide, a fast current, and a coral-lined beach. The rubber boats could not reach the shore and the cargo had to be back-packed by manpower to the beach from the coral heads that lined the shore. It was a tough job. Bontier tried to ease it by hauling the boats via a waterproof jute line. But the line did not float and was useless. Unidentified lights down the beach disturbed the natives, but they kept working. Bontier felt sorry for them. Before daylight, they had to move the cargo from the beach into safe hiding. Despite fears and difficulties, the unloading went well and soon the *Seawolf* was en route to her next port of call, which was reached two days later.

This second landing spot was also a tough one on a coral-lined beach. Even so, it was accomplished by the *Seawolf's* crew with amazing speed. Five tons from sub to shore in three hours was far from bad.

The first day en route home, 10 August, the *Seawolf*, always hunting for action, chased smoke that turned into clouds and masts that always developed into floating debris. The next two days passed like beads strung on a too-thick string. But at 0016 on 13 August, while surfaced in the middle of a rain squall, the radar got a pip at 7,000 yards. Next, radar reported the pip at 5,000 yards and closing fast. Now a plane could be heard coming in on the port beam. Just as the sub was diving, the plane let go a light flare that went off directly over the sub's after battery room and cast a ghostly white light. The last man off the bridge in a flying run, Captain Bontier was in the act of closing the upper hatch when a couple of small bombs came down; both were near-misses.

"No damage," reported the captain, "except a jangled nerve here and there. No more bombs followed so we decided that he carried only two, but since we also believed that it would be best to clear that area before he could call in too many pals, we departed for home at best submerged speed."

The mission was completed without undue incident. CTF 72 radioed: "Well done *Seawolf* for snappy work on first two jobs."

Al Bontier's next run was not to be as uneventful.

11

THE TRAGIC LOSS
OF SEAWOLF

The pages were flying off the calendar like leaves off a tree in the fall when Admiral William F. Halsey succeeded Admiral Raymond A. Spruance to command of the old Fifth Fleet, which then became the Third Fleet, largely to confuse the enemy. While Halsey took command on 26 August, he did not actually catch up with the main core of his interest—Fast Carrier Task Force 38, commanded by Vice Admiral Marc A. Mitscher—until 11 September. On that date Halsey came aboard Mitscher's flagship, the heavy carrier *Lexington*, just as the carrier force had completed a very disappointing series of air strikes on the southern Philippines. Instead of meeting up with the strong Japanese resistance expected, only 6 enemy planes were sent aloft to fight over Mindanao; on the ground, 58 Japanese planes were destroyed. The answer was that General Kenney's army fliers, MacArthur's air arm, had scrubbed the air over Mindanao clean of Japanese airmen. Mitscher suggested that attention be shifted to the central islands. Halsey agreed. During the next few days, some 300 enemy planes were either shot down or smashed on the ground by "Pete" Mitscher's carrier fliers, and some shipping in island waters was also hit.

Aboard his flagship, the battleship *New Jersey*, Halsey followed events and decided that the much-advertised Japanese wall around the Philippines was a hollow shell. Instantly aware of the vital significance of this discovery and always on the trigger, the admiral sent identical radio messages to Admiral Nimitz and General MacArthur suggesting that the program for landings on Peleliu, Angaur, Yap, Morotai, and Mindanao be cancelled and that General MacArthur should land his forces on Leyte directly. To shorten the story, the plan, somewhat changed by Nimitz and MacArthur, was approved by both and forwarded to the Allied Quebec Conference just before its final adjournment. No action had been taken by the high and the mighty on the invasion project. The new MacArthur-Nimitz plan stimulated quick action by the Joint Chiefs of Staff present at the meeting. On the recommendations of Admiral Nimitz, invasions by his Central Pacific force were limited to Peleliu, Angaur, and Ulithi. General MacArthur would cut out island-hopping in the southern and central Philippines, take Morotai, and land on Leyte on 20 October. This proposal was approved by the conference.

With this plan given the go signal, Admiral Nimitz at once pitched in to help where he could. Naval attack forces at Pearl Harbor and destined for Yap Island were sent to MacArthur's base at Manus in the Admiralties instead. The same swift shift was given an attack unit already at sea and bound for the western Carolines. Transports, supply ships, and landing craft, even whole escort carrier groups with their fire-support units of warships, were transferred bodily from Halsey's Third Fleet to General MacArthur's Seventh Fleet, commanded by Vice Admiral Thomas C. Kinkaid.

MacArthur was naturally jubilant. That the road to Tokyo would be by way of a free Philippines was now assured. His ringing promise to the Filipinos, "I shall return," would be redeemed. When all transfers had been completed, Halsey's fleet had been reduced to "Pete" Mitscher's carriers and their gun-support groups. To be sure, this was a powerful task force of 17 heavy and light carriers whose airplane complements totalled 1,178 aircraft, from fighters to torpedo-bombers. In addition to the gun-toting fire-support vessels attached to each of the four carrier groups, a separate support unit of battleships, cruisers, and destroyers acted as bodyguards for the vulnerable flattops. A new element had been added to the fleet in the guise of a refueling unit of tankers, baby flattops, and destroyers that provided the fleet with fuel, ammunition, planes, and even pilot replacements at sea. The officers and men on the carriers and warships would now seldom see port. No more Pearl Harbor liberty parties. The new fleet base established on Ulithi

Atoll in the western Carolines had only sand, sun, and suds (beer) to offer. But if everyone was not happy over this new girl-free paradise, no one sounded off about it very loudly.

In line with programming, a small MacArthur force, supported by a carrier task group, landed and took Morotai, just south of Mindanao, on 15 September. It was a walkaway and a suspiciously easy, as well as false, example of things to come. Work was begun at once on an airfield on Morotai to serve planes en route from SoWesPac bases to Leyte.

Submarine skippers in the gunrunning trade learned that numberless Filipinos had enjoyed watching Kenney's and Mitscher's airstrikes on the Japanese from their sanctuaries in the hills. Planes and shipping had been hard hit, but best of all, enemy infantry had been seriously unnerved. At this period, American army planes patrolled the land and waters over the central and southern Philippines, as well as the Indonesian Islands. Navy planes, on occasion, were also quite common over the area. The submariners learned to dislike even thinking about "Yankee" airplanes and aviators, especially army fliers, and for reasons that will soon become evident.

Stingray's September guerrilla run was to land a heavily armed reconnaissance party on Majoe Island. Let Captain Sam Loomis tell his own story.

This landing was to be made at night, undetected. A 25 or 50 mile radius around Majoe (I forget which) was designated as a restricted area for aircraft for this particular top secret mission.

The reconnaissance party was composed of about 25 Dutch officers and men who were to set up a radio station on the island.

We were to land them one night and pick up those who were not staying on the island the next night.

We reconnoitered the beautiful sandy beaches of this small mountainous island by close-in periscope observation during the day. If there ever was an island paradise this looked like it. Well built native girls (topless) were observed walking along the beach. I jokingly offered to go ashore myself.

The Dutch were prepared for the worst, for upon boarding in Darwin their C.O. gave me a packet of rubber coated potassium cyanide pills to keep in my safe until debarking. Each man was to carry one of these deadly pills in his mouth, biting down on the rubber coating if captured; thus ending the prospect of cruel torture. Their fears turned out to be unfounded as we found out later when we picked up the returning party. The Japs earlier had set up an observation post on the island but had departed a few days before the landing. To get back to the aircraft hecklers:

In addition to being pestered en route by Army aviators, darned if while making our final "undetected approach" within the restricted area one of our "friends" dropped a bright flare that made us feel awfully naked on this dark tropical night. The Dutch C.O. was all for postponement but finally agreed to go ahead with the landing after waiting a couple of hours.

When we picked up the returnees the next night they said Majoe was truly an island paradise. Beautiful "coffee and cream colored" natives and very friendly. No insects on the island and fruit and food plentiful.

I have since often wished I could cruise these waters on the surface and in particular make my own personal "undetected landing" on Majoe Island.

After completing this mission Loomis returned to Darwin, his usually genial face overcast by clouds of wrath. Out of 18 aircraft houndings, some of the most persistent had been by friendly planes.

In his report, Loomis observed gloomily: "We have schedules to follow and places to go ourselves and just because an aviator thinks it is fun to force a boat down, we have to put up with a lot more of the inconveniences of war, which are not a Hell of a lot of fun to begin with.

"I have talked with many airmen who are ignorant of bombing restriction in safety areas and recognition signals. Many have said that it gives them a big kick to force pigboats to dive. Most of these have been Army fliers.

"Carrier pilots seem to have seen the light and are generally cooperative. I believe that is because they know some of their shipmates, downed at sea, have been rescued by lifeguard submarines on duty with the carrier fleet."

The observation was noted by hard-bitten Submarine Force Commander in Brisbane, Captain J. M. Haines, who added that the mere presence of planes hampered submarines in the performance of their special missions and passed the comment upstairs to higher authority.

The next mission of the *Narwhal* turned out to become —in its closing phase—one of heartbreak, sadness, and hatred of war.

After delivering 35 men and 35 tons of cargo on the southwest coast of Mindanao and 3 men and 20 tons on the north coast of the same island, Captain Titus, in line with orders, surfaced near Sindangan, Mindanao, where he was met by Captain Thomas, AUS. At his request, the submarine moved into nearby Siari Bay to pick up 80 rescued American prisoners of war and one American medical officer. All the POW's were in bad shape; 4 were stretcher cases.

They had been prisoners aboard five transports, in a seven-ship convoy sunk by a submarine—obviously American—off Sindangan Point, Mindanao, on 6 September. The stories told by the grateful men as they came aboard were truly terrifying testimony to enemy cruelty. After the torpedoings, the guards butchered hundreds of helpless prisoners, mowing them down in the holds or slaughtering them in the sea with machine-gun fire. Some 20 men, "rescued" by the Japanese from the sea, were lined up on deck, their hands tied behind them, and shot.

One enemy officer had previously told his prisoners that if their ship was torpedoed, he would personally annihilate them. Antisubmarine drills were staged during the voyage in which the guards would assemble, armed with guns and grenades, and surround the hatches, ready to use their weapons on prisoners crowded into the cargo holds.

The men rescued from the sunken hellships by guerrillas responded well to food, kindness, and medical care. These poor wretches, ridden by tormenting nightmares, were horrible testimony to the "glory" of war.

On 30 September, the home-bound *Narwhal* and all aboard were in a tight jam as the sub submerged in a runaway dive that could have ended too far in the depths of the sea for survival. She was submerging from a float-plane attack coming in from a distance of some 12 miles, with the stern diving planes set for a 20-degree diving angle. Suddenly all power was lost. The planes could not be moved by power or manually. To stop the dive,

Captain Titus blew all main ballast and backed engines at emergency speed. But the *Narwhal* was running wild, going down, down, down. At last the skipper stopped her at about 300 feet, the fastest and dizziest dive the old girl had ever performed. Now the action reversed.

Venting all main ballast tanks and going ahead emergency did not prevent her from broaching stern first when she surfaced at 1525 into blessed sunlight, which many aboard had never expected to see again. Unruffled, radar reported the enemy plane at a range of one mile. Taking a long chance, in spite of his lack of proper diving control, Jack Titus went down to 90 feet and changed course.

"No bombs," he recalled, "so *Narwhal*, bursting out of the sea, must have surprised the pilot as much as she did ourselves."

What did Titus think about during his vertical "Nantucket sleigh ride?"

"This condition must be rectified," was the cool answer.

No truer words were ever uttered. En route home, while surfaced, the skipper determined that the stern plane failure was due to partially seized bearings that resulted in the need for more than usual power to work the planes—an old flaw.

A few days later, the sub sighted a Japanese hospital ship, *Hikawa Maru*. The captain took photographs and let the conning-tower watch look at the untouchable target while they thought about their 81 passengers, their hapless shipmates, and their cruel fates.

On 2 October, Captain Titus informed Fremantle about his diving troubles and requested that our aircraft be ordered to keep clear of the *Narwhal*. He could still dive if he had to, but only very slowly, and there was no assurance with respect to the eventual outcome. The *Narwhal* might bounce back to the surface or she might plummet to the bottom for keeps.

During the night of 2-3 October, main engine No. 1 went out of commission from a cracked liner. Eight minutes later, radar interference on his own frequency led Captain Titus to conclude that it was either the USS *Paddle* or *Seawolf* outward bound. The *Narwhal* was proceeding slowly on the surface.

"I put the contact abeam to open track and at 9,000 yards a lookout reported a dark spot similar to a submarine. I could not see this object. Shortly thereafter, tracking indicated that the contact also had changed course to open track with a slight increase in speed. Later information disclosed that this was an enemy submarine which we misjudged."

Just to liven things up for the ex-POWs, when *Narwhal* crossed the equator on 4 October, Titus made all his passengers "shellbacks," with appropriate ceremonies.

With typical thoroughness, Captain John M. Haines, Commander Submarines, Brisbane, read the sub's patrol report and noted, as a faint reprimand, that "only one worthwhile target was encountered on the patrol and that was a probable Japanese submarine which the *Narwhal,* believing it to be friendly, avoided."

This complicated business of selecting friend from foe among submarines took a tragic turn early in October when the *Seawolf* was sunk by a friendly destroyer escort or aircraft on her third guerrilla run. She had departed from MacArthur's base on Manus on 29 September to carry 17 soldiers and 6 tons of stores to Samar Island. There she was to pick up Major Sabarre and 11 men to be landed secretly on Bataan Island with 9 tons of cargo, on 6 October. On her way north, she entered a new submarine safety lane* that had been defined north of Morotai, which was now in American hands. On 2 October, *Seawolf* told Fremantle she was a day behind schedule because of high seas and strong winds. In accordance with rules, Seventh Fleet Headquarters received this information to be passed on to carriers and other ship units concerned.

Before noon on 3 October, a Seventh Fleet task group was attacked by an enemy submarine and the destroyer *Shelton* suffered severe damage from a torpedo hit. The task group went on, but the destroyer *Rowell* was ordered to stand by the *Shelton.* While *Rowell* circled her wounded companion, the latter detected a submarine on her sound gear and reported it to the *Rowell.* About 1130, aviators from the jeep carrier *Midway* sighted a sub and reported her position to the *Rowell.* One plane dropped a couple of dye bombs as markers while the other let go two

---

*A restricted attack area, a moving lane usually about 25 miles wide and 100 miles long along a predetermined axis (course) which gave the submarine sanctuary if unable to keep up her scheduled speed of advance, or get ahead of it.

325-lb. bombs as the sub dove. The surfaced sub had not given any recognition signal and neither carrier flier knew that they were over a safety lane, which showed that the channels of information in the Seventh Fleet were, to say the least, slow. The *Rowell* reached the area about 1310 and almost instantly detected a submerged sub. The destroyer attacked with a deadly hedgehog projectile pattern after which she heard underwater sounds that could have been an attempt at sonar transmission. On the other hand, they could have been attempts to jam the destroyer's sound gear. To the *Rowell*'s skipper they sounded like the latter. He promptly tripped off four more hedgehogs and added a depth charge for good measure. He was rewarded by several heavy underwater explosions and the appearance of debris on the surface. The latter included a section of periscope. This he tried to recover but failed to reach before it sank again. The board of inquiry that followed determined that *Seawolf* had been sunk by "friendly" forces but could not decide if her loss was caused by aircraft bombs or hedgehogs. However, that was slight consolation to fellow submariners who could well visualize the frantic last minutes of those aboard the *Seawolf* trying desperately to make their attackers understand that they were friends, only to be blown to kingdom come seconds later by fellow Americans.

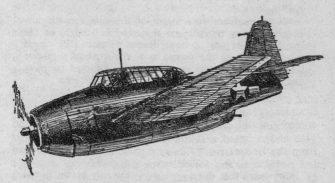

Grumman TBF Avenger

The danger of pushing submarines around in active war zones infested with our own forces was also demonstrated on the same day that *Seawolf* died, when the *Stingray* was attacked in the same safety lane. On this patrol, the sub's vital IFF equipment, which identified her as friend or foe, was out of commission. Not enough time between patrols to fix it. Captain Loomis wrote that, at 1222 on that date, "An American TBF crossed the *Stingray*'s stern at about eight miles. An attempt to exchange recognition signals failed." In providing the authors with an account of this hair-raising incident, Captain Sam Loomis, now retired, recently wrote:

The morning of 3 October dawned bright and clear, with a choppy white-capped sea. Our large U.S. flag was flying and looked beautiful in the bright sunlight.

Stingray, heading south, had just entered a newly established submarine safety lane and expected to pass *Seawolf,* heading north. A classmate of mine, Al Bontier, was C.O. of the *Seawolf* and I was looking forward to exchanging pleasantries via signal light. We had no information that a friendly hunter-killer group was nearby.

At 1222, an American TBF was sighted visually and by radar on a crossing course eight miles astern. Recognition signals were flashed by searchlight which apparently attracted the pilot's attention for he immediately turned, and headed toward us at low altitude. When the range had decreased to about five miles, at 1226, we pulled our port recognition flare, cleared the bridge and dove. Ordered depth to 120 feet. As we passed 100 feet, heard a very loud thud.

We submariners were aware of the new acoustic torpedoes and my thought was that this thud might be the splash-down of one of these deadly weapons. We rigged for silent running and slowed to 40 rpms. About a minute later, we heard a loud explosion which knocked off paint and later found that it shattered our searchlight lens.

    1318: Came to periscope depth and observed a TBF circling at range of about four miles.

    1324: Plane headed toward us. Went to 150 feet.

    1405: Periscope depth; nothing in sight.

    1410: Heard series of distant explosions.

    1550: Surfaced.

    1625: Sighted a TBF at ten (10) miles.

Convinced that there were many friendly planes in the vicinity, I decided to stay on top and fight a recognition battle, rather than take our chances with friendly acoustic torpedoes.

A short time later, four F8F fighter planes came roaring in from astern. Pulled both recognition flares, flashed the light and waved the flag, in addition to the one flying from our mast. At the last second, they veered off and circled close aboard. Established voice radio communications with the leader who said his "base" was 20 miles astern, same course and speed at ours and headed for Manus as were we.

During the same course of our conversation, I learned the following:

(1) That "Base" was a hunter-killer group, composed of two escort carriers and four or six destroyer escorts.

(2) That one of the groups, a *DE*, the *Shelton*, had been torpedoed shortly after 0800 that morning.

(3) That a "successful" attack had been made against a submarine that forenoon.

(4) That a TBF was missing.

I requested that he ask his base to furnish us an escort to keep his "friendly pals" from using us as a target.

The answer came back that they would furnish us air cover until sunset and that, at dawn, we would have a *DE* escort during the remainder of the passage to Manus.

Bright and early the next morning, the *DE Rowell* showed up and, during the voice radio chit-chat, learned the following additional information:

After the torpedoeing of the *Shelton*, a TBF had straddled a diving submarine with two depth charges, just as the submarine's periscope shears were going under.

The *Stingray* attack by a TBF occurred shortly after the sinking of the *Seawolf*, about five (5) miles away.

The *Rowell*, our present escort, was called in and launched depth charge and hedgehog attacks that were considered highly successful.

I voiced apprehension for the *Seawolf* as all during the night the Southwestern Pacific submarine command was asking her and *Stingray* to report our positions immediately. I had heard nothing from *Seawolf*.

This bit of information to the C.O. of the *Rowell* seemed to deaden his previous elation over what he thought to be the sinking of the Jap submarine that had torpedoed the *Shelton*.

Stingray arrived at Manus about an hour after the hunter-killer task group the morning of 5 October.

The Admiral in command must have had his doubts by then about the *Seawolf* incident, for, within a few minutes after we anchored, his barge came alongside with orders that I report to his flagship, the escort-carrier *Midway*, (name later changed to *St. Lo*, so that a new, large attack carrier could bear that name).

When I arrived in the Admiral's cabin, the pilot of the

plane that initiated the attack on the sunken submarine was present, as were several other pilots and, I believe, the C.O. of the *Rowell*.

I noted a large chart showing the old submarine Safety Lane displayed on the bulkhead, but not the new.

At the conclusion of our conversation, it was my opinion, by deduction, that:

A TBF and the *Rowell* had sunk the *Seawolf* and that the missing TBF pilot had attacked the *Stingray*. At the last second he had realized we were friendly and, in his attempt to abandon the attack, he must have dipped a wing, or made some maneuver that caused him to crash over us.

The loud thud we had heard was the plane hitting the water and the heavy explosion about a minute later, were his two depth bombs going off when they reached their pre-set depths.

If this unknown pilot did in fact abort his attack upon recognition, thereby causing his fatal crash, it's too bad his efforts could not have been rewarded, for his loss, undoubtedly, prevented *Stingray* from meeting the same fate as *Seawolf*.

All in all, this fourteenth war patrol had not been a pleasant one for *Stingray*, and Loomis was glad when it ended at Brisbane, for a much-needed refit, on 14 October. There had been seemingly unnecessary delays at Spot One on Mindanao Island, where 35 tons of supplies had been put ashore. At Spot Two, on Suluan Island, huge breakers had prevented a landing. The submarine had crept to within 1,800 yards of the reef, with its crashing and thunderous breakers, but dared not go in closer because of the uncertainty in the accuracy of the charts and the state of the sea. After hours of anxious waiting a launch finally appeared through the treacherous surf and took the three Army officers and their equipment off and away. With relief, Captain Loomis turned to deeper and safer waters only to find the air full of friendly planes bent upon killing friendly submarines.

There must, thought Loomis as the patrol ended, be easier ways to fight for victory and survival in combat, but if there were he did not know them.

Captain George A. Sharp took the *Nautilus* on her twelfth war patrol on 17 September out of Darwin, with two army enlisted passengers and 106 tons of cargo. En route north, she practiced quick dives to avoid, mostly, friendly plane attacks, but just south of Timor Island she began to dodge the real thing. By the time the *Nautilus* reached Cebu, her first objective, she had made 11 plane contacts and had avoided them thanks to the training in quick dives to best Houdini standards in speed and adroitness. While Sharp was making a periscope reconnoiter of the landing spot on 25 September, the twelfth plane contact was made at 8 miles. He didn't even bother to lower his periscope because he had become annoyed by this type of activity. That night at sunset, after security signals had been shown on shore, *Nautilus* surfaced. Colonel James Cushing came aboard. Soon many small boats, about 25 in all, came alongside and took off the cargo. The sub was about 600 yards from the beach and had to maneuver constantly against the current to keep in that position.

The *Nautilus* had received 11 evacuees and had just gotten under way on the surface to clear the area under cover of the pitch-black night when she suddenly came to an abrupt, jarring halt. She was aground on a shoal in 18 feet of water. In the twinkling of an eye, Sharp blew all main and variable ballast. He also rang for full back emergency speed. But the *Nautilus* remained aground. The off-duty crew was roused and rushed topside to run from port to starboard and back repeatedly in an attempt to rock (sally) the ship afloat. That too was futile. What with enemy planes, patrol boats, and troops all around, Sharp was pressed for time. He took a chance and shot off a message to Brisbane to explain his predicament—that he would probably have to take his men ashore and destroy the *Nautilus* with her built-in demolition charges. The message was acknowledged; headquarters wished Sharp and his men good luck and began to make plans for the rescue of the submarine's crew, as well as ways to complete the destruction of the great old sub, a job which dynamite might fail to accomplish. But George Sharp was not one to give up easily. Taking an even longer chance, he decided to hang on and to lighten the ship in the hope of taking full advantage of the high tide due at 0400. Captain Sharp sent all evacuees, mail, and captured documents ashore. Next, some 40 tons of cargo, all that Cushing's men could handle in that time, were also sent to the

beach. It was a tense race against the hands of the
clock. Just before 0400, Sharp burned all confidential
papers and blew all reserve fuel and gasoline tanks dry.
Some 190 rounds of 6-inch ammunition also went over
the side. At 0400, the tide changed but actually went
out instead of in. Coral heads and a sandy bottom now
became clearly visible around the ship. Sharp was ready
to send his crew ashore and destroy the *Nautilus* if she
could not be taken off the shoal after a reasonable try,
but, with low water, he did not have much hope.

The four main engines were started one by one; gradually they built up to full power and, with an unspoken
prayer on the captain's lips, they were thrown on full
back. The sub trembled and shook. Then slowly, ever so
slowly, to the happy surprise of all aboard, she backed
off the shoal and floated unharmed into deep water.
When underway, Sharp compensated for the weight which
had been jettisoned by removing manhole covers and
flooding the gasoline and reserve fuel tanks. Meanwhile,
an all-safe message was flashed to Fremantle where rescue and demolition projects were happily abandoned. The
process of flooding the regular ballast tanks was initiated
promptly and the *Nautilus* soon had a diving trim. That
was great consolation later when plane contacts popped
up that afternoon. It was a narrow escape but all in a
day's (or night's) work so far as the Silent Service was
concerned.

This situation points up one of the most troublesome
problems encountered by subs on secret missions.

ComSubPac, having been informed of *Nautilus'* predicament, diverted *Mingo,* which was en route south to
Australia from patrol, to stand by the stricken vessel.
This meant that *Mingo* had to enter the Mindanao Sea
to get to Cebu. In the meantime the *Cero* was on patrol
in the same area, guarding Surigao Strait, but free to
roam the whole body of water. Her mission was top
secret and known only to ComSubSoWesPac. The skipper
of *Cero* was unaware of the *Nautilus* mission, or her
predicament, nor was he informed that *Mingo* was entering his area. It must be recognized that *Mingo* belonged
to ComSubPac, Pearl Harbor, and *Cero* was under the
operational control of ComSubSoWesPac in Australia. So
was *Nautilus.*

There was considerable confusion that dark night in

the Mindanao Sea. *Cero,* patrolling on the surface, made radar contact on a single target and went to battle stations. Closing for a surface torpedo attack she suddenly picked up radar interference. Commander Dissette, the CO of *Cero* dared not attack under these circumstances unless the target was positively identified as enemy. So how to do that?

The submariners had developed a method of "keying" the surface search radar so that brief recognition signals could be transmitted. It was risky business because the Japanese were believed to know our radar frequency. Nevertheless, Dissette challenged. His target turned out to be *Mingo.* In the meantime *Mingo* asked, via radar, "Who are you?", both subs keeping their bow torpedo tubes aimed at each other. Both skippers heaved a sigh of relief when the muddied situation was cleared up.

Mingo and *Cero* drew abreast of each other at close range and in the silent black night the captains, old friends, exchanged information by bullhorn (electric megaphone). That was the first time Dissette learned about *Nautilus* and *Mingo*'s mission. He offered to stand by to assist. Not long thereafter came the happy word that Commander Sharp had shaken *Nautilus* loose. Relieved, everybody turned and went about their business.

The moral of this recitation is "How much does any one else have to know about a submarine's movements and particularly, about special missions?" To broadcast submarine activities, even in code, to one's own forces could be disastrous for two reasons: 1) the code might be compromised, and therefore the information become known to the enemy; and 2) because of the communication system (blind broadcasts) imposed on the submarine force by the nature of their business, many people, especially submarines and aviators, who did not need to know, would have knowledge of secret operations, and if captured and tortured might be forced to divulge that information.

The fact that no submarines were lost while in direct contact with guerrillas is mute evidence that the decision to maintain as much secrecy as possible was the best of several choices. Nevertheless, many submarines went through moments of anxiety and frustration on many occasions. Was this contact friend or foe? Most times they never found out.

Nautilus proceeded on her second mission and on 29 September reached Spot Two on Panay, where Colonel Garcia came aboard. Several large sailboats took what remained of 75 tons of cargo aboard. In return she took off 47 evacuees, including 28 women and 9 children.

By the time the patrol ended at Mios Woendi Lagoon in the Padaido Islands off New Guinea, on 6 October, the sub had sighted 36 planes and made fully as many sudden dives. Captain Sharp did not know it then, but the *Nautilus*, at that time, was the only submarine in service on the guerrilla line. The *Seawolf* along with Al Bontier, USNA graduate number 11887, class of 1935, his loyal crew, and unsuspecting passengers were gone forever. The *Narwhal* and *Stingray* were either laid up or scheduled for essential repairs. Commodore Haines congratulated Commander Sharp on his "coolness and good judgment . . . in saving the *Nautilus* to fight again," and extended similar compliments to his stouthearted crew.

12

LEYTE LANDING

On 5 October, when Commander Parsons stepped ashore from a submarine that had carried him to Mios Woendi from a tour of inspection in the Philippines, he was startled to be informed that a plane, sent by General MacArthur, was waiting for him with orders to report to MacArthur in Hollandia without delay. On his arrival at the General's headquarters, he was at once ushered into a meeting of the staffs of General MacArthur and Lieutenant General Walter Krueger, commander of the Sixth Army.

General MacArthur's opening statement to Parsons was so surprising to Chick that he literally had to hang onto his seat. The General said, in effect, that Parsons had exactly ten days to get up to Leyte and pave the way for a major landing to be made on the island from Leyte Gulf. Some 170,000 troops would go ashore on 20 October, but prelanding saturation bombings would begin with daylight four days earlier and continue round the clock to D-Day.

This, briefly, meant that the friendly civilian population in the area had to be warned to get away and to stay away until they were told it would be safe for them to return; that guerrillas had to be placed along escape routes used by the Japanese and cut them down, and that the waters along the proposed beachheads had to be searched for obstructions placed there by the enemy. Parsons, because of his guerrilla contacts and superior knowledge of Leyte, had been selected for the job. He was to be given a navy code book and a decoding machine so that he could provide prompt and up-to-date intelligence to the General and the Seventh Fleet. He would be accompanied by Lieutenant Colonel Frank

LEYTE AND SAMAR
CENTRAL PHILIPPINES
Nautical Miles
0 10 20 30 40 50

Rowall of Sixth Army Intelligence who would keep General Krueger's outfit informed.

To say that Chick Parsons' world was turned upside down by this order was putting it mildly.

Up to that very second he had believed and prepared for the initial landings to occur on the beaches of Sarangani Bay in southern Mindanao. In accordance with orders, he had had Colonel Fertig build a landing strip deep in the interior of the island on a plateau that lies atop a mountain near Kolambugan and another airfield at Kolambugan itself. The former could be reached and serviced only by plane; the second was close to the sea. It had been back-breaking work for the guerrillas who worked on the mountain airstrip. All material and equipment had to be carried up by carabaos (water buffalos) or by men, up steep and winding trails through thick mountain jungle. The strip, just completed, was large and strong enough to handle B-29 bombers. As things turned out, the airfield was never used because Leyte had been

B-29

selected as the landing site. But Parsons was not informed of this change and Fertig's work was not stopped because to do so would have been an open revelation of a change of plans. Before he left Hollandia, Parsons was warned that the real reason for his mission to Leyte could not be told to anyone, including Colonel Kangeleon, commander of the local guerrilla forces, whose cooperation would be desperately needed.

It was evident that General Krueger placed great reliance on the participation of the guerrillas in the forthcoming Leyte operations. For that reason, Parsons went out of his way to make certain that it was understood by all Sixth Army staffers that the guerrilla was a well-equipped, effective, and loyal jungle fighter trained in guerrilla warfare, such as ambush and demolition, but was in no sense a soldier able to execute specialized and difficult military operations. Parsons, to his great relief, discovered that he spoke to an understanding audience that actually did not need his well-meant warning with respect to the military limitations of these brave and loyal fighting men.

Time being precious, and knowing that submarines were too slow to meet his needs, Parsons obtained, through Admiral Kinkaid, an order to the Air Officer, Seventh Fleet, to place a Catalina flying boat at his disposal for an eight-hour mission so secret that its destination would only be disclosed by Lieutenant Commander Parsons to the pilot on the day of departure.

On the Spyron radio net he sent word to Colonel Ruperto Kangeleon to be prepared to meet him on Leyte on short notice to discuss important business. He would contact him on arrival.

The island of Leyte and its gulf presented some formidable, or at least challenging, topographical and navigational problems. Leyte Gulf, a surprisingly large spread of water, is formed by the east coast of Leyte which is some 55 miles long. The gulf is about 40 miles wide. To the north it runs east–west along the shores of Samar Island, while to the south it is funneled down between Dinagat and Panaon Islands through Surigao Strait into the Mindanao Sea. This waterway provides the back door from Leyte Gulf westward to the South China Sea by way of the Sulu Sea.

Admission into Leyte Gulf from the Pacific Ocean is through two rather narrow entrances between which lie two islands. These are Homonhon, a large mountainous island, and Suluan, a small dab of woods, earth, and rock which lies directly to the east of, and only 8 miles from, Homonhon Island. On the southern coast of the latter is a small fishing village called Pagbabacnan. The entrance to the gulf north of Homonhon is narrowed down by a long peninsula, pointing south-southeast from Samar like a long, crooked finger. The entrance was further whittled down by thin and narrow Candolu Island, which projected like a long mandarin nail from the fingerlike

peninsula. This reduced the width of the northern gulf
entrance to a mere 10 to 12 miles; moreover, it was
hard for large ships to navigate because of the nature
of its channel.

The distance between Homonhon Island and Desola-
tion Point on Dinagat Island to the south is about 20
miles, thus providing a commodious southern entrance to
the gulf with at least two big-ship channels. This is
Surigao Strait.

Most of the long strip of Leyte Island coastline that
runs along the gulf is the same wild jungle country it
was during the era when Columbus landed far across the
world in the Caribbean. The only town with any port
facilities worthy of the name was Tacloban, the pro-
vincial capital. Near that city was also an airplane landing
strip. Along the entire rest of the coastline there were
only four ports worth naming—San Jose, Dulag, Tar-
raguna, and Bito.

If American army and navy leaders had visualized
miles on miles of broad white beaches for their myriad
landing craft to land upon, they would have to revise
their opinions when cold facts informed them that the
only acceptable landing beaches on Leyte ran some 20
miles between Tacloban to the north and Dulag near the
center of the coastline.

From the waterline, heavily wooded mountains soared
upward in ragged ridges broken by valleys and deep
ravines. The beach was a narrow stage on which to
unfold a dramatic assault, and the jungle-clad mountainside became a threatening theater from which a hostile
audience could annihilate the actors on the stage. It was
up to Parsons, and to Kangeleon's guerrillas as well, to
do what they could to lessen the impact of enemy resistance.

As the hours of preparation sped on, Parsons became
increasingly aware of the weight of the responsibilities
placed upon his shoulders. These realizations did not cause
him to shrink away from them, but rather increased his
determination to meet them head-on.

After delays, caused by tropical storms over the route
to be flown, a "Black Cat" (night-flying Catalina), took
off from a New Guinea naval air base on 11 October.
The plane's pilot was Lieutenant James Shinn. Aboard,
besides the crew, were Lieutenant Colonel Frank Rowall,

attired in jungle garb and loaded with combat gear, and Lieutenant Commander Charles Parsons in his standard guerrilla outfit of shirt, shorts, and shoes. As usual, he carried no weapons. Aboard, they had an inflatable rubber boat for landing on the gulf south of Tacloban, and carried little other equipment except for Parsons who had been entrusted with a navy code book and a decoding machine.

That first flight, which found Leyte the center of a heavy tropical storm that shut out all sight of land and sea, was a wash-out, and Shinn was lucky to get back to base with his passengers on the last pint of fuel. There was but one thing to do—hope for better weather and arrange another flight. This time it fell to the lot of Lieutenant Henry Nelson to make the flight. Shinn insisted on going along as copilot. Since takeoff time was set for midafternoon, the northward course ran well away from the Philippine coast so that the plane could not be observed by Japanese aircraft spotters or tracked by radar. Only when he was opposite Homonhon Island did Nelson turn west toward land. It was now late in the afternoon and the narrow beaches were barely visible in the fading daylight as the great thunderbird roared in over the gulf, fairly close to the Leyte shore, with great mountain masses rising beyond its port wing tip. The plane's machine gunners were at their stations, as there seemed every probability that Japanese would soar up to meet them. But none did. At the appointed spot, Nelson throttled down his engines and let the aircraft down gently on the water. The flying boat slowed down. At that instant the inflated rubber craft was tossed overboard; Parsons and Rowall scrambled aboard with their gear. The plane's engines immediately sounded a full-throated roar as Nelson and Shinn lifted the plane aloft and out of sight. With the departure of the Catalina came one of those episodes that usually are the fruit of a divided command. Fearing opposition, Rowall did not want to land until after dark. Hoping for help ashore, Parsons wanted to hit the beach at once.

The arrival of two friendly Filipinos in a canoe settled the issue. They towed the rubber boat ashore, where the visitors were taken to a small village. There they were given a warm, hospitable reception. Hungry and tired, the two Americans ate heartily and slept well.

The next morning two of Kangeleon's guerrillas appeared, by accident, on the scene. They told Parsons, with much pride, that they had seized a Japanese launch that Parsons could use if he liked. He certainly did. By means of the boat he reached a well-hidden Spyron radio station equipped with local, as well as long-range, transmission sets. Parsons and Rowall sent safe-arrival messages to their respective headquarters. Also, Parsons sent a local signal to Colonel Kangeleon and dispatched the launch to carry him to their place of meeting. At this time, Colonel Rowall went about his own business, aided by a pair of guerrilla guides provided by Parsons.

So far as an American invasion was concerned, the general belief, among Japanese and Filipinos alike, was that one was in the offing. Moreover, the feeling that Mindanao would be the scene of MacArthur's return still prevailed. But the Japanese, having plenty of manpower, increased their forces on Leyte and neighboring islands, so as not to be caught unaware if Leyte was an alternate American invasion point. During the next few days, Parsons was to discover the full extent of Japanese preparations for welcoming the Americans to Leyte, just in case they should happen to come that way.

In his meeting with Parsons, the elderly guerrilla leader was cooperative and did not ask any questions his American friend could not answer. Colonel Kangeleon was told that it was vital for all loyal Filipinos in the area to leave their homes not later than nightfall of 15 October because, starting the following day, and for many days to follow, there would be a full-out, round-the-clock air bombardment of enemy installations in the Leyte area.

Kangeleon, knowing about recent Japanese troop buildups in the area, which amounted to fully 24,000 men, could well understand the American operation and readily agreed to cooperate. He was also aware that the withdrawal of the civilian population must be made in such a manner that Japanese suspicions would not be aroused. Parsons need not have worried about Kangeleon's understanding and cooperation. The wise Filipino leader was not only cooperative, but way ahead of Parsons.

"The people will be attended to," said Kangeleon. "Now, what can the guerrillas do?"

Carefully the two men discussed the areas of guerrilla cooperation. How the various local units could locate

and report the personnel strength, the gun power of
Japanese positions, and troop movements, and how they
could put their active or negative reports on their local
radio network at hourly intervals, day and night. At the
radio station from which he had sent out his own messages, Parsons would evaluate the decoded guerrilla messages for long-range transmission in the navy code. Bearing in mind the new Japanese policy of fighting only
holding actions on invasion beachheads, instead of the
bloody do-or-die banzai battles that had been the style
in the earlier days of the war, Parsons asked Kangeleon
to place guerrilla groups along routes of retreat that the
Japanese might use, with orders to kill as many of them
as possible.

During the next few days, Parsons was busy encoding
radio reports to GHQ, all tagged "Parsons sends." He
spent much time roaming mountain trails looking for
information or exploring the dark waters near the beach
of the gulf at night in search of landing obstructions or
mines. Actually the only mines discovered were in the
channel near Homonhon Island, and there were no landing obstructions along the beaches other than those provided by Mother Nature in the form of coral formations
and rocks. This was determined by the use of drags
hauled by sailboats and other small native craft.

One morning it seemed as if Parsons' luck had run
out. He was scouting a trail with four guerrilla guides,
all dressed as local farmers and unarmed, when a Japanese patrol of 18 soldiers filed out of the tall grass on
a crosstrail and brought our quintet to a sharp halt. As
the Japanese went by in Indian file, Parsons placed his
right hand on the shoulder of one of his companions
and engaged him in idle conversation. They paid no
attention to the Japanese and the Japanese paid no attention to them. But, as he said later, "That was really
the stiffest scare in my life. Had one of those Japanese
compelled us to doff our hats and to bow, as they often
did, they might have noticed that neither the shade of
my skin, nor the color of my hair were exactly right.
Nor were my facial features exactly those of a Filipino."

But the soldiers did not take a peek and thereby
passed up an award equal to $100,000 in gold placed
on Chick Parsons' head by the Japanese.

As Parsons had told Kangeleon, the air bombardment

began on 16 October and for four days, without letup, the bombs rained down from the skies over Leyte.

As the invasion fleet approached Leyte, wrapped in unbroken radio silence, Parsons did not know if his messages were received and understood. He was particularly bothered by one message he had sent urging that Tacloban be spared from bombings and shelling because the Japanese, after evacuating the city, had prevented the residents from escaping. To Chick's great relief the bombers left Tacloban carefully untouched as did the gunners aboard the fighting ships when the fleet arrived. To the guerrillas, this was quite a feather in Commander Parsons' hat.

On 17 October, the 6th Rangers, 500 strong and led by Lieutenant Colonel John Mucci, were landed on Suluan Island where they disposed of the small Japanese garrison as the natives cheered. The rangers also advanced to Looc Bay on the northwestern tip of Dinagat Island. There the Japanese had flown the coop. The same proved to be the case on Homonhon Island, where the rangers landed on the 18th.

The weather over Leyte had, on 17 October, been stormy and rainy, and the seas, even in the gulf, had been rough. But 18 October brought better weather, as well as the advance guard of General MacArthur's armada. This force was Vice Admiral Jesse Oldendorf's powerful gun-support unit of 6 prewar battleships, 8 cruisers and 26 destroyers. To them had been added, to meet the needs of the immediate situation, several jeep or escort carriers, minesweepers, and destroyer-transports, for carrying underwater demolition teams and the 6th Rangers. With minesweepers leading the way, the force steamed into the gulf via the southern entrance and came into battle position opposite the proposed beachheads between Tacloban and Dulag. While minesweepers paravaned the channels and the gulf, and the UDT swimmers explored and measured the slopes of the four landing beaches, Oldendorf's large and small guns probed the mountain sides that faced the water for enemy artillery and other positions. What with the roar of the guns, the explosions of the shells, and the booming of the aircraft bombs drowning all other sound, it was not a restful day for anyone in the area, especially the Japanese.

Seldom in the history · of even modern war has a
greater fund of important intelligence been reported from
a battle area to headquarters in such steady flow as in
this, the Leyte campaign. The exact effect of the
devastating bomb and shell fire was reported day to day,
hour by hour, as was every Japanese movement, almost
as quickly as it was executed. And so it went on October
18 and 19. Guns and planes, bombs and shells. And,
under the constant pressure, Japanese defenses crumbled
and defenders died where they stood or melted away only
to meet fresh onslaughts along roads they had believed
led to safety. The guerrillas were indefatigable and
everywhere. When American fliers complained that they
could not spot the source of antiaircraft fire because the
Japanese used smokeless and flashless powder, guerrilla
fighters graciously disposed of the gun crews with whatever was handy, from dynamite to the cold, sharp steel
of bolo knives. Those Japanese defenders of Leyte, well
entrenched as they believed themselves to be, never really
had a chance. They lost the game without ever taking
a single trick.

On the night of 19–20 October, General MacArthur
arrived with the rest of his fleet and his army of 174,000
troops. Slowly, the warships, transports, and landing craft
—some 700 of them—entered the gulf during the black
and cloudy morning hours. By the magic of fine seamanship, each vessel headed for and occupied a predesignated
place in the gulf. Among the last to enter were the
cruiser *Nashville*, the General's flagship, and the command ship *Wasatch*, flying Admiral Kinkaid's flag.

As the rising sun peered over the eastern rim of the
Pacific Ocean, a thunder of guns was released from
thousands of ships' batteries as if triggered by a single
finger; formations of planes roared over the beaches and
mountains of Leyte and dipped into their bombing dives;
rocket launchers aloft and afloat sent off their missiles,
which left long white vapor trails in the murky sky. On
the mountainside, fountains of earth and rock rose as
bombs and shells erupted in violent explosions that seemed
to make even the waters in the gulf tremble. Japanese
resistance continued, but it was now reduced to mainly
rifle and small-caliber automatic fire. This would soon
be wiped out by landing forces.

Meanwhile, landing craft of all kind were streaking

Bolo

toward shore, opening the great maws in their bows
and discharging all the sinews of combat from infantry
to artillery, from tanks to supplies. As General Mac-
Arthur, with President Osmena of the Philippines and
General Carlos Romulo, watched the first landing wave

reach and take hold on Red Beach, south of San Jose, another party of six men sat on a more remote shore on Leyte Island with their backs to the mountains and their eyes on the gulf. They were Colonel Kangeleon and three staff offices—Major J. C. Fernandez, a former Tacloban lawyer who was Kangeleon's chief of staff, and Lieutenants Silvestre Moame and Jose Rifaneal. The last was also a signal officer who, according to orders, had brought along his guerrilla network code book and call signals. Present also was Colonel Rowall and Commander Parsons. Parsons was under orders to deliver Colonel Kangeleon aboard the command ship as soon as possible. But getting transportation to the invading fleet proved a very difficult matter. Time and again Parsons flashed a signal light at a passing vessel but none of these, mostly destroyers, paid any attention to his call.

Finally, the DD *Hale,* Commander D. W. Wilson commanding, passed by and caught Parsons' signal. "Can you send boat for Commander Parsons?" read the message.

The destroyer stopped her engines, while the inquiry was forwarded to the task-force commander. The immediate reply was: "Send boat for Commander Parsons."

Now it seems that the whole blooming Navy knew about Parsons without knowing more about him than just the name. But for days on end the name Parsons had come over the air in dozens of coded messages and no one in the fleet knew if he was a general or an admiral; if he had an army or a navy. He was a man of mystery and now, here the crew of the DD *Hale* was to meet him in the flesh. All officers and men of the destroyer offered to go ashore in an armed boat to fetch Parsons. Captain Wilson selected Lieutenant George R. Fahnestock and seven men to bring back the shore party. But first the skipper warned them of possible trickery and interception by the Japanese.

"Approximately 500 yards off shore," reported Lieutenant Fahnestock later, "we met Commander Parsons in a native outrigger canoe paddled by three Filipinos, accompanied by another banca. Parsons came hatless and shirtless to facilitate recognition. But even so, he was carefully inspected, and not until he hailed us was he taken aboard. Both boats then headed for shore to pick up the rest of his party."

"Those sailors of yours trust no one," Parsons later

told Captain Wilson on the *Hale*. "I thought they would never lower the guns they had aimed at me."

While aboard the destroyer, they heard General MacArthur's famous landing speech broadcast to all the Islands on the Spyron network. He and his Philippine friends had walked ashore on Red Beach with the third landing wave.

"People of the Philippines," those aboard the *Hale* heard him begin, "I have returned!"

The speech was short, to the point, and strongly inspirational. When it ended there was not a dry-eyed man aboard the *Hale*. Presently, the destroyer transferred her passengers to the *Wasatch*. There, General Krueger at once greeted Colonel Kangeleon on behalf of General MacArthur. Before that eventful day was over, General MacArthur was to pin the Distinguished Service Cross on the guerrilla colonel, and President Osmena was to name him governor of the province of Leyte. And, while on the subject of honors dealt out, Lieutenant Commander Parsons received the Navy Cross and his first combat command.

During the conferences aboard the *Wasatch*, Parsons had let it be known that he believed Japanese still occupied the towns of Maasin and Malitbog on the southern tip of Leyte, in the region of Taacan Point. He was promptly given the job of driving the Japanese out with the aid of his guerrilla forces. Knowing what we already do about Parsons' belief that guerrillas had not been trained as regular soldiers and could not be used for such purposes, it is surprising that he accepted the offer. Perhaps it was pride in the job the guerrillas were doing that led him to believe they could handle this task. At any rate, he did not plead their inadequacy as soldiers to handle the job, although he tried, unsuccessfully, to get out of it.

The sun was still below the eastern horizon the next morning when Commander Parsons landed by plane in Sogod Bay, which cleaves the southern end of Leyte Island like a huge V. His only concession to naval formality was a navy officer's white-topped and black visored cap. Here, at Santa Cruz, he found Captain Juan Escano, the local guerrilla chief, and two rocket launchers (LCR) waiting for him. The latter were regular landing craft that had been converted into hard-hitting rocket ships.

Parsons looked at the LCRs and their alert crews with warm approval and felt more secure in his new job than he had up to that moment. He introduced himself to the two young skippers of the ships, and without further formalities, he outlined the situation, which was that Escano's guerrillas would enter the old Spanish-style compound that housed the Japanese garrison at Malitbog as soon as the demolition rockets had knocked down a part of the wall that surrounded the building.

Escano said he would be ready with 200 to 300 men at dawn the next day. Without prearranged signal, the rocket boats appeared off Malitbog the next morning and at daylight began bombarding the wall of the structure that faced the beach. The work of knocking the old adobe wall full of holes was of short duration because of the high destructive power of the rockets, which were launched from racks on the decks of the LCRs in multiple salvos. As soon as the rockets stopped exploding, the guerrillas stormed the citadel, which they found unguarded and unoccupied. The Japanese had fled during the night, probably as soon as the LCRs had been sighted off shore. Only three Japanese were found in hiding on the premises. They were taken prisoner.

With this action over, the two-boat flotilla, flushed with victory, headed south toward Naanean Point and proceeded to Maasin. The target there was a school building surrounded by a jungle of barbed wire, with the added protection of pillboxes that housed machine gunners. The attack would begin at daylight the following day, when the guerrillas would surround the building. Commander Parsons and his guerrillas would go overland from Malitbog ahead of the boats. When his ships were in firing position, he sent a note to the Japanese commandant urging him to surrender. Parsons received a curt refusal.

Since Maasin faces the islands of Cebu and Bohol across the narrow waters of Canigao Channel, it was natural for Parsons to suspect that the Japanese at Maasin might have radioed the Japanese garrisons on Cebu or Bohol for reinforcements. For that reason, he did not drag his feet after the surrender offer was refused.

The LCR crews at once sent heavy salvos of their fiery missiles into the Japanese positions and blasted open the barbed-wire barricades, and pillboxes. This was followed by incendiary fire directed at the roof and second story of the school building. The Japanese ran out of the structure like rats from a burning ship, only to be met by guerrilla bullets and bolos. Inside the building there was furious, but ineffective, resistance by some enemy soldiers who finally killed themselves by using hand grenades. In a very short time, Parsons could send a "Mission completed" signal to the Seventh Fleet. He was very proud of the guerrillas. They had acted with exemplary soldierly behavior throughout both actions. Some very valuable and complicated radio equipment in the school building confirmed the suspicion that it had been a very important wireless station.

Meanwhile, all over the Islands south of Luzon, in response to orders issued by Colonel Kangeleon on General MacArthur's instructions, guerrillas had risen, fully armed, against their Japanese enemies. Where there were American forces they cooperated with them to the utmost. Where they were on their own, the guerrillas destroyed bridges and wrecked supply depots, ambushed enemy troops and made life shorter, as well as miserable, for the Japanese at every turn. Those who sought safety in the woods and mountains were hunted down and destroyed like animals. The proud old banzai cries had died down to hoarse whispers of distress.

Unfortunately, these events did not win, at the time they began, the public attention they deserved. The four separate, yet coordinated, suicidal attempts by the Imperial Japanese Navy to turn defeat into victory at Leyte demanded priority attention.

First—on 24 October, Admiral Kurita, with 5 battleships, 8 cruisers and 13 destroyers, entered the Sibuyan Sea from the South China Sea. He was bound for San Bernardino Strait to do battle with Admiral Halsey. The Japanese fleet commander would have had four more cruisers if two of them had not been sunk and two more heavily damaged by torpedoes fired by American submarines while the fleet was approaching the Philippines from Borneo. The Japanese, utterly without air protection, were heavily pummelled by Admiral Mitscher's fighters, bombers, and torpedo planes during daylight hours throughout their passage of the Sibuyan Sea on 24 October, and appeared to reverse course before sunset. This caused overenthusiastic pilots to make wild guesses in reports about damages inflicted by them upon Kurita's fleet that day. They saw it beaten and in retreat. As a matter of fact, the air-inflicted damages were, all considered, amazingly light. But the reports received by Admiral Halsey showed many battleships and cruisers sunk or damaged. All stuff of which dreams are made. True, Kurita had a badly beaten-up superbattleship unfit for action, a cruiser or two in the same situation, and some limping destroyers. But retreat was not in his mind; he simply wanted sea-room for his fleet, until sunset, before he entered the narrow channels that led to the San Bernardino Strait.

In the meantime, regarding Kurita as a dead duck, Halsey's entire carrier task force steamed north at full speed to contact a Japanese carrier task force under Admiral Ozawa. It was standing south to threaten MacArthur and the Seventh Fleet. That his task force was merely bait to lure Halsey away from San Bernardino Strait the Americans had no way of knowing. There were four Japanese carriers, but they had barely a baker's dozen of planes aboard. During the afternoon, Halsey had been considering the idea of creating a Task Force 34 out of his gun-support group and leaving it to stand guard at the strait.

Both Admiral Nimitz at Pearl Harbor and Admiral Kinkaid at Leyte Gulf believed that the guns of Task Force 34 guarded the strait. Such was not the case. TF-34 was merely a plan in Halsey's mind and it was discarded because he did not believe there was any need for it. What Nimitz and Kinkaid had regarded as a reality never came into existence and they were misguided by too close and too "iffy" monitoring of Halsey's interfleet messages. When Admiral Kurita's fleet slipped into the Philippine Sea via San Bernardino Strait soon after midnight on 25 October, there was not a single American vessel or weapon on hand to oppose him.

Meanwhile, other Japanese threats were aimed at Leyte. During the afternoon of 24 October, Admiral Oldendorf received word through coast-watchers that two separate enemy fleet units were approaching Leyte Gulf by way of the Mindanao Sea and Surigao Strait. The first of these units was commanded by Vice Admiral Shoji Nishimura and consisted of two old battleships, the *Yamashiro* and the *Fuso,* the modern cruiser *Mogami,* and four destroyers. The second, commanded by Vice Admiral Kiyohide Shima, contained two heavy and one light cruiser and four destroyers. The two units were about 40 to 50 miles apart. As Nishimura approached Leyte Gulf, where Oldendorf's battleships and cruisers were in position to deliver heavy broadsides into the enemy ships, he was subjected to PT-boat as well as destroyer attacks. The DDs' torpedo hits mauled him badly. But, despite exploding shells and deadly torpedoes, Nishimura steamed doggedly on toward Oldendorf's waiting and slowly circling battle line. When the Japanese were within 23,000 yards, the American admiral pressed the firing button aboard the old *West Virginia* which let go the first eight-gun salvo of armor-piercing projectiles from her long 16-inch rifles. Other battleships fired in turn. The shooting lasted only 18 minutes, when there was nothing left to shoot at. Nishimura's fleet had literally been blasted out of the water. Only one destroyer, the *Shigure,* survived the battle. Vice Admiral Shima, after having a light cruiser damaged by a torpedo in a PT-boat action and having seen, as well as heard, the fate of Nishimura's fleet, reversed course and headed for Borneo.

When the sun rose on 25 October, the situation was well in hand at Surigao Strait, but Admiral Kinkaid had a quiet hunch that all was not as it should be at San Bernardino Strait. He sent a squadron of "jeep" carrier pilots north to investigate. They returned with the information that they had seen neither hide nor hair of Task Force 34.

Since 0412 on 25 October, Admiral Kinkaid had been trying to contact Rear Admiral Willis A. Lee, supposedly commander of Task Force 34, but without success. Next, he tried to reach Admiral Halsey to learn from him what had happened to Task Force 34. When he learned from the latter, about 0645, that TF-34 had never been created, he could also inform Halsey that Kurita was on the prowl in the Pacific Ocean. This did not bother Halsey a great deal at the moment. Had not Kurita been beaten to a pulp by Mitscher's aviators? Kurita had no air strength and Oldendorf had plenty of gun power.

Besides, the important job just now was to knock Ozawa's fliers down before they could do any harm.

Ozawa had been discovered just northeast of Luzon. Eventually Halsey was to rush back to San Bernardino that morning with part of the fleet's fastest gun-support vessels, leaving Admiral Mitscher to deal with the Japanese, which he did in great style. At 0800, the first of six attack waves of American carrier planes hit Ozawa's fleet, and by the time they had run their course, Ozawa's four remaining carriers had been disposed of. A cruiser had also been crippled by a torpedo and several destroyers had been sunk. Some of this work was by the guns of the screening warships commanded by Rear Admiral Laurence T. DuBose. Admiral Ozawa was lucky to escape into the South China Sea with what little was left of his task force.

Meanwhile, just east of Samar Island, a group of six jeep carriers had made regular morning launchings of planes, starting at 0530. The carriers were the *Fenshaw Bay, Gambier Bay, Kalinin Bay, Kitkun Bay, St. Lo* and *White Plains,* each carrying about 28 aircraft, ranging from fighters to torpedo-bombers, some of which, at times, had to squeeze extra hard to take off or land on the jeep carriers' rather short 500-foot flight decks. The jeep's only armament consisted of one single 5-inch popgun placed aft on the hanger deck and eight twin 40-mm machine guns.

For added protection the jeeps had an escort of three destroyers and four destroyer escorts.

These flattops were commanded by Rear Admiral C. A. F. "Ziggy" Sprague. The group was one of three similar ones assigned to the Seventh Fleet under the command of Rear Admiral Thomas L. Sprague. As circumstances would have it, Ziggy Sprague's group, known as Taffy-3, was the one closest to San Bernardino Strait on the night of 24–25 October. Shortly before 0700, the boss of Taffy-3 received a report from Ensign Brook, a torpedo-plane pilot on antisubmarine patrol, saying that he had been fired upon by a hostile fleet some 20 miles north of the group.

On this news, Admiral Sprague sent signals to Admiral Kinkaid advising him of the situation, roused all his pilots, readied all his planes, and headed Taffy-3 into the north-northeast wind for takeoffs, although this brought him closer to a vastly superior enemy. Kurita was heading toward Taffy-3 ready for battle and all guns bearing on the jeeps in the mistaken belief that he was engaging Halsey's fleet. The day was cloudy and visibility bad.

Having launched planes, Taffy-3 reversed course. Now began a deadly serious game of hounds and hare in which the jeeps and their escorts revealed sublime seamanship and superb courage. The battle actually started at 0730. It began suddenly by a salvo of 14-inch Japanese shells. The engagement ended when the Japanese withdrew to the north two hours later. Just why Kurita broke off is not known. But it could be that slowed-down Japanese communications had caught up with Kurita; that he had learned how Nishimura was defeated and Shima turned back at Surigao Strait; also that, strong as he was, the situation demanded more strength than he was able to produce with lack of air support. In addition, he had suffered severe losses that morning in his encounter with the jeeps. From bomb and torpedo action, the Japanese had lost three heavy cruisers sunk, and one cruiser badly damaged. On the other hand, the losses inflicted by Kurita were one carrier, the *Gambier Bay*, the DD *Hoel*, and the DE *Samul B. Roberts*. In the early afternoon, Kurita was attacked by planes from Vice Admiral "Slew" McCain's task force, which had made a hasty turn-around from a refueling and repair trip to Ulithi. They did no great damage but probably firmed Kurita's decision to leave Leyte alone and expedite his westward return through San Bernardino Strait. This saved him from a gun-to-gun confrontation with Admiral Halsey who, as mentioned, had left Mitscher early that morning accompanied by a task force of fast, new battleships, cruisers, and destroyers but would not reach the strait before Kurita's exit.

Thus 25 October 1944 went down on the calendar as the day when the status of Japan as a high-ranking naval power officially died. But on that same day a new and terrible weapon of war came into existence, namely, the kamikaze, or suicide, pilots. The first of these death-seeking pilots struck the jeep carrier *St. Lo* at 1051, in a Zeke with a bomb under each wing, and sank her. Others of this weird and unearthly breed followed, and before the day was over, similar attacks had been delivered on several jeep carriers. The *Suwanne* and *Santee*

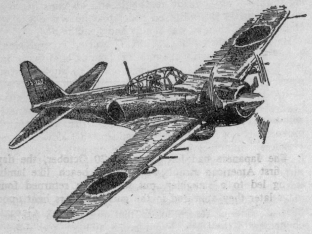

Zero A6M5 "Zeke"

were damaged, as was the *Kitkun Bay*. But that was only the start of a new brand of air warfare against surface ships that was to challenge America's grip on the Far Pacific Ocean.

13

WHERE ARE YOUR COMPANIONS?

The Japanese had left Leyte on 20 October, the day the first American assault wave hit the beach, like lambs being led to a slaughter, but when they returned four days later they appeared in the guise of tigers bent upon making kills. The counterattacks, ordered by General Tomoyuki Yamashita, Japan's best combat soldier, and now in command at Manila, were delivered in the air and on the ground. The Seventh Fleet and Tacloban airstrip were the targets of intensive and protracted air attacks. These were pressed with vigor despite serious losses from heavily concentrated anti-aircraft fire on ships and ashore, as well as counterattacks by Admiral Kinkaid's carrier planes and General Kenney's army aircraft. At the same time, and in quick succession, 50,000 Japanese troops were landed at Ormoc, on Leyte's west coast, from Luzon and neighboring islands despite stiff aircraft opposition.

"The Japanese will fight the decisive battle on Leyte," General Yamashita had declared. Taking the Japanese leader at his word, General MacArthur brought reserves up from New Guinea and launched a two-pronged drive northward from the gulf. One prong crept up along the east coast of Leyte and Samar; the other followed the island's west coast. Although each prong was a powerful military steamroller, obstinate Japanese resistance and continuous tropical rains slowed American progress to a mere crawl. MacArthur had to wait patiently, because of lack of aircraft and landing equipment, before he was in a position to change the situation by a bold but breathtaking leapfrog surprise. When the opportunity came in early December, things changed radically and with stunning rapidity. On 6 December, a convoy carrying the 77th Division, commanded by Major General Andrew J. Bruce, slipped around the southern tip of Leyte and steamed north toward Ormoc. There, on 9 December, the division landed in shipshape order 3½ miles south of the city, despite persistent Japanese air attacks. Two days later, after taking Ormoc, General Bruce was in contact with MacArthur's main force. The drive against the Japanese now expanded to its full thrust and fury. Having cut the enemy's main line, General MacArthur was able to chop up the pieces right and left, like meat in a gigantic grinder. Enemy soldiers fought fanatically without thought of surrender. By 26 December, when all organized opposition had been smashed, only 798 Japanese had been taken prisoner, while the enemy dead numbered more than 80,000.

General Yamashita, according to General MacArthur's estimate, had suffered the greatest defeat ever inflicted on the Japanese army. Between their navy and army losses, Leyte had been a costly battle ground for the Japanese.

But Douglas MacArthur did not rest to enjoy his victory, nor battle honors, which included his fifth star and promotion to General of the Army. The Philippine government awarded him the Medal of Valor, equal to the U.S. Medal of Honor.

"We have our hold [on the Philippines] now," he said in closing a general order to his forces, guerrillas, and other native civilians who had fought for that victory, "and I shall not relax the grip until Bataan and Corregidor once more rise into life!"

Whereupon he began the complicated job of setting up the operational program for the next target: Luzon.

In the meantime, there were many little dramas that were obscured by the bigger picture. It is a fact of life and war that whenever there are air operations in a combat zone, there will be a certain number of downed aircraft. But nowhere else in the world was there ever a deal like the air war over the Philippines. American pilots would come plummeting out of the sky, only to be plucked from the jungle, or the seashore, by friendly islanders. They were Filipinos, and they were either guerrillas or knew some that were. So between them and Spyron, most of the downed airmen were gathered

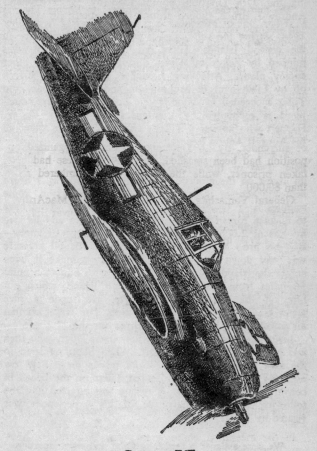

Grumman F6F

together and shipped back home, usually via guerrilla submarines.

Two incidents, one that occurred over jungle wilderness and another on the surface of the sea, are related here, not only because each is true to type in its respective field, but also because they reveal that guerrillas were ever present and always helpful to Americans, including Americans who literally fell out of the skies.

The first of these incidents happened to Ensign Thomas
C. Tillar, one of Mitscher's carrier pilots, on 12 September
1944, during the softening-up period of air resistance in
the central Islands. Tillar, an F6F fighter pilot, was
jumped by Zekes off Cebu during an attack on other
enemy planes. Attacking Japanese aircraft were driven
off by Lieutanant B. McLaughlin and his wingman, and
Tillar succeeded in shooting one down. What next transpired is recounted by Lieutenant Commander C. W.
Harbert who answered Tillar's call for help. He stated in
his Aircraft Action Report:

"I had circled Mactan Island to look over the airfield. Two or three minutes after my group launched
an attack on the grounded planes on the airstrip, I heard
someone scream that there were Zekes attacking. Some
minutes later 'Ginger Eleven' [Tillar] said he would have
to make a forced landing. I talked with him and he said
he was at 2,000 feet and able to maintain 110 knots—
that his prop had gone into low pitch. His oil pressure
was way down and he said he couldn't make it back
across the islands. Skon and I stayed with him to a point
36 miles from the center of Mactan Island, which put
him off the west coast of Leyte. He made a nice
water landing. I reported his position. The target combat
air patrol circled him after we left for our ship."

Lieutenant (jg) W. A. Skon flew over Tillar, who then
was safely in his one-man raft. When Skon returned to
the area to assist, a USS *Wichita* rescue plane flew low
over the reef island and observed Tillar on the beach in
conversation with natives. A rescue was effected and the
following interesting narrative of his experiences was
related by Tillar:

We were assigned a target on Cebu and were escorting
the TBFs and SB2Cs. We were high cover at seventeen
thousand feet. The bombers had completed about half of
their runs and still were bombing the field. Our division
leader, Lt. McLaughlin, led us down in a strafing attack
on Opon Field, Mactan Island. The last two planes in the
formation, Lt. (jg) C. P. Spitler's and mine, passed them
on the way down. At four thousand feet Spitler spotted
two Zekes and we started after them. Then I was jumped
—tracers went by the cockpit and I looked back and saw
a Zeke on my tail, riding me down at very close range. I
turned left under him and continued diving. McLaughlin

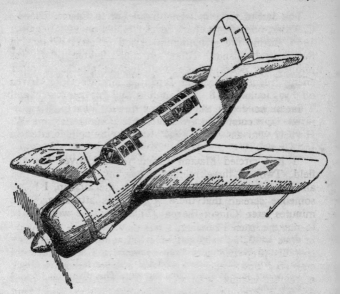

SB2C Curtis Hell Diver

chased one of the two. My Zeke turned left and I chopped throttle. He over-ran me and I got in behind him; we were then about one thousand feet. He levelled off and headed south, I after him with water injection turned on. I was overtaking him in level flight indicating 210–220 knots. He apparently was aware of this and when I was within two thousand feet range he went into a wing-over to the left. I turned inside him and followed him around in the turn, firing at five second bursts. One-half his wing and part of his tail came off. By that time we were going straight down to the water from two thousand feet. I pulled out at about one hundred feet off the water and saw him splash—he did not bail out or burn; he just crashed.

I was then at one hundred feet, indicating about two hundred fifty knots and two Zekes made a formation run on me from my starboard bow. They were shooting at me from head-on. I turned into them and fired at them as they went by. I smoked one but do not know what happened to them. I put on full power and climbed to 9,000 feet without difficulty. My windshield started to cloud up as I climbed due to an oil film. I flew around for about ten minutes with Ens. H. J. Stockert, who noted a large

hole in the port side near my oil line. I noticed my oil
pressure was down to forty and dropping gradually. I cut
down the power immediately. The plane was not over-
heating. I called Stockert and told him I thought I would
have to make an emergency landing. I flew about fifteen
more minutes in formation, even joining them in a strafing
run because I did not dare to lose them.

We headed home and I asked Stockert to lead me to the
rescue point as I had no vision forward. We headed toward this point from five thousand feet; my speed dropped
off to one hundred ten knots. I was losing altitude all the
time and when I increased throttle my oil pressure dropped
off. Lt. Cdr. Harbert called and told me to try and get
over Leyte and if not, to make a water landing. I was
about 1,500 feet then and my prop went into low pitch,
and my plane began to overheat. I had only fifteen pounds
of pressure. I knew I would have to make a water landing. I jettisoned belly tank and hatch. I had difficulty getting the hatch off because I was only indicating one hundred knots. I finally pushed it off using both hands. I
tightened my shoulder straps, lowered my tail hook and
flaps, which came down easily. I felt the tail hook drag
the water just as the engine cut out. The plane made an
easy landing.

I got out easily with my gear strapped to me. The plane
remained surfaced for approximately twenty seconds, during which time I was in the water in my Mae West. After
the plane sank, I unbuckled my gear and got out the
rubber boat. The sea was calm. Just before I opened the
boat I pulled one of my dye markers. There were friendly
planes flying over me all the while until I was safely in
the boat. I kept my chute, which I held in one hand,
while climbing into the boat, which added somewhat to
the ordinary difficulty of climbing in. I had tried previously to climb into the boat with the back pack and
chute on me but I was unable to do so. I bailed out water
in the boat.

Once in the boat, Tillar determined that he was about
10 miles west of Amogotada Point, Leyte. He decided
to stay away from the beach and wait for rescuers to
pick him up. He was about 600 yards north of a little
hilly volcanic island with a 100-foot shelf dropping down
to the sea (later identified as Apid Island), and was
drifting away from it very slowly. His first thought was
that this island, with its scrub trees above the gray shelf
rock, was deserted. To the north of him there were some

fishing boats. He had seen them before he went down but guessed they probably were friendly and decided not to strafe them. They stayed where they were and did not seem to be aware of his presence.

After I was out there about an hour, in which time I had drifted only about 200 yards, I noticed several outrigger canoes coming from the north side of the island [continued Tillar]. There were three at first, but, as they came half way out, three more followed them. An elderly man and boy were in the leading canoe and a single man in each of the others. They seemed suspicious of me and I was more so of them. They stopped about twenty yards from me. They were jabbering away in a foreign tongue which I was unable to understand. All this time I had my revolver in my lap as I was unable to understand whether they were native or Jap, friendly or unfriendly. I made a lot of motions to them, none of which were of an unfriendly nature. They gained confidence and came within ten to fifteen feet of my boat. When they got that close the young boy, about 15, stood staring at me while the old fellow, a man about 50, talked. I decided to curry their favor by offering them razor blades which I kept in my emergency belt kit for that purpose. I opened up a razor blade and offered it to the young fellow and he showed it to the old man. Meanwhile, the others tangled up their outriggers trying to get close enough to study the packet. They passed it around, continuing to talk among themselves and occasionally to me.

They evidently decided to take me ashore as they motioned to me to get into the largest canoe. Then they threw me a line with which to tie my raft to one of the canoes. I spent my trip to the shore bailing water as the canoe leaked badly. I had decided that they were friendly and had no hesitancy in going with them. My only concern was to make them understand me. I would look at them with a dumb look when they addressed me and they laughed. Half-way back to the beach a formation of our planes approached from the east. They started to row like mad and I could make out the word Japanese as they pointed toward the planes. I made hand signals to the old man indicating they were friendly planes; they seemed to understand. We went almost right under the shelf of the island and around to the south side where there was a beach. There was a native village and about 200 people were waiting for us. The whole population had turned out. They were scantily clothed; those with anything wore a tough type of cloth that resembled burlap. The men were about five-feet-four inches tall, a dark yellow complexion, with almond shaped Filipino type of eyes and straight, black hair.

I waded ashore in two feet of water and a boy who looked about 18 (actually he was 26) met me at the beach and said 'Hello sir,' and shook hands. He could speak broken English mixed with Filipino. He engaged me in conversation. From then on I used him as my interpreter. I told him I was an American flier. They did not know what Navy meant or what aircraft carrier meant. I told them the planes were American. They could see and detect the approach of planes long before I could. They kept asking the question, 'Who are your companions' and 'Where are they?'.

I kept telling them: aircraft carrier, which I think they failed to understand. I told them my companions were those fliers up there and I think they understood this. They brought all my gear ashore and put it in a big open shed which the Americans had left there a long time ago. The shed had 'Apid Water Tank' written on it in English, but the water tank was gone. There was a good concrete foundation remaining. I handed out some more razor blades; then I opened my chute which was soaked and covered with dye marker. The chief's wife felt the texture of the silk and mumbled something. She told the interpreter she would like to hang it up and dry it out and the chief indicated a desire for it. He told me, through the interpreter, that they did not have much clothing. I immediately gave it to the chief's wife. She took it to the house and hung it up to dry.

The chief's house was made out of board with a thatched roof while the other huts were thatched affairs on four inch wooden poles. Their floors were made of split bamboo. One of the men cut his finger with one of the razor blades and he winced in pain. I took out my first-aid kit and wrapped it up for him. They appreciated this immensely. They seemed curious about the rest of my gear so I opened my back and seat packs to show them their contents and held the mirror in front of the chief's wife; she turned away and laughed.

The boy, who could speak broken English, told me to wait and came back in five minutes with his identification papers to show that he was a member of the Philippine Army. They gave his name as 'Sosa' and rank of PFC. He told me that he had been in Cebu and had escaped about a year and a half ago. I gathered that he had been a prisoner. He then asked me if I had eaten. When I said No, he sent someone to bring me food. One of the women brought back three raw eggs and gave me them. I ate them, although they almost gagged me; I guess because I thought I would offend them by refusing.

They hung all my gear on a line between two trees and took me back to the chief's house where we sat down on bamboo seats, the interpreter sitting next to me. I asked him all the questions I could. He told me they had had no contact whatsoever with the Japs, that the natives in the area had no personal hatred for but were unfriendly to the Jap, partly because of what they had heard and partly because they knew their supplies had been cut off from the time the Japs came. I asked him whether the Japs were around and he said there were none on any of the small islands. He further stated, pointing westward, that a seaplane went over their village every two or three days. During our conversation, a carrier strike came over from the east. They heard it long before I did; everyone started jabbering and they suddenly became quiet. It was at this moment that I heard the planes for the first time. We went down to the beach and I tried to signal the formation. The planes were between eight and nine-thousand feet. I used my mirror but apparently it was ineffectual. After the strike had passed over we heard the bombing of Cebu.

We went back to the chief's cabin and were sitting there, they staring at me during a lull in conversation. Someone asked me if I liked fish and, when I said I did, brought me two fish about eight inches long, which were highly colored in purple, red and pink hues. These were not recently cooked, entrails and all. I broke one and gave half to the interpreter and we each ate some. He ate the head and tail as well, but I just the fillet. At the same time, they brought me a big plate of rice which was very dry and garnished with two fried eggs served on top of it. I ate about half of this. They then brought me four more raw eggs and insisted I eat them. I did so although I nearly gagged.

We then heard another plane and went to the beach. I could barely see it but it was very apparent to them. It disappeared to the north. We came back to the chief's home and the interpreter said he was going to take me somewhere but not to be afraid. The warning was unnecessary as I was completely at ease by this time. We walked about one-half mile to the other end of the island. A large group of people were gathered around a shed and when I looked in, I found it contained my belly tank, in perfect condition except for a slight dent in one side. It still contained about ten gallons of gas. The natives thought it was a bomb and I opened the cap and showed the interpreter its true nature. He seemed to understand what it was after smelling the gas. Then we went back to the chief's cabin and I opened my back pack and took out the emergency rations. I gave out the chewing gum, vitamin tablets and candy. One of the natives who had not spoken a word of English exclaimed 'Sweet.' I gave the interpreter the rest of the razor blades which pleased him immensely. I also gave him the rubber sail in the life raft, my sea anchor and bailing bucket.

About this time, the strike that had passed over was returning and again I tried to contact it with a mirror but failed. The next planes we heard were a couple of F6Fs which came over and circled at three-thousand feet [Lt. (jg) Skon and Lt. (jg) Sipes]. I used the mirror again. They came down close; then I shot a thirty-eight tracer right in front of them. Evidently they saw the tracer because they joined up and came down closer. The interpreter exclaimed 'tracer' when he saw it. I then ran back to the chief's cabin and got the verey pistol out of my sea pack. I fired a verey shell which they saw.

Just after I fired the verey pistol, an outrigger came over from a little island to the south. The interpreter recognized the occupant and said he was a Lieutenant in the Philippine Army. This man was a Filipino about five-feet-five inches in height. He looked better fed than the others and was fairly well dressed in civilian clothes—pink sport shirt and trousers. I think they sent over for him. I was given to understand that he made regular trips to and from Apid. He introduced himself in pretty good English and did not mix Filipino with it. I told him I was an Ensign, a pilot from an aircraft carrier. He asked how many carriers we had out there and I said a great many. He seemed pleased with this. He told me, in answer to my question, *that there were no Japs on Leyte.* He inquired as to how many bombs we had dropped on Negros and Cebu. I told him over three hundred on Cebu and as many more on Negros that morning. He repeated it to the natives and all were greatly impressed, repeating several times in amazement the word '300', throwing up their hands and jabbering. He represented the guerrilla forces and told me they were badly in need of arms and medical supplies.

Just then I saw the SOC coming in from the south. I ran and got my back pack and helmet. Skon and Sipes directed the SOC over to me. I fired another thirty-eight tracer at the SOC which he did not see. He flew over the island once without sighting me; then he flew back around the island and when he returned I fired a verey shell which he saw. The plane landed and taxied within 75

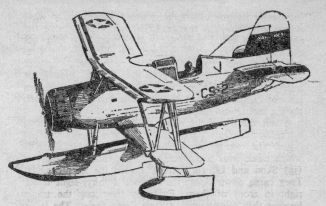

Curtiss SOC "Seagull"

yards of the beach and I paddled out to it in my rubber raft.

The experience of Ensign John P. Richardson, a Hellcat flier on a jeep carrier in Admiral Kinkaid's Seventh Fleet, ran along different and more difficult lines.

Richardson's squadron flew up from Leyte, at about 1400 on 25 October, to attack a Japanese cruiser in San Bernardino Strait. First, another fighter unit went in to draw antiaircraft fire and confuse the enemy. Then Richardson's gaggle came in, dropped 500-pound bombs and made strafing runs to clear things up for the torpedo bombers that followed at deck level.

They tell me, [said Ensign Richardson much later] that I scored a direct hit. I don't know. I didn't look back. Anyway, my radio was shot out. When we started to join up with the other planes, I noticed Zekes all around. One right in front of me, with one of our boys on his tail, burst into flames.

I noticed one lone Zeke circling about 3,000 feet above us. We started climbing up after him when we saw he wasn't coming down. While still 2,000 feet below him, he started a straight-away dive to outrun us. In about a minute we overtook him, one plane directly on his tail, two out to the port side, and myself out to starboard. The man on his tail shot a quick burst. The Jap turned quickly, which caused one of our pilots to overrun. When

the Jap turned he made a beautiful target for me. My port
guns jammed, but I gave him all I had with my three
starboard guns, and the shells appeared to be going right
into the cockpit. After a moderate burst, he rolled over
and went into a mountain.

I joined the pilot that had overrun. He signaled that
the Jap had crashed, and asked how much gas I had.
I signaled back that I had 55 gallons, and that my radio
was dead.

The lead plane and I started back in a slow circle on
the outside of the cruiser, the other two planes on the
inside. Suddenly the lead pilot pulled into a wing-over
because there was another Jap on our tail. Due to my
gasoline shortage, I went into a tight circle to starboard,
allowing the Jap to come in on my tail and shoot at me.
All the bullets fell way behind my plane. Within a very
few seconds, my leader shot him down in flames, but the
pilot bailed out.

We then started down the eastern coast of Samar, in an
attempt to reach Tacloban airstrip on Leyte Island. When
I got down to 35 gallons of gas, I signaled the lead pilot.
About that time, we turned on our running lights, so that
if we flew over friendly territory we wouldn't get shot at.

I got down to five gallons and signaled the lead plane
with my wing lights. He acknowledged, but there was
nothing he could do. Shortly after, we headed in towards
Tacloban. Over Samar my motor cut out. I immediately
cut off my lights, so if there were any Japs below they
wouldn't spot the crash. With all precautions taken, I dove
down into a valley and then started climbing uphill until
the plane hit a tree and stalled. The plane went on through
the trees to the ground. The crash ripped the left wing,
smashed the canopy, and ripped the fuselage off just behind the pilot's seat.

The jar of crashing snapped both my shoulder straps.
My head hit the instrument panel, and I was cut, but not
knocked out. However, both my feet were paralyzed from
the shock, and I couldn't leave the plane for a while.

When the use of my legs returned, I climbed out of the
plane through all the equipment. I noticed I had cuts on
both legs, and my left ankle was almost useless with a
sprain. My back seemed to be wrenched, and my left
wrist was quite weak. I opened my parachute, climbed
under the plane and went to sleep. There was nothing else
to do. The time was 1908. Of course, I woke with every
little sound of the birds and animals all night.

Next morning, at sunrise, having proven the truth of
the old Army Air Corps wheeze that any landing you

can walk away from is a good one, Richardson opened his back pack and put iodine on his cuts. He wrapped and taped the ankle and started to walk uphill to get an idea of the terrain. However, after about 15 minutes of stumbling in the jungle, he realized that he was making no headway, and reversed his course. Two hours later he reached a river and started walking downstream. After an hour's walking he stopped to rest. All this time, in fact, all during the days he was on the island, it rained and rained.

At sunrise I got up and started walking again [the ensign continued]. My food for the whole trip was malted milk tablets and some other tablets called Charms, which taste just about the same. I knew I could go for six days on these, and then I could eat leaves and things. At about 1500 that second day, I got tired of walking through the steady rain, so I stopped to build a bamboo shelter. It didn't prove very effective, but I did go to sleep finally, and slept till daylight again.

I started walking, paralleling the coast, which I knew the Japs held. In the afternoon, I built another shelter from the rain, but it caved in on me while I slept.

The next day, the fourth, he started out the same way and had to swim across the river four times. After the fourth swim across, about 1430, he saw a native house.

I couldn't be sure whether it belonged to a Filipino or a Jap, but a man came out just then and saw me. When he started to talk, I knew he was not a Jap. Neither of us could understand a word the other one said, but I was so glad to see him that we talked for 15 minutes.

He put me in a canoe and took me to the next house. Nobody there spoke English but, by sign language, I let them know I was hungry and they gave me some food. Then they took me on down the river to another house. A girl there could speak some English, and she told me her father was in the guerrilla forces and that it would be safe to recuperate at their home. They sent for the father, who was in town. Then a woman massaged my ankle and my back for a long time, and made me feel a lot better.

The next morning the father arrived. He spoke English. He asked me about the plane, and we decided to send natives to salvage it. On the third day of my stay with them, I felt well enough to get about, and we went up by boat to find the plane. When the river got too rough to go any farther, I told the men where the plane was and they went on by land while I came back to the house by boat.

A day and a half later the father returned and said they had found the plane and were salvaging it. The natives knew of a U.S. Army man, who operated an army radio station somewhere near there. They had sent for him the day the pilot's host got home, and he got there the day after Richardson's host got back from the plane.

This man—whom I'll call Bill—and I made plans to leave the next afternoon [reported Richardson]. The natives came back from the plane, bringing the machine guns, ammunition and radio gear. We took that and started off by boat. Next day, about 1100, we stopped at an island because of extremely bad weather, and remained until the following afternoon. The natives had a dance in our honor during the night, and everybody came. Bill had a fine time dancing the Lube-lube with the native girls, but I stuck to the good old-fashioned waltz.

In the afternoon, we started off and rode in the boat until noon the next day. We got word in a village that there were four other survivors nearby. We decided to go there. The night before we arrived, the guerrilla forces cleared out the town for us. On the way, we stopped at each island and village and rendered first-aid to the natives in any way we could. There wasn't much we could do about sores, diseases, children's illnesses, etc. with our small medical kit, but they had been so good to us that we wanted to do whatever we could for them.

When we arrived, we found four men safely in the care of the natives. They were survivors of ships sunk in the sea engagement. Bill left the next morning to return to his radio station.

The morning after Bill left, Lieutenant (jg) Doy H. Duncan, an FM-2 pilot off one of the carriers, arrived with word that surface craft would arrive that night off a prearranged point to remove us and to bring in guns, food and clothing to the Filipino guerrilla fighters.

They went to the place and waited until 0900 the next morning, then got another message that the rendezvous had been cancelled. They stayed around town two days waiting, then decided to return to the place they had been staying. There they found a buck sergeant es-

Grumman FM-2

capee from Clark Field. He had been on the island for three years and had had 37 gun exchanges with the Japanese. First lieutenant's bars were pinned on him before the little group left the island on 15 November.

On 14 November, they received word that the second rendezvous had been arranged for that night. The rescue party brought supplies to the natives, and they also brought five newspaper correspondents who remained with the natives to watch them fight. While the supplies were being unloaded, the natives went aboard with piles of freshly cut branches and did a beautiful job of camouflaging the ship.

We went to Leyte Gulf, where I was immediately put into sick bay. I was released from sick bay in time to get to New Guinea, where I found orders to return to my ship by air. I found out that my ship was, by that time, back in the United States so, believe me, I hurried to rejoin her. I met up with her finally in Seattle on 2 December.

I'll never forget the natives on Samar [concluded Ensign Richardson]. "Nobody can believe how much they mean to us, or how much damage they are doing to the Japs. One Filipino boy, about 23 years old, has already killed 145 Japs himself. He was Bill's righthand boy and he worshipped Bill.

The natives think the Americans are wonderful, and they wouldn't let us do any work at all. Even when I felt fine, they wouldn't let me touch an oar to row the boat. If we had to wade a few feet through inch-deep water when we beached the boat, the natives insisted on carrying us on their shoulders.

The plane instruments, engine and two props are at a warehouse on Samar waiting for the Navy to pick them up. I gave the bullets and guns to the U.S. Army on Samar for the guerrillas to use.

In the meantime guerrillas on other islands were far from idle.

On Panay they rounded up 20 downed aviators and reported this via Spyron to GHQ-Brisbane. The SS *Gunnel*, Lieutenant Commander G. E. O'Neil, Jr., on combat patrol in the South China Sea, was ordered to pick up the airmen. Unfortunately no contact was made at the rendezvous and after several days of fruitless waiting the rescue mission was abandoned. The fate of these fliers remains one of those mysteries of World War II that will probably never be solved.

Gunnel was then directed to rendezvous with guerrillas on Palawan, where they had assembled 11 airmen. This rescue was a success.

Subsequently, SS *Hake*, Commander F. E. Hayler, was ordered to pick up 19 people from Panay, some of whom turned out to be downed American pilots. It has never been determined whether the men were part of the original group which *Gunnel* was to rescue, or whether they were recent additions to the guerrilla rescue net. No matter, 19 American fighting men got off Panay—thanks to their loyal compatriots, the guerrillas, and the submarines that made them an effective organization.

When Parsons finished his business in southern Leyte, where he and his guerrillas had wiped out the small pockets of Japanese resistance in Maasin, he returned to HQ, now established ashore, in Tacloban.

General Krueger gave Commander Parsons a hearty welcome and congratulated him on the soldierly qualities shown by the guerrillas, which pleased Parsons to the core. He also called on Colonel Whitney but did not notice that his boss watched him with thinly guarded concern. To Whitney, Parsons looked thin, drawn, and near the point of complete exhaustion. Chick had carried on at Leyte Gulf despite frequent attacks of malaria, little sleep, and inadequate food. Before he knew it, Parsons was in the hands of medicos, given leave, and packed off by plane to the United States. There he was

hospitalized at Asheville, North Carolina, where he had
established a home for Katsi and the boys before he left
for Australia in early 1943.

Like a battery responds to an electric charge, Chick
Parsons—now a commander and also holder of a gold
star in lieu of a second Navy Cross—bounced back to
good health. Like all wartime leaves, it seemed to end
almost as soon as it began, and in January 1945 he returned to Leyte for duty.

But he knew Leyte was not the end of the line. Somehow, sometime—way up ahead—lay Luzon and his old
home, Manila. He'd get there, by God, whether it be by
submarine or banca or aircraft, and he'd get there before
MacArthur.

14

LUZON WATERS

Toward the late summer of 1944, the curtain of silence that had shrouded the guerrilla situation on Luzon was raised by the infiltration of men from AIB brought in by submarine. The guerrilla forces there were found to be strong and stable. And Luzon waters were added to submarine gunrunning schedules. For these highly vulnerable ships to venture into Luzon territory, where the Japanese had concentrated their naval defense forces on a last ditch stand, was to invite trouble with a capital T. But the submariners who ran the Japanese gauntlets on the guerrilla runs did not shrink from this opportunity to serve, no matter how great the dangers that awaited them.

The first submarine to hit this dangerous circuit was the *Stingray*, commanded by Lieutenant Commander Sam Loomis, Jr. She left Darwin on 16 August 1944 for Saddle Rock, Mayraira Point, on the northwestern coast of Luzon. If captain and crew expected to encounter trouble, truth is that they ran up against more than their share of it.

On the morning of 21 August the *Stingray* was well on her way to Luzon with 15 military passengers and 20 tons of cargo when a sight to stir a submariner's heart met her captain's eye from the bridge. On the horizon, the tops and superstructures of three vessels became plainly visible. Captain Loomis had worked his way into position for a submerged torpedo attack when he took another look. He now discovered a decrepit old tramp steamer of about 1,200 tons escorted by a destroyer on each quarter. To Loomis it was a trap—even the veriest landlubber would have smelled something fishy. It looked

PHILIPPINE ISLANDS
Nautical miles
0 30 60 90 120 180
Ocean depth
less than 3000 feet
more than 3000 feet

N

Balintang
Channel

Mayraira Pt.

Pasaleng Bay

LUZON

Darigayos Inlet
Lingayen Gulf
Santiago Cove
Dagupan

Capas
Cabanatuan
San Fernando

PHILIPPINE SEA

SOUTH
CHINA
SEA

Polillo St.

Zambales Mts.

Bataan Pen.
Corregidor I.
Batangas
Manila
Olbut Bay

Verde Island Pass.
Cape Calavite
Patuan Bay
Calapan

Catanduanes I.

Lagoney Gulf

MINDORO
Sibuyan
Sea

Busuanga I.

VISAYAN
ISLANDS

SAMAR

PANAY

LEYTE

Bombay Shoal
Palawan Strait

NEGROS

Cebu

PALAWAN

SULU SEA

Brookes Pt.

Ramos I.
Balabac I.
Balabac Strait

Cagayan

MINDANAO

Davao

BORNEO

Sibutu Passage
Tawitawi I.

CELEBES SEA

like the old Q-boat game.* The Captain decided to pass up this questionable group and hauled clear.

On the evening of 25 August Japanese activities seemed nervously intense, of the shoot-first-and-ask-no-questions caliber, as *Stingray* approached Saddle Rock. Things looked none too good for reconnoitering the landing spot. Evidently the damaging of a tanker by a submarine torpedo attack the previous day forced the Japanese ship to take shelter in Pasaleng Bay, with a destroyer for protection. This was much too close to *Stingray's* spot for comfort. The sea was flat calm and the presence of debris yelled to the high heavens of torpedo action. The destroyer dashed hither and yon like a nervous terrier.

Loomis decided to spend the night in quieter waters and retired three miles off shore. He noted that he found himself "off the rock-bound coast of Maine with many strong tide rips and currents."

As he had anticipated, the landing spot proved a sticky bit of business. The *Stingray* cautiously approached Mayraira Point on the surface in the pre-dawn hours of the appointed day. She passed debris and oil slicks. When four miles off the point, radar picked up a small contact between the sub and the shore at a range of 5,300 yards. Captain Loomis dove and, in the dawn's early light, discovered that his contact was a two-masted schooner. Some 15 other sail boats were seen in the area. The sub was closing the designated spot, at periscope depth, when a single-engined plane, probably having sighted the 'scope's small wavefeather, came at *Stingray* in a steep, fast dive. Loomis pulled the plug for the deep deep and he got there quickly. No bombs.

With these developments, Loomis decided he was wasting his time trying to land his passengers and cargo at this point, so he crossed the 100-fathom curve and went periscoping for a likely looking beach. After a long search, he found one; however, there was one drawback—there were a number of nipa shacks clustered

---

*A Q-boat is a ship which appears to be a harmless old tub but in reality is a combat vessel equipped with modern anti-submarine weapons and manned by naval personnel. The trick is to lure a submarine to the surface on the premise that the target is not worth a torpedo and could be destroyed by gunfire. With the submarine on the surface the Q-boat unmasks her batteries and lets go with everything she has.

among the coconut palms just beyond the beach. The Filipino officer in charge of the party on board looked the situation over carefully through the periscope. When Loomis took the 'scope away from him because of the lengthy exposure, the Filipino shrugged his shoulders and said, "It looks all right to me."

Soon after, about one mile off the beach, the Fathometer indicated a hard, smooth bottom at a depth of 219 feet, so Loomis sent *Stingray* down to lie dogo until sunset. Coastal shipping passed noisily overhead. The sub was probably right under a traffic lane. But no one complained to the management about the noises coming from above. From 1525 to 1610 all aboard heard very distant depth charges. Forty minutes later *Stingray*'s sonar picked up fast screws coming in. The noise had the characteristic high pitch of a destroyer. The intruder passed between *Stingray* and shore and had almost faded out when he dropped a depth charge. Next, the ship cranked up high speed and headed back. She passed overhead, slowed to 40 rpm, speeded up and once again passed overhead. Sound conditions were such that every man aboard the hunted submarine could hear, through the hull, every speed change of the hunter. It wasn't particularly enthralling. Again the DD slowed down, then speeded up. He dropped a depth charge, and then another, but for some strange reason none were even close to the submarine. Slowly his screw noises faded out.

Quiet reigned thereafter. Then *Stingray* surfaced and approached the beach flooded down and taking soundings. Four hundred and fifty yards off shore, in about 8 fathoms of water and just about to anchor with bare steerageway, the *Stingray* ran aground. With three heavy jolts forward she rolled over about 10 degrees to port. Much of the sub's glistening forward hull shone in the silver moonstreak under a starlit sky. Loomis ordered all engines back, emergency, and blew main ballast. After a few anxious moments for all hands, *Stingray* bounced a couple of times and clumsily clawed her way off, like a stranded whale wriggling off a sandy beach. She reached deep water without damage. Loomis backed to 14 fathoms and let go the anchor. As if this had been a signal, natives built a bonfire on the beach and raced toward the *Stingray* in canoes. As soon as Loomis was sure of his contact, he sent a boat ashore with a hauling line to be secured to a coconut palm to overcome the strong current in moving the boats between ship and shore.

When Captain Loomis got word that all was well on the beach, unloading began. The operation went well for some two hours, when the radar operator sounded the alarm. "Contact!" Off-loading ceased immediately while Loomis and the bridge watch strained to see whatever it was. At first it seemed to be a convoy of three or four cargo ships led by three escorts with more small ships astern. Radar tracked them on a course that would pass close aboard *Stingray,* if not right into her.

It was not a healthy situation for a sub in hostile and shallow waters on a bright, moonlit night, her deck piled high with stores and the anchor out.

"If we dive," mulled Loomis, "the escorts will hear us and will be all over us. The stores will be a wonderful marker and the completion of the mission will be really completed. If we heave round on the anchor or slip it and try to shoot it out on the run, with one 3-inch gun and four machine guns, the mission is also completed.

"And what speed can these escorts make? I decided to sit tight and play at being a native sail boat, since our stern-to position presented only a small target to the enemy. All deck guns were manned and all hands topside told to lay low on deck.

"As the minutes dragged by and the ships opened out from overlapping, we could at last see that they were an assortment of large and small sea-trucks. The first group of ten chugged by at 450 yards, outboard of us. The land background saved our identity but surely not their sighting of us."

About midnight, 14 more sea-trucks came around the point. Again action on the submarine's deck froze as it passed inspection at 300 yards. They were crowding closer; Loomis did not like it but what could he do?

During these tense moments, the captain overheard two seamen bellying down close to the foc'sle deck.

"Are you praying?" said one to the other.

"Nope!" was the reply.

"Then why in hell aren't you?"

The gunnery officer found the ship's cook rummaging among the stores on deck. On asking the cook what he was doing, the cook replied, "Sir, I am looking for something that will float."

About now the group of 14 sea-trucks had the sub completely boxed in. The loose formation broke up and the ships began to mill around. It looked as if they were going to anchor all around the *Stingray*. Loomis decided that enough was sufficient, loaded two more rubber boats as he heaved around on the anchor, and slowly crept out to sea.

"We would have liked to have opened fire on the whole damn bunch," said Captain Loomis, "but I figured that the security of the landing spot, our own vulnerability with stores still on deck and hatches open, did not warrant gun action. So striking the remaining stores below we sneaked out and away."

While homeward bound, the *Stingray* picked up a red and white raft. In it were four Japanese who said they were from the Japanese cruiser *Natori*, which had been torpedoed on 18 August by a submarine.

"All were in serious physical condition from exposure and lack of water and food," observed Captain Loomis. "I have never seen a lousier looking group of human beings."

In his patrol report, the captain gave the staff of ComSubSWPac a morsel to chew on when he observed: "We were certainly sighted by all hands in the sea trucks; they were neither blind or asleep. Undoubtedly we passed as one of their own type or as a native schooner. I think it entirely reasonable to equip subs, in this type of business, with a portable sail to be mounted forward. Never have we wanted to try sailing a submarine as much as we did on this occasion. This sail would be used, only, of course, when the decision is made to stay up and either get away with it by playing possum or fighting it out on the surface."

The suggestion was never acknowledged, which probably did not surprise skipper Loomis.

The decision by the U.S. high command to take the road to Tokyo via the Philippine Islands (there had been proposals to bypass them and go directly into Okina-

wa instead) led to the acceleration of submarine deliveries
to Luzon.

In late August the *Narwhal* pulled out of Darwin on
a threefold mission to Luzon with 45 passengers and
20 tons of cargo. Aboard was the ubiquitous Commander
Parsons, accompanied by Ensign Sinclair, USN, and Private Courtney Whitney, USA, two of his most trusted
Spyron bodyguards. Parsons and his two men left the
Narwhal on the night of 29 August at Dibut Bay. His
plans were to scout the lay of the land, confer with
guerrilla leaders and contact Spyron radio operators. The
trip north was uneventful.

With barely time for a breather after the conclusion
of her eleventh and nearly last war patrol, the *Nautilus*
headed out to sea again on 10 October from Mios
Woendi to discharge a party of 12 men and 20 tons of
cargo on the northeast coast of Catanduanes Island, east
of Lagoney Gulf off Luzon on the Pacific Ocean side.
Two other landing spots, quite close to each other, were
on Dibut Bay, some 50 miles east of Manila.

En route to Spot One, *Nautilus* was informed that
the landings had been scrubbed. This time, not because of
enemy activities, but because on the scheduled landing
date, "Pete" Mitscher's carrier force would deliver massive air strikes on Manila and its vicinity. Captain Sharp
decided not to stick around to see the show. At dawn
the next day he found the proper signal at Spot Two on
Dibut Bay. On surfacing he found no one to greet him.
Waiting impatiently, Sharp saw, shortly after sunset, some
unreadable signals and a red light about half a mile down
the coast. Smelling a rat, the skipper suspected that the
reception party had been ambushed and that Japanese
lay in wait for him. He stood off shore to report and
await instructions. None arrived, so he took off for Spot
Three. There the security signals were correct and Major
Anderson came aboard when the sub surfaced after dark.
It was then that Captain Sharp first learned of the assault on Leyte. The guerrillas were elated, as were all
aboard the submarine.

Unloading completed, with only one interruption by
enemy aircraft, *Nautilus* nosed homeward, dodging planes
and surface patrols, but before she reached her base she

was ordered to proceed to Bombay Shoal in the Palawan Strait and destroy the U.S. submarine *Darter*.

On 23 October the *Darter*, Commander D. A. ("Dave") McClintock, attacked the First Striking Force of Admiral Takeo Kurita's fleet on its way to smash the American invasion of Leyte. With *Darter* was her sister ship, *Dace*, Commander B. D. Claggett. McClintock torpedoed and sank the heavy cruiser *Atago*, Kurita's flagship. Within minutes Kurita lost another cruiser, *Maya*, which succumbed to a torpedo spread fired by *Dace*. Next, *Darter* crippled the heavy CA *Takao*. About this time SS *Bream*, another SoWesPac boat under the command of veteran "Moon" Chapple, joined the action and stopped the cruiser *Aobo*.

All in all it had been a busy day for McClintock, Claggett, and Chapple, and a very sad one for Kurita.

Unfortunately the action ended abruptly and unexpectedly when *Darter* rammed head on onto Bombay Shoal at full speed. She had been making an end around on the surface in an attempt to get into position for further attacks when, to McClintock's great surprise, he found himself virtually high and dry, naked as a jaybird, on an inaccurately charted shoal. Japanese destroyers stood off at a considerable distance, afraid to close because of the poorly charted shoal waters, and lobbed shells toward the hapless sub, but to no avail. McClintock went about the depressing business of burning codes and other classified material, and the destruction of sensitive equipment such as radars, sonars, the TDC, and the like.

Dace stood by, submerged, herself wary of the dangerous waters until the discouraged Japanese suddenly left the scene. Claggett surfaced, launched a rubber raft, and after many shuttle trips, took off *Darter's* entire crew. According to tradition, McClintock was the last to abandon his ship. Not a man jack was lost or even slightly injured.

With the rescue completed, Claggett tried to do with his 3-inch deck gun what the Japanese had failed to do. McClintock stood on *Dace's* bridge and winced with every hit. It was useless to keep on, they agreed, so *Dace* departed the area and headed for Australia.

A week later, *Nautilus*, the old reliable gunrunner, was on hand to act as chief executioner in the death of a magnificent submarine that had served her country with distinction by sinking 20,000 tons of enemy shipping in her first few months on combat patrol.

On 31 October Commander Sharp approached Bombay Shoal cautiously, submerged so as to make his sonar more effective in locating reefs and also to make periscope observations of enemy activity. There were no Japanese ships or aircraft to be seen. No doubt the almost complete destruction of the IJN in the naval battles of Leyte Gulf and off Samar, 24–25 October, accounted for their lack of interest in the *Darter.*

Commander Sharp surfaced and went about his melancholy chores with precision. First, he fired ten rounds of common projectiles from each of his two 6-inch deck guns. Next, the No. 1 gun fired 26 rounds of high-capacity projectiles while the No. 2 gun slammed off 18 of the same. These were followed by 24 more rounds of common ammunition. The *Darter* shuddered and shook like a living thing. It was painful to watch but submarines die hard and she did not distintegrate. Large explosions, with yellow flames, rose from the vessel. A huge oil fire burned aft.

"It is very doubtful that any equipment was left intact aboard the *Darter,*" wrote Captain Sharp in his log. "Nothing aboard would be of any value to Japan except as scrap!"

The *Narwhal* had nothing new and noteworthy aboard except a new skipper when she left on her next mission. He was Commander W. G. ("Bill") Holman, an old hand at submarining with ten war patrols under his belt.

With 37 military passengers and 60 tons of cargo, he departed for Tawitawi and Negros on 11 October and found the air full of planes ready to fight any sub, friend or foe, at the drop of a bomb.

On Friday, 13 October, Captain Holman had two radically different experiences with aviators. At 1116, just as he was surfacing from a dive to repair the trim pump, a plane was discovered coming in at a range of 3 miles. The sub dove and released two red smoke bombs as a sign of friendly feelings. When Captain Holman returned to periscope depth for a cautious peek, he saw the same plane, a PBY, American, circling the dye marker it had dropped.

The picture did not look too good, but Holman fired another red friendship bomb and, taking a long chance, surfaced beneath its crimson glare. Plane and sub exchanged messages but they were garbled. Then a string of the usual "IMIs" and "W's." The plane, standing on its port wing tip, circled the sub in a tight, steep bank and ended by zooming the sub three times. Thereupon it dipped its wings and flew away; all very palsy and jolly.

An hour later, another plane, also supposedly friendly, approached the *Narwhal*. Encouraged by his good luck with the PBY, Holman let this one, identified as an army aircraft, come within 4 miles before he dove. Going down, he felt and heard two light bombs go off as he passed 90 feet. He did not pause but went deeper and rigged for depth charge, and decided that not all army pilots were friendly fellows.

"All of today's troubles," commented Commander Holman sadly, "could probably have been avoided if we had had IFF* equipment and an air search radar. I feel that equipment of this sort is needed more on this vessel than others that operate, in the main, outside the range of our own planes. All hands agree that we will be glad to get to an area where the Japs have control of the air."

On the night of 16 October Holman completed his first mission with only minor inconvenience in the form of three Japanese coastal patrol boats who didn't seem to know what they were patrolling for, or how to do it. A few days later *Narwhal* was off Calipapa, Negros, and landed her 37 guerrillas and 60 tons of cargo despite a drenching rain. To compensate, Holman took aboard 6 men and women and 14 children ranging in age from 18 months to 14 years.

The 2nd of November found *Narwhal* happily steaming into the harbor of Brisbane proudly flying from her signal halyard not the customary call sign, but a dozen clean white diapers. Everybody ashore knew who she was.

Narwhal had had more than 100 positive aircraft contacts and made twice that number of dives during this patrol, and Holman prayed that the powers that be

---

*Identify Friend or Foe by coded signal.

would provide him with an IFF and aircraft search radar during an upcoming refit.

In his comment on this patrol report, Commodore Haines endorsed Holman's recommendations, but as usual the old workhorses, farmed out to a business not as glamourous as direct combat, were relegated to the low end of the totem pole when it came to getting the most modern equipment. *Narwhal* never did get any.

A surprised Commander Dissette, commanding *Cero,* found himself pressed into service on the guerrilla circuit when he pulled into Woendi in early October to replenish after a month at sea on combat patrol. A special mission to Luzon had been assigned to *Pollack,* another line submarine, but she had developed serious engine trouble and could not make the run on time. Overnight, *Cero* was transformed into a guerrilla gunrunner. Off came all torpedoes save for two forward and two aft in the tubes for defense, and ship's carpenters swarmed aboard all night building wood platforms in both torpedo rooms. That finished, aboard came 17 tons of cargo consisting mostly of small-block TNT demolition charges. At daybreak 16 army men filed aboard.

When briefed that night by Commodore Peterson aboard the submarine tender, the skipper of *Cero* learned that he was to land a hand-selected demolition squad onto Luzon only a few miles north of Manila at a place that was already a veritable hot spot and destined to get hotter. His orders were to not attack anything but a major warship until he was rid of the TNT and demo squad. As the skipper prepared to leave, the commodore, a kindly man, almost fatherly toward his young submarine commanders, cautioned Dissette to be wary of the "new" safety lane. Then Peterson told him about the *Seawolf* and Al Bontier.

Al Bontier and Ed Dissette had spent their last R & R together in Brisbane only a month before. For two weeks the war had seemed to go away.

Cero arrived on time off Spot One, Darigayos Inlet, on the west coast of Luzon, after running the usual plane and patrol obstacle course. That night she was almost run over by a convoy being chased by the submarine *Cod,* Commander J. A. ("Caddy") Adkins, skipper, a

Pearl Harbor boat unaware of *Cero's* position or mission. Dissette managed to draw off one escort, inadvertently, because he got nosy and wanted to divert the convoy from Spot One. Shaking the escort after a crazy Mack Sennet-type of stern chase, *Cero* returned to the rendezvous at dawn. There were no boats, no signals, no people, at Spot One. The skipper set up a methodical periscope patrol and turned the duty over to the watch officers. There were so many aircraft sightings that he began to wonder what was going on. There was a steady stream of Japanese aircraft, some going north and almost an equal number going south. He was puzzled because the planes seemed to be in transit and not bent on molesting U.S. submarines.

What the skipper didn't know was that the battle for Leyte was raging to the south. Submariners were seldom cut in, for security reasons, on plans of impending major operations unless they were directly involved in them.

That night he went offshore to charge batteries and returned again to Spot One at dawn. Same deal. Nothing, except at noon, conducting a submerged reconn of the beach, he ran into a amusing incident. He wrote:

"We passed close aboard a banca containing two brown brothers busily engaged in fishing. Wanting very badly to find out if one of them might be our contact I raised the periscope a full 10 ft. above the surface while abeam of the canoe at a range of about 50 yards.

"At that moment we missed the picture of the year. The two fishermen obviously saw us, frantically hauled in their lines and lit out for the beach, leaving a wake astern like that of a PT-Boat. We had made contact alright, but with whom?"

Another day and another night produced nothing. The skipper wrote later: "Major Vanderpool [the senior Army officer aboard] and the demo squad were becoming restless—no action, no contacts, just a few distant depth charges. I felt the same way, so one night we picked a fight with a couple of seatrucks we found skirting the beach. With the Major as spotter we opened up with our 3-inch deck gun and the 40 mm. Oerlikon and poured it on. The Major admitted later that he wasn't an artillery

man (his spotting was terrible) but he allowed as how
our gunnery was lousy, too.

"Anyway we relieved some tension aboard and, incidentally, drove two small enemy vessels ashore—afire
and exploding."

Cero kept moving northward along the west coast of
Luzon but could not make contact with the guerrillas
ashore. With the high-explosive load she carried aboard,
Dissette wanted the cargo and passengers off as soon as
possible. The Army aboard was in complete agreement.

Finally, CTF 72 came up with orders. *Cero* was to
proceed to Spot Three, the mouth of the Masanga River,
in Polillo Strait, on the east coast of Luzon. It was the
back door to Manila. The passage through Balintang
Channel was slowed by headseas and heavy weather.
Most of the passengers were violently seasick.

Once through Luzon Strait and into the Pacific the
seas abated and *Cero* reached her destination at dawn.
Making a periscope reconn off shore, the proper recognition signal was sighted on the beach in the late afternoon.
He headed in, submerged and with all hands in life belts
(Dissette had been warned that Polillo Strait was probably mined), relying on his sonar gear to detect mines
ahead. After a few alarms, which proved false, *Cero*
surfaced at dusk, a short distance from the beach. Instantly a small boat, flying a spanking new Stars and
Stripes, stood out from the beach. Major Anderson, area
guerrilla commander, came board. Anderson indicated
where he would like to have the sub anchored to facilitate off-loading. He was an old hand, he said, at this
business (actually this was only his second experience with
a G-sub) but the sharp-eyed navigator of *Cero*, Lieutenant
Commander "Chuck" Nace, spied a pair of rocks near
the spot Anderson had designated and suggested that
Cero anchor between them. Being surfaced, the sub's
conning tower added a third "rock" to the scene as
viewed from sea. It apparently worked, because Japanese
patrol boats that wandered by occasionally never went in
to investigate.

There was a brilliant moonrise and flat calm sea, a
good break following the heavy weather of the past few
days. The unloading went like clockwork. Four evacuees
came aboard—two were Navy pilots who had been shot
down while raiding Manila, one was an escaped POW,

and the fourth a young American boy about 12 years old, who was adopted by *Cero*'s crew, promptly nicknamed Charlie and put to work as a messboy.

About midnight *Cero* got underway eager to return to base. When clear of the area Dissette attempted to radio a message reporting the results of his mission, but continuous Japanese jamming blocked the transmissions. At dawn the next morning it became apparent that the radio jamming was deliberate. She was greeted by a single torpedo. It missed.

The enemy submarine's presence was announced by a torpedo trail that passed close aboard. *Cero*'s lookouts sighted it at about 150 yards. Fortunately for the *Cero*, the other submarine was badly handled. She broached like a killer whale, apparently at the firing point, about 1,500 yards on the *Cero*'s port quarter. An alert Officer of the Deck, Lieutenant Joe Hokr, maneuvered the *Cero* smartly to avoid the solitary torpedo. Thanks to the broaching, there were no more torpedoes. A counter attack was out of the question.

After firing the torpedo, the other sub surfaced at a distance of about 8 miles, about long enough to summon a plane by radio. Anyway, half an hour later, the *Cero* had a hostile aircraft contact at 6 miles. Dissette pulled the plug and vanished on the double to avoid it.

For a pinch runner on the guerrilla beat, the *Gar*, Commander M. Ferrara, drew a rather tricky task of multiple deliveries of military personnel and cargo. To add to his difficulties, the delivery points were in the Manila area where sharp enemy eyes were everywhere and trigger fingers ever ready. The *Gar* was an elderly lady with 13 war patrols and 20,000 tons of sinking to her credit. This was a new experience under a new skipper. She left Brisbane on 3 November for Mios Woendi where she took aboard 16 army men and 30 tons of cargo. These were destined for a selected spot off Darigayos Inlet on the west coast of Luzon where Colonel Wendell Volckmann, USA, and his cargo handling party would be waiting. But as the time approached for *Gar*'s arrival Volckmann became increasingly aware that the Japanese patrols in the area were acting very jittery. He advised ComSubSoWesPac to abort the rendezvous with

Gar at Spot One. Ferrara was diverted to Spot Two—
Santiago Cove—also on the vital west coast of Luzon but
apparently a much quieter area.

In the morning twilight of November 20th Ferrara
approached the new rendezvous with caution. He saw
flickering yellow lights along the beach. They looked like
torches. Otherwise all was quiet—no ships, no aircraft.
As the morning twilight gave way to daylight he dove
to periscope depth and began the monotonous offshore
patrol watching the beach continuously for any signs of
activity. There was nothing until at sunset when the beach
seemed to erupt with people. Up went the security signal
—two white panels side by side—and within moments a
banca paddled by two little brown men stood out from
shore. Seated amidship was a passenger waving a small
American flag. Ferrara was convinced. He surfaced *Gar*.
A few minutes later Volckmann stepped aboard. How
he got to Santiago Cove from Darigayos before *Gar* Ferrara never asked.

The next morning, after unloading, the weather was
clear and the sun was bright when *Gar* lookouts sighted
a floating island in the distance. The submarine went
down and discovered the island to be a well-camouflaged
sea-truck of about 1,000 tons. Tree branches and other
foliage covered the ship completely topside. Ferrara decided the enemy was too small for a torpedo, so he
surfaced, battle stations, about 3,000 yards on the sea-
truck's starboard beam. Since the target was heavily
ladened and offered very little freeboard to aim at, *Gar*
closed the distance to 1,800 yards. The machine guns
chattered away angrily but the *Gar*'s 3″/50 deck gun
spoke with slow, well-aimed precision. The sixth shot hit
amidships and produced a tremendous explosion. In the
twinkle of an eye, the target disintegrated completely.
Flame and smoke shot hundreds of feet into the air.
The explosion came as a complete surprise to all hands
since no one expected to find a sea-truck loaded with
ammunition. There were no survivors.

On Thanksgiving Day the *Gar* was glad to escape a
friendly plane, although the IFF was going full blast.

A lightning-quick dive saved her from a PBY dropping
three bombs to make the kill. Later in the middle of the

night, sonar reported fast screw sounds, which proved to be noises made by schools of fish. No further incidents jarred the *Gar*'s journey home and she anchored in Mios Woendi Lagoon without meeting any troubles, except engine headaches.

At about the time *Gar* was in the Verde Island Passage, the *Blackfin*, Commander G. H. Laird, Jr., skipper, entered the same waters on the shortest and last of her guerrilla runs. What with American forces spreading over

PBY

the Islands and pushing the enemy into the north—except for isolated units—the gunrunning business was drawing to a close.

The *Blackfin*'s run to Mindoro was the ticklish one of making a contact just west of the Camurong River on the island's north coast. The sole purpose of the mission was to pick up some captured cryptographic and other secret enemy documents, plus equally secret and important technical equipment. To risk a submarine and its crew on such a mission, the material must have been of great value.

After marking time offshore for two days, contact was

made on the night of 18 November, and a captain of
the 105th Paratroop, USA, delivered three huge sealed
sacks of documents. The bags were tightly sealed to
protect their secret contents but the lips of the paratroop-
ers were not. On the deck, within hearing of the entire
bridgewatch, the paratrooper told Commander Laird
about the contents of the three bags while Laird listened
painfully and prayed the soldier would stop spilling top
secrets as if they were common gossip. After the paratrooper departed, Laird lectured the entire crew about
the utmost secrecy of the information and warned each
man to forget that he had ever heard about it.

The skipper felt relieved of a great burden when, on
24 November, he delivered the three sacks aboard HMAS
Kiama at sea and stood home for Fremantle.

The submarine *Gunnel*, Lieutenant Commander G. E.
O'Neil, Jr., skipper, received orders, while on patrol at
sea, to proceed to a chart position that was identified as
the town of Libertad on Panay Island. The mission was to
pick up 16 American aviators in friendly hands. On arrival off Libertad about dawn on 30 November, Captain
O'Neil began to reconnoiter the beach. The town was
largely hidden behind the trees that grew, in spots, to
the water's edge. That night, Commander O'Neil received
orders to meet a sailboat the next afternoon between the
50- and 100-fathom curves, about a mile off Libertad.
There would be about 20 aviators in the boat, which would
fly an American flag. O'Neil was also told that a second
party of American aviators awaited pickup near Flecha's
Point on Palawan Island. It seemed to O'Neil to be raining aviators in that part of the Islands. Nothing occurred
at the spot designated on the appointed day. What
could have happened to 20 U.S. aviators? The disappointed men aboard the *Gunnel* never learned the
answer.

After two days of constant and vigilant waiting off Libertad, the *Gunnel*, on orders, steamed westward to
Palawan to pick up 11 naval aviators led by Commander
Justin Miller, USN. They were to be in position off Flecha's Point at dusk on 2 December. The boat, or boats,
were to show a torch at ten-minute intervals and shout
the password: "Ballast." A word with double L's in it

would be particularly difficult for Japanese to use without unmasking themselves.

On the night, at the time and place specified, the *Gunnel* was in position in waters full of shoals, reefs, and coral heads. The submarine was flooded down and kept her Fathometer running to be warned of shoals and the like. A 1.7-knot current made it hard for the ship to maintain position and keep from being pushed on a reef. At 1848, Captain O'Neil began a search along the coast. It was smart, because eventually a light, that came on at ten-minute intervals, was sighted. O'Neil spotted a small boat in the black night. He thought it was his contact. So he blinked a plain-language "keep coming." This was a good hunch because those aboard actually had concluded that they were on the right spot, had dropped their sail and were waiting. At 2019, after shouting "Ballast" repeatedly, the men were taken aboard. Their welcome, at first, looked far from hospitable. The passengers approached a submarine whose deck was lined with armed men, their carbines pointed at them and machine guns ready to clatter. Combat scowls changed into broad grins as the word "Ballast" came across the gap of water loud and clear.

Aboard with the airmen came guerrilla leaders Colonel Jacinto Cutaran, Major Pablo Muzco and Lieutenant Alberto Sandoval, a medical officer.

"The highpoint of the evening for the rescued aviators and the guerrillas," noted the skipper, "were servings of pie and ice cream with chocolate cake and coffee, the first they had tasted in a long while."

Captain O'Neil, having reported the completion of his mission, received orders to bypass Panay and complete her regular patrol, which gave the hungry airmen an excellent opportunity to enjoy submarine chow, which stood second not even to that of carriers.

In December 1944 *Hake,* Commander F. E. Hayler, was called off combat patrol to pick up another group of aviators whose wings had been clipped. No problems. Twelve more happy birdmen were delivered to Perth in time for Christmas.

The honor of making the final officially recorded guerrilla run fell to the venerable *Stingray,* now commanded by Commander Howard F. Stoner. He completed his mission on New Year's Day 1945. With that, the Special Mission Unit was dissolved and the submariners went happily back to the business of destroying Japanese shipping, what little was left of it.

15

THE WINDUP

With Leyte conquered, all that remained to complete
the harvest of victories in the Philippines was Luzon.
Leading to it, Mindoro was seized and occupied by Amer-
can forces in mid-December. The landings were relatively
uneventful, but later Japanese suicide pilots raised havoc
with the ships, inflicting considerable losses. Only a narrow strait lies between Mindoro and Luzon. General
Yamashita at once visualized southern Luzon as General
MacArthur's prospective landing area. The American
commander did all he could to nourish this belief because
his selected landing place actually lay a short distance
north of Manila. In the shadow game that followed,
MacArthur hoodwinked Yamashita into the firm conclusion that the Allied troops would land south of Manila.
This was done by means of a feint to plant Eighth Army
troops ashore, by staging bomber attacks and photographic
air missions, as well as by intensified activities by central
and southern Luzon guerrillas and their submarines. The
show they put on was so realistic, well-armed, and ably
led that the Japanese general threw a majority of his
troops into southern Luzon to meet the oncoming assaults, which was just what MacArthur wanted. Under
cover of night, the Allied landing expedition stole up
the west coast past Manila and came to anchor in
Lingayen Gulf before the Japanese leader was aware of
their presence. In the meantime the guerrilla subs kept
up a constant supply train.

The landings began at dawn on 9 January 1945 and
ran off without a hitch. GHQ was established at Dagupan and the drive on Manila began under the leadership
of General Krueger. In the mountains to the northeast a
heavy concentration of Japanese troops was immobilized

by the I Army Corps, under Major General Innis P. Swift, in front, and Colonel Volckmann's guerrillas on the flanks and in the rear. Thus an enemy force, variously estimated at from 120,000 to 150,000 men, was permanently removed as a threat to MacArthur's march on Manila by the continuous pressures applied by Swift and Volckmann. The Americans moved at high speed all over Luzon. Just below the Zambalas Mountains the battle line swept out in a wide and bulging front, anchored at one end near Cabanatuan and at the other on the coast near San Felipe. Here the enemy opposition changed from merely stiff to outright fierce; but, strong as it was, it could not stop the Americans who now received timely reinforcement by the addition of various Corps of the Eighth Army. This was about 29 January–1 February. With the Eighth Army attacking Manila hammer and tongs from the south, and the Sixth hitting hard from the north, General MacArthur finally had Manila in his grasp. In this victory drive, Luzon guerrillas served with distinction from start to finish. In fact, the peak of their services was reached when they, with Ranger troops, liberated the prisoners in Manila concentration camps and saved them from brutal eleventh-hour slaughter by their Japanese guards. Thus, mass murders were prevented, just before Manila fell, by heroic men who dared to enter the city and its environs while Japanese power still held sway. Many months would pass before the last pockets of Japanese resistance would be cleared out, but the heavy fighting was over. Among troops that did not surrender easily were those penned in the Luzon mountains and now headed personally by General Yamashita. On 1 September the Japanese general, accompanied by members of his staff, walked into Volckmann's guerrilla camp. Yamashita gave up. Later, in promoting Colonel Volckmann to brigadier general, General MacArthur said that the work by his guerrillas alone was equal to that of a front-line division.

Yes, the guerrilla forces had served with distinction throughout the Philippine Archipelago. The Filipinos were a proud people, and they never lost faith in the submariners who ran the rough risks on the guerrilla runs to supply them with technical experts, weapons, and other necessary sinews of war. The mutual respect between the two totally different type of fighters—the men in the field and the men in the boats—is what welded the guerrilla units into a fighting force.

The supplies and trained personnel brought in by sea played a major role in organizing the originally scattered guerrillas into formidably effective units in combat and reconnaissance operations. Thanks to the submarines, Parsons and his people . . . the central and southern islands were covered by a network of coast-watchers, plane spotters and weather observers. While submarine cargo provided mainly military supplies and some rations, they could not include enough food needed by the guerrillas, most of whom were on starvation diets, nor enough medical supplies for many who were in dire need of medical attention. Their clothing was often reduced to mere rags, and to many shoes were an unknown luxury. The submarine skippers always gave all the food and medicines they could afford from ship's stores, and the officers and crews willingly ransacked their own belongings for garments to give away, even the shirts off their backs.

Lastly, but far from least, there were the evacuations of refugees from Japanese persecution, entire families who, but for the submarines and the guerrillas, would have perished in enemy hands or died of starvation or disease.

"A full quarter of a century has passed by since these events transpired," wrote Commander Parsons from Manila, "yet some of them, and the people who played parts in them, are engraved upon my memory as if the events occurred only yesterday. The people I worked with were driven, as I was, by a passionate love of the Islands and an urgent desire to help set them free. They were real patriots. I knew scores of them personally, but thousands who served the guerrilla cause loyally and well were nameless to me."

As for the submariners who brought new life and hope to the some 65,000 men and women who elected to resist the enemy rather than surrender, it can only be said that without them the guerrilla movement would have collapsed long before Allied forces could return to the Islands.

Appendix

SPECIAL SUBMARINE MISSIONS

Period Covered: Approximately 1 February 1943 to 23 January 1945.

Total number of Missions   41
Number of Submarines   19

Bowfin	9	Gar	2
Narwhal	9	Blackfin	1
Angler	1	Gunnell	1
Crevalle	1	Hake	1
Harder	1	Ray	1
Redfin	2	Gudgeon	2
Nautilus	6	Grayling	1
Seawolf	2	Tambor	1
Stingray	5	Trout	2
Cero	1		

Missions involving apparent attack by enemy   4
    1 with complete success (*Seawolf*)
    3 without damage to our subs
Missions involving attacks upon enemy   4
    2 with complete success
    2 without success
Partially unsuccessful missions   3
    1 all personnel and 60% cargo delivered
    1 all personnel and virtually all cargo delivered
    1 mission as modified, accomplished. No supplies delivered. Returned to Australia.
Completely unsuccessful missions (sub lost or presumed lost)   1
Missions involving delivery of important mail (in addition to personnel and cargo delivery)   4
Missions involving pickup of important captures or secret documents of intelligence value   7

Approximate Number of Persons
   Delivered   331
Approximate Number of Persons
   Evacuated   472
Approximate Number of Tons Supplies
   Delivered   1,325

Bibliography

Haggerty, Howard, *Guerrilla Padre*. Manila, People's Publ., 1946.

Harkins, Philip, *Blackburn's Head Hunters*. New York, Norton Co., 1955.

Ind, Allison, *Allied Intelligence Bureau*. New York, David McKay, 1958.

Ingham, Travis, *Rendezvous by Submarine*. New York, Doubleday, Doran, 1945.

Keats, John, *They Fought Alone*. Philadelphia, J. B. Lippincott, 1963.

Lichuco, M. P., *Roxas*. Manila, Kilko Press, 1952.

Lockwood, C. A., *Down to the Sea in Subs*. New York, Norton Co., 1967.

Lockwood, C. A. and Adamson, H. C., *Battles of the Philippine Sea*. New York, T. Y. Crowell, 1967.

Ney, Virgil, *Notes on Guerrilla War*. Washington, D.C., Command Publications, 1961.

MacArthur, Douglas, *Reminiscences*. New York, McGraw Hill, 1964.

Recto, Claro M., *Enemy Occupation*. Manila, People's Publ., 1946.

St. John, J. T., *Leyte Calling*. New York, Vanguard Press, 1945.

Volckmann, R. W., *We Remained*. New York, Norton Co., 1954.

Wolfert, Ira, *American Guerrilla*. New York, Simon and Schuster, 1945.

Yay, Panlilio, Colonel, *Crucible*. New York, MacMillan Co., 1950.

Combat Patrol Reports by all U.S. submarines engaged in Filipino guerrilla operations made available by the U.S. Navy History Division, OCNO, Washington, D.C.

ABOUT THE AUTHORS

EDWARD F. DISSETTE served on submarines from 1936 to 1946. After the war, he was assigned various posts ashore and afloat. Highly decorated, he retired as a captain in 1960 and took a position in the aerospace industry. He has published several magazine articles, both fiction and nonfiction. Captain Dissette took over the task of completing *Guerrilla Submarines* when Adamson died suddenly in 1969. He lives in Largo, Florida.

HANS CHRISTIAN ADAMSON was born in Denmark and came to the United States after several years at Oxford. A naturalized citizen, he served as an officer in the U. S. Army Air Force during World War II. He is the author and coauthor of many books on military and naval subjects. These include historical works and a biography of the late Eddie Rickenbacker, with whom he was closely associated. Mr. Adamson lived in San Francisco until his death in 1969.

BANTAM WAR BOOKS

Now there is a great new series of carefully selected books that together cover the full dramatic sweep of World War II heroism— viewed from all sides and representing all branches of armed service, whether on land, sea or in the air. All of the books are true stories of brave men and women. Most volumes are eyewitness accounts by those who fought in the conflict. Many of the books are already famous bestsellers.

Each book in this series contains a powerful fold-out full-color painting typifying the subject of the books; many have been specially commissioned. There are also specially commissioned identification illustrations of aircraft, weapons, vehicles, and other equipment, which accompany the text for greater understanding, plus specially commissioned maps and charts to explain unusual terrain, fighter plane tactics, and step-by-step progress of battles. Also included are carefully compiled indexes and bibliographies as an aid to further reading.

Here are the latest releases, all Bantam Books available wherever paperbacks are sold.

AS EAGLES SCREAMED by Donald Burgett

THE BIG SHOW by Pierre Clostermann

U-BOAT KILLER by Donald Macintyre

THE WHITE RABBIT by Bruce Marshall

THE ROAD PAST MANDALAY by John Masters

HORRIDO! by Raymond F. Toliver & Trevor J. Constable

COCKLESHELL HEROES by C. E. Lucas-Phillips

HELMET FOR MY PILLOW by Robert Leckie

THE COASTWATCHERS by Cmd. Eric A. Feldt

ESCORT COMMANDER by Terence Robertson

I FLEW FOR THE FÜHRER by Heinz Knoke

ENEMY COAST AHEAD by Guy Gibson

THE HUNDRED DAYS OF LT. MAC-HORTON by Ian MacHorton with Henry Maule

QUEEN OF THE FLAT-TOPS by Stanley Johnston

V-2 by Walter Dornberger